The Beautiful Lost

The Beautiful Lost

LUANNE RICE

Point

Library of Congress Cataloging-in-Publication Data available

ISBN 978-1-338-11107-1

10 9 8 7 6 5 4 3 2 1   17 18 19 20 21

Printed in the U.S.A.   23
First edition, July 2017

Book design by Abby Dening
Hand lettering by Baily Crawford

For Diana Atwood Johnson, with love

Chapter 1

MAY 20
CRAWFORD, CONNECTICUT

The day everything changed, I shouldn't have been at school. I had to institute The Plan, and I couldn't do it here.

I sat in the third row of English. *One Hundred Great American Short Stories* lay open on my desk, and I was just waiting for the period to be over. It was second to last in the day. Maybe I could go to the nurse and get excused. Or I could just walk out the front door, down the school's wide steps, and head toward my destiny.

In the meantime, Mr. Anderson's voice droned on about "Chicxulub" by T. Coraghessan Boyle. It was May, we had an end-of-semester test coming up, and I'd liked the story. It was about sublime disaster in a family. I knew I should take notes for the exam, but I was distracted by several things.

My mind was stuck, like tires in snow, spinning and spinning. It scared me because this was how I always felt before IT—capital *I*, capital *T*—started. The classroom windows were open, and I tried to focus on the present, on the sound of spring leaves swishing in the wind, the way I'd learned at the hospital, but it wasn't working.

Another distraction: the back of Billy's head. His brown hair was cut short and badly, as if someone had used nail scissors on it. He had freckles on the backs of his ears. All winter long he had worn the same sweater, navy blue with a hole in the cuff of his right sleeve. He lived in a group home, where I imagined everyone relying on hand-me-downs. But now, in spring, he seemed to have a few different shirts. Today's was dark green, short sleeved with a frayed collar, and I could see his arms. Pale, because Connecticut in May was just slightly removed from winter and we hadn't had much strong sun yet, and freckled, of course.

As if he could feel my intense gaze, he turned around. Our eyes met with a jolt and I looked down. But that didn't last long. I looked back up and blinked at him, focused on his serious expression, his wide mouth, the way his hair fell across his eyes, and then the bell rang.

Clarissa and Gen, my best friends, stopped at my desk. I loved them but was slightly jarred, because I'd felt Billy getting ready to say something. I leaned toward him, choked up with the fact that this would be my last time speaking to him, ever, ever. But with Clarissa and Gen standing there, he stood up and backed away.

"We're going downtown after school," Clarissa said.

She had short wavy brown hair, big round brown eyes, and she was a little heavy, one of those rare girls who didn't seem to care, who ate what she wanted and called herself "just right with a little left over."

"A little late lunch action at the Burritt?" she asked.

"You skipped lunch?" I asked, and I had, too. School food was basically swill.

"Of course," Gen said. Gen was Korean American, slim with straight black hair. She had taken ballet lessons since she was four and had danced in *The Nutcracker* at the Garde theater in New London. Right now, she stood on her toes and twirled around. Her mind was always on dance.

"I'm craving the Fresco," Clarissa said, licking her lips.

It was our favorite sandwich: tomatoes, fresh mozzarella, and basil on panini bread. We didn't do it often, but we loved going to the oldest hotel in town, sitting beneath the chandelier in the big dining room, eating Frescos, and having tea afterward. Then we'd go to the library for homework or Walnut Hill Park to hang out with our other friends.

"I can't today," I said, thinking of The Plan.

"My father told me it won't be the Burritt much longer," Clarissa said. "They're turning it into condos."

"I still can't," I said, but the news drove tears into my throat. Something else that mattered to me, that was part of my life, about to be gone.

"Okay," Gen said, raising her eyebrows. They worried about me. I smiled to let them know I was fine. I'd gotten good at reassuring people so they wouldn't stress that I'd do something rash, and so they wouldn't bother me—even my best friends. I pretended to look for a book so they'd leave the room without me. I knew, but they didn't, that this was good-bye. I couldn't look them in the eyes much longer.

Clarissa leaned down, giving me a quick hug, squishing me into her body. "We love you anyway, even if you're ditching us. *Jusqu'à la prochaine classe!*"

Until the next class. Which was French, my favorite subject, and the one I did best in. I sometimes wondered why I thrived in foreign languages—French and the language of depression. I excelled in both.

"See you," I said.

I stood up, grabbed my books to run out. But the weird dizziness—a combination of my dark mood and excitement/fear about The Plan—made me drop the books on the floor.

I bent down to pick them up, and so did Billy. I hadn't realized he was still there. I practically jumped. Our heads bumped slightly as we grabbed the books, and I felt a lightning-bolt spark down my spine.

"Sorry," he said.

"It's okay," I said, watching him gather my books. The sight of him helping me, crouched at my feet, made my heart beat so fast, and for just a few seconds the tide of approaching depression stopped.

Billy picked my books up one at a time—English, math, biology, French—placing each in my hands, his fingers brushing mine each time. It was accidental, I was sure, but every touch felt more intense.

We were the last two kids in the room.

"Um, why did you . . ." I wanted to finish the sentence

with *come back?* But I just couldn't; I suddenly had a major attack of shyness.

"What was that?" he asked.

"That?" I asked.

"Yeah. At the end of class. When I turned around. It looked like you wanted to say something." He looked as cool as ever, completely detached.

"Ha," I said, panicking. He was so totally correct it was scary. "I was just exerting my magical powers. I can't help it. My eyes bore into people's hair and, well, I bend them to my will. You just happened to be there. Right place, right time. Ha-ha."

"Oh. Okay."

"Yep." I felt like an idiot.

"So, you're okay?"

Why would he ask that? How did he know I wasn't?

"Oh," I said, trying to sound normal. "I'm fine."

"Gorman, Collins, get moving, you're going to be late for last period," Mr. Anderson said, barking our last names as kids for his next class filed in.

I straightened up, arms full of books. But I was totally rattled because, whether Billy knew it or not, we'd had a psychic interlude. Such was the power of my crush. It wasn't magic at all—just the magnitude of my emotions for him that had made him turn around.

Would he even notice when I was gone?

We walked out of the classroom, and there was an awkward moment in the hall when we had to decide whether we were going to walk to French class together or separately. Things like that mattered. Everyone would notice. He wouldn't want that.

The group home where Billy lived crested a distant hill visible from my bedroom window. At night, when I was alone, I had a consoling ritual that involved kneeling and binoculars. *That* seemed like a magical bond. The problem was at school, seeing him in real life and sensing his indifference to me, my crush seemed absurd and futile.

This year he'd been new to school, and rumors swirled about his life before, what had happened to him. He was distant, seemingly unknowable, and everyone wanted to solve the mystery of Billy. Why would he like me anyway? There were lots of girls who were normal, who hadn't been to a mental hospital. And they all wanted him to take them to the prom. Sit with them at lunch. Text them all night long.

Two of them passed now: Elise Bouchard, with her cheerleader's bounce, always wearing short skirts and a smile that made her turquoise eyes crinkle. Life for Elise was a perpetual football field filled with applause—for her. She was walking with her best friend, Leslie Brooks, who had transferred from a boarding school in Massachusetts, spoke in an almost-English accent, and wore preppy everything—French sailors' striped shirts, pink alligator dresses, cashmere sweaters around her neck—in a way that hugged her perfect body and made everyone, or at least me, feel like a low-class blob in comparison.

I saw Billy glance at Elise and Leslie. They walked straight over to him, and he fell into step beside them. I heard the girls' flirty voices and Billy's low chuckle as they walked him into French class.

Instead of following them and going inside, I passed the classroom door and ran out of school, heading toward home.

My house was about five miles from school. I had daggers in my stomach. I could have waited till the end of next period for the bus—but I was too charged up.

I had a mission. The Plan was clear in my mind. But the pull of depression: It wanted to thwart me. It felt like an opposing force, something that should be taught in physics. It was the opposite of rising, an internal gravity pulling me down. I tasted it in my throat, felt it all through my body. My bones wanted to dissolve and turn me into a puddle. I forced myself to walk fast, to counteract the force.

But every step made me feel I was stepping into a hole or sliding off the earth. The thing about depression: It collides with even the best plans.

I could have called my father, and he'd have picked me up in a heartbeat, but I wouldn't do that: It could mean another trip to Turner.

My grand plan involved not leaning on him, not anymore. I could have called Astrid, my stepmother, but only in another universe and if I was a completely other person or if *she* was.

The air smelled like spring. There were tulips in the gardens, wilted blossoms falling from the magnolia and apple trees, twinkly new-green leaves on the spreading maples and massive oaks. It had rained the day before, and a warm fragrance rose from the still-soaked ground.

My street didn't have sidewalks. We lived in the smallest house in the fancy part of our old factory town, where all the rich industrialists had built mansions around the turn of the last century. That meant no paved walkways, because they preferred their gracious sloping lawns, unsullied by a concrete path, to childhood safety. I was sixteen now, and had been walking home on this street since first grade. I'd learned to tread just enough on the moneyed people's yards to avoid being mowed down by passing traffic. But right now I felt the ground giving way beneath my feet.

I had to hurry. My mission would cure everything—I was sure of it. Once I really got started, over the worst hurdle (i.e., Astrid), I would feel better. My actions would stab depression right in its withered, nasty heart.

I got to my house, a small Cape Cod in a sea of rambling estates, and sure enough, Astrid's car, a white Mercedes, was in the driveway. I straightened my spine. This was do-or-die.

I let myself in through the side door to the weathered barn my parents had turned into a garage. My mother's old green Volvo was just sitting there; I should say *my* Volvo. Mom had left it for me to drive once I got my license, which I had, no problem, but as my father put it in his serious, worried-about-Maia voice, my driving would have to wait until I could prove I was *completely stable.*

Step One of my plan was to sit in my mother's car—it comforted me to call it *her* car, it reminded me of all the rides we'd taken together—until after school got out, when I could saunter into the house as if everything was fine, as if I were *completely stable.*

I reached into my backpack for the key they didn't know I had and unlocked the car door. They assumed they'd taken the only copy from me, but long ago I'd found the one my mother had kept in the little magnetic box in the left rear wheel well. I climbed into the driver's seat.

"Mom," I said out loud. "I'm here. The letters aren't enough . . . I need you, Mom."

But my words were like an incantation gone horribly wrong. The door to the breezeway between the garage and the house flew open, and there stood Astrid.

"Maia," she said, aghast to see me sitting in the car in the closed-up garage. "Who are you talking to? Get out of that car—now."

"Not yet. I just . . . need to stay here for a while," I said, mortified that she had heard me talking.

"The school called to say you missed your last class."

"My stomach hurts a little," I said, hoping to mollify her and nip her annoying faux concern in the bud.

"You mean you're depressed," she said—a statement, not a question. "Do I need to phone Dr. Bouley?" My psychiatrist.

"It's nothing, please drop it," I said.

"Why didn't you call me? I'd have come to get you! Why didn't you tell the office instead of just leaving? You know we worry so terribly, Maia. I see you in this car, the garage sealed up like a *tomb*, talking to your mother . . ."

"It's not like I think she's *here*," I said. "I was just mulling out loud!"

Astrid raised her perfectly shaped eyebrows. She didn't believe me for a second, and it made me furious that she'd intruded on anything to do with my mother, that I had to justify myself to her.

"Get out of that car. Your father would feel the same way—don't you remember last spring?"

Attempted suicide, that's what she meant. No matter how often I'd told them I'd never kill myself, I'd just been starting up the car—it was mine, after all, they hadn't taken it from me yet—to listen to the radio for a few minutes, the exhaust had given them the wrong idea. It was a month before their wedding.

They put me on perpetual, never-ending suicide watch. Don't ever start a car in a sealed garage and then, if you wind up being held in a locked psychiatric facility for a major depressive episode, happen to mention you just wished things would end, just wanted the lights to go out. Especially if your father's about to get married to someone you don't exactly like. Okay, can't stand.

"It's cramps," I said, getting out of the car and walking into the breezeway. "Or something I ate. I just need to lie down, okay?"

She reached out, as if to touch my forehead and feel if I had a fever, but I jumped back. My mother used to do that.

Astrid pursed her lips, hands on her hips. She had short highlighted hair and wore camel-colored wool pants and a white sweater. I knew it was cashmere because Astrid always wore cashmere. She had a thick gold necklace around her neck, with a single square emerald in a heavy setting hanging from it. My dad had given it to her on their wedding day.

"I'm calling your father," she said.

"Don't bother him," I said. "I'll be fine. I'm just tired."

She let me go, up the stairs to my room, and although I walked slowly, appearing to be calm, I clutched the car key in my hand.

Astrid was an accountant and worked from home. *Our* home, my dad's, my mom's, and mine. I passed "her" office—actually my mother's whale room, as I had always called it because it had been lined with bookshelves filled with material about marine mammals, the Arctic, whale communication, textbooks from her days as a grad student in Woods Hole, where she'd studied to become a marine biologist, and from Mystic Seaport, where she'd been the whale-song expert in residence. Her walls had been covered with photographs of humpback, minke, gray, fin, blue, and beluga whales taken on research cruises, and a few framed photos of my dad and me.

Everything of my mother's, except those family photos, had been torn down, thrown out, or stuck in the garage next to the old Volvo wagon—other than the few posters and books I'd rescued—and replaced by Astrid's modern desk, computer, calculator, tax codes, all the things accountants needed. She'd left up my mother's old photos of my dad and me, a fact that dug into my soul. Those pictures had been my mom's—they had been taken during our family times together—and Astrid had no business keeping them.

When I got into my room, I rushed around, packing, ready to bolt. But when I glanced out the window and saw the big brick mansion on a distant hill, I stopped dead.

Billy.

Could I really leave? My father and Astrid—yes, because I was going somewhere better. But Billy. Some would say it was only a crush, but it felt like love.

That hulking estate had once belonged to one of the richest factory owners. When he'd died, he'd left it to the state of Connecticut to be a home for foster children. It was named after him, the benevolent industrialist, the Lytton Stansfield Home. I thought of it as "Billy's Home."

Outside my door, I overheard Astrid on the phone. Obviously she had called my father. Words and phrases like "somatic," "depressed," "talking to Gillian," "the garage," "that damned car," and—naturally—"suicidal" burned my ears.

"Of course it's psychosomatic, Andrew," she said. "It's just like the last time. She had the stomachache, and she started up that car, and that night she was in the hospital. Let me call Dr. Bouley right now and get her admitted. Walking out of school *with just one period left to go*, Andrew. That's another sign."

She talked on and on, her voice clipped and efficient, as if she knew better than my father what was best for me.

Hesitating could be my downfall, but I knew I couldn't leave town, not yet. School was out by now; the buses would be dropping everyone off. I lay the car key on my bureau and reached into the top drawer for my binoculars.

I trained them on the Home. Billy's room was on the second floor, all the way on the right. At night, when the lights were on, I could see him clearly. The Home had always pierced my heart. Even before I knew him I would turn off my lights before bed, kneel by the window with binoculars pressed to my eyes, gaze at the Home, and whisper good night to the parentless kids.

Nine months ago, the night before school started in September, I looked up and spotted a boy I hadn't seen before. He stood at a window—second floor, all the way to the right—staring over the hills with unbearable longing. I kept the binoculars on him for a long time. He was tall and lanky with such tension in his body I felt as if he might fly out the window, to wherever—or whomever—he was thinking about.

The next day a new kid showed up at school: the boy I'd seen in the window. It was Billy Gorman. He had no idea, but I'd claimed him that night. The more I watched him—not that I got to know him, he never let anyone in—the more I cared. I'd see him in that upper right window, sleepless just like me, staring out with a silent yearning that matched my own.

Only mine was for him, and his was for . . . I had no idea. His terrible story was on the news, whispered in huddles outside lockers.

Billy's mother had been murdered. By his father.

It was in all the papers, and on TV, and talked about by everyone in school, town, all through the state. Billy had grown up on the Connecticut Shoreline, but after what happened, he got sent to Stansfield.

Our classmates acted one of three ways toward him: as if he were a celebrity and they wanted to get close to him and learn all the dirt; as if he were a wounded bird and they wanted to heal him; or as if he were a pariah and they were afraid the crime and his tragedy would rub off on them.

But Billy was quiet and kept to himself. He didn't react to any of the kids who sidled up to him or spurned him. Girls of the "wounded bird" school of thought circled around, wanting to draw him close. Clarissa called him "poor Billy." Other kids called him "the murderer's son" behind his back. It made me mad because it reminded me of things kids said after my family fell apart and I wound up in the bin. But Billy just did his schoolwork.

As the school year went on I begged my father—could we adopt him? He needed a real home; could it be ours?

Shocker: The answer was no.

One day in December, just before the first Christmas without his mother, Billy and I stood next to each other in choir. Our music teacher had arranged everyone according to the way we sang harmony. So Billy and I being side by side was accidental, and no one had any idea what it made me feel inside. Not even Gen and Clarissa.

Music books rustled as we prepared to sing "The Birds' Carol."

The audience was packed with parents. My dad and Astrid were there. Billy's arm accidentally brushed mine. I blushed like mad and forced myself to stand stiff instead of leaning into him.

I wanted to say: *I miss my mother so much. Christmas is hard. It must be for you, too.*

Mrs. Draper, the music teacher, rapped on the podium to get our attention, shot us a raised-eyebrow glare to get us to start singing, so we did.

"From out of a wood did a cuckoo fly . . ."

"Ha, cuckoo like Maia," Jason Hollander said under his breath, and he and a few other kids snickered as the song went on.

"Crazy girl!" Pete Karsky said.

Billy cleared his throat—was it a chuckle? My heart practically stopped. It was bad enough being teased by stupid Jason and Pete, but having Billy join the mental-patient bashing made me want to disappear.

My mouth moved, but no words emanated.

Then Billy did something strange. He stared at me with such intensity I felt it in my blood.

"Don't let them get to you," he whispered, looking stern, almost angry. He didn't look away until sounds came out of me again.

Had he been mad at me for screwing up the song by shutting down? Or was he reacting to the boys' meanness, their borderline bullying?

I thought about all that now, in my room, revving up to leave.

My dad was very protective of me. Especially when it came to boys. I'd never even been on a date. He'd been that way since my mother left—when I was thirteen, prime time for me to start really liking boys. He didn't mind my going to dances or the movies with groups, but he kept saying he didn't want me getting hurt.

After I got depressed, forget it. His overprotectiveness went into high gear. Then it became about stability. I might crash at any moment. I wasn't emotionally equipped to handle a boyfriend. If someone wanted to come to the house for snacks while he and Astrid were home, that would be fine. Get this: Astrid said we—this imaginary boy and I—could have those little cocktail hot dogs impaled on frilly-ended toothpicks along with Bugles and her famous cream cheese clam dip, the recipe direct from some supermarket magazine.

I would sooner stick a frilly-ended toothpick in my eye than have Billy come over and sit in the living room while my dad and Astrid sat there summing him up and passing plates of gross snacks.

It was seventy-two-going-on-seventy-three months since my mother had left and eleven and three-quarters months since my father had remarried. I wanted things the way they'd been when it had been just the three of us, pre-Astrid. Cocktail franks had played no part in our lives. My mother was real, deep, and couldn't be bothered making recipes from the Food Network.

Now she wrote me every two weeks, sometimes more often, on cream vellum stationery sealed with red wax.

I'd just gotten a letter from her. She'd sent a picture of herself outside her cabin, on the banks of one of the only fjords in North America. She looked exactly as I remembered her the last time I saw her: just like me, but twenty-five years older, with straw-colored hair, a slightly long nose, and eyes that crinkled when she smiled. Our need for braces was undisputed—we each had two crooked bottom teeth and a space between our front teeth. I'd gotten braces the week before she left and pulled them off myself a month later.

I didn't want my smile to change, to be different from hers.

I loved her letters, and she always said how much she missed me. Everything should have been fine. There were no major triggers in my life. So why was I going off the deep end now? I'd been seeing Dr. Bouley faithfully, once a week. I took my antidepressant every morning, never missed a dose. But I was crashing.

Astrid was still on the telephone. Her voice was nasal and grating; it bothered me all the time, even when it wasn't talking about me to my father.

"Andrew, just look at the calendar if you need to be convinced. Do you think the timing is an accident? Hello, one-year anniversary, sweetheart."

Silence while she listened.

"Yes, you've got it," she said, continuing her rant. "She wanted to spoil it for us, she couldn't help herself, and now, well, it doesn't take Freud to tell us she can't stand the fact of our anniversary."

More silence; my dad must have been talking.

"Yes," Astrid said, lowering her voice. "Talking to Gillian, I heard her. Yes, out loud. Come home now. I'll call Bouley and get things started."

She might as well have said she was calling the men in the white coats. Trust me, there was no way I was going back to the Turner Institute. Never, ever again. Ever.

I knew Astrid would be guarding the stairs, so I locked my bedroom door from the inside, grabbed my duffel, opened my bedroom window, and climbed out onto the roof. My mother had shown me the way when I was seven.

She and I would sit here at night—it didn't matter the season, winter, spring, summer, or fall—and she'd teach me celestial navigation. She let me hold the sextant she'd had since grad school.

"We're the Whale Mavens and Construction Crew," she said. "And my fellow whale maven had better learn how to patch a leaky boat and how to steer by the stars. Show me Polaris."

I pointed at the North Star, and she gave me a long, strong hug that made me feel like I'd gotten straight As, discovered a new constellation, and shown her a rare whale.

"Identification is good, but navigation is hard. Here's how you hold the sextant," she said, positioning my hands on the delicate instrument, made of brass, with a handle and wheels and a long scope. She showed me how to rock it, how to bring a sky object down to the horizon. During the day we did it with the sun, and I thought of what an amazing mom I had: She could tame the sun.

When she had been out at sea on the *Knorr*, her favorite research vessel, she'd learned how to navigate by the stars at night, shoot sun lines at noon, and determine the ship's position at sea.

I couldn't think about that now. A white pine grew close to the house, thick with long needles and smelling of pitch, and I took a leap and landed in the middle branches. I scrambled down the trunk, my hands sticky with pine tar, and slunk around the corner of the house. Reaching into the pocket of my jeans, I found nothing.

That's when I realized: I'd left the car key upstairs, on the bureau next to the binoculars.

Chapter 2

MAY 20
CRAWFORD, CONNECTICUT

Standing by the pine tree empty-handed, tears began leaking from my eyes. That always happened—not actual crying or sobbing, just an inside sorrow pushing itself up through my tear ducts—before I got *really* depressed, when I stood at the top of the slide.

That's how I thought of serious depression, the Real Thing, not just sadness. I thought of it as a big, tall, stainless-steel slide slicked with ice, and once you let go of the supports and started down, there was no stopping or going back till you hit the bottom.

My dad found me standing by the pine tree. He must have sped home to get here so fast. He wore his office clothes, a tweed sports coat and the striped tie I'd given him for Christmas a few years ago. He was the most mild-mannered dad ever, but his expression was wild. Worry, panic. That made my eyes stream even more.

"Maia," he said, freezing in place before lurching forward and grabbing me in a hug.

Then I really started to cry. He smelled like our family, the way we had been: the woods, a salt marsh, the cabin of a sailboat, and a breaching whale. Having him hold me so close made me think of the three of us, our little unit that was never supposed to break apart.

"What's wrong, honey?" he asked. "What happened?"

I mumbled something, not real words, because there *were* no words—nothing had happened. Not one thing I could point to and say, "That's the reason!" If I could, then I could fix it. But this was more like a gigantic, unending, ugly swamp reaching out as far as my eyes could see. I couldn't tell him that because he'd be driving me to Turner before I knew it.

"Come inside," he said, arms still around my shoulders, practically carrying me up the back porch steps and into the kitchen door. When I saw Astrid standing there, in the middle of the room, her hands clasped at her chest as if she was both praying and feeling left out, I closed my eyes.

My dad made me sit down at the kitchen table. *Bad idea, Dad,* I wanted to say. There was my mother's empty chair directly opposite me.

"My stomach hurts," I said, bending over so my head touched my knees. "I told Astrid, and that's all it is. You didn't have to come home."

"She was sitting in the garage, Andrew," Astrid said. "Talking to Gillian as if she was right there."

"Trust me, I knew she wasn't 'right there.' And you don't have to speak as if I'm not here," I said.

"I'm sorry," Astrid said. "Maia, I just can't bear to think of you hurting yourself. That's why I called your dad."

"I told you what I was doing."

"I firmly believe," Astrid said slowly, addressing me but with her eyes locked on my dad's, "that we have to take your cries for help very seriously."

"It wasn't a cry for help!" I said, jumping up.

"They take such good care of you at Turner," she said.

That was so typical, I thought, Astrid wanting to get rid of me so she could be alone with my dad. She probably hoped I'd stay there forever. I pictured those snake pit movies where the patients were in straitjackets and had lobotomies—even though Turner was nothing like that.

"They do, sweetheart," my dad said, sitting beside me, taking my hand. "Do you think you should go in?"

"I don't," I said. "Please don't send me."

He was silent. He stroked the back of my hand with his thumb. It comforted me so much the tears began streaming harder—a paradox. I stared at him, his face blurred. He had hazel eyes, curly graying brown hair, and a long nose. That's something he, my mother, and I had in common: our noses. Seeing the gray in his hair hurt my heart. I didn't want him to get old.

"Please, Dad," I said. He nodded slightly; I saw him relenting.

"Andrew," Astrid said in a firm, insistent voice that

made me want to scream. As if she knew better than my dad and me.

My father held up his hand toward her—to make her stop talking. Victory! That actually gave me a small feeling of happiness.

"I won't take you right now, Maia," he said. "As long as you see Dr. Bouley. We'll do what he recommends. Will you agree to that?"

I nodded. What choice did I have?

Thirty minutes later my dad and I were in his Jeep SUV, an off-road relic from his short-lived bachelor days after Mom left. He had dabbled on Match.com where he'd sought out women who, like us, enjoyed sailing the Atlantic or kayaking or cross-country skiing in New Hampshire.

None of the dates bothered me too much because other than their love of the outdoors they were all wrong: one smoked, one was in the middle of a divorce she wasn't too sure she wanted, and one had six kids, including a daughter who was a persistent shoplifter, who took up most of her time.

The Jeep had come in handy for transporting supplies and duffel bags as my dad and I continued our love of chartering sailboats every chance we got. Then he'd settled down with Astrid. She got seasick and had never learned to swim. That meant no more sailing, no more time on the water.

Dr. Bouley had cleared an hour for me. He always did when I had an emergency, and I felt bad for the patient who got bumped. His office was downtown in an old brownstone behind the library. My dad stayed in the small waiting room with austere black-and-white photos of Crawford on the walls—deserted factories, crumbling smokestacks, the band shell, Walnut Hill Park in winter. The doctor across the hall from Dr. Bouley had taken them.

Dr. Bouley's taste was much different. It was warm.

He greeted me at the door. Tall, skinny, young, with the best smile ever—it filled his eyes and showed his teeth and made him look like a wolf, but in a really good way—he nodded at my father as he let me pass.

His office was cozy.

I sat in my usual seat, a brown leather chair across the office from his. A big Navajo rug covered the hardwood floors, and there were rust-red and pueblo-gold geometric images that reminded me of buffaloes with their mothers, herons with their mothers.

Dr. Bouley always placed fresh flowers on his bookcase. Today he had a tall bouquet of white lilacs. On the walls were framed watercolors he'd done himself: coastal scenes from Newport, Rhode Island, mangroves in the Everglades, and plazas in European towns. He had bright, fluffy blankets—in colors of rose, emerald, azure—folded on the couch in case you got cold.

"How are you?" he asked. He never just sat in his chair. He folded himself into it, and then leaned forward, elbows on his knees, all long limbs akimbo, as if he were a heron himself. His hair was black, his eyes were brown, and his face was always filled with kindness.

"Not so great," I said.

"Tell me what's going on."

"Didn't they tell you?"

"Yes, of course," he said, his face opening in one of his wonderful trademark wolf grins. But it quickly slid away and was replaced by grave concern. "But that's them. I want to hear from you."

"Well, it's true, I walked out of school before last period. I have a horrible stomachache." Although I noticed that, sitting there with Dr. Bouley, the pain was gone, replaced with a wave of guilt, because I knew I wasn't going to tell him about The Plan. "And yes, I was sitting in the car in the garage. And yes, I was talking to Mom. But I knew she wasn't there, I wasn't being delusional. Astrid has no idea what she's talking about. I just miss my mother and wanted to feel close to her. That was my mom's car! I wasn't going to *start* it or anything. Or *do* anything."

"Do?" he asked. Of course he knew what I meant, but he was going to make me say it.

"To kill myself. It wasn't like last year."

"It's almost a year to the day," he said.

That shocked me—he was right, and I hadn't thought of it. I'd heard Astrid mentioning their anniversary, and of course I had that date, June 2, carved into my heart as if it were a piece of granite—a gravestone in my chest. But I hadn't realized that yes—my suicide attempt had been three weeks before their wedding; I'd done it a year ago tomorrow—May 21.

"Huh," I said.

"Are you having suicidal thoughts?"

"No. Honestly."

"Okay. But how does it feel? Is it really just an upset stom-ach? Or are you sad? Or does it feel like depression?"

I shrugged, thinking of the slide.

"On a scale of one to ten . . ."

"I'm not depressed, not really. But I might be on the way there. I've got that slipping feeling. So, maybe a five." Even though it was at least a seven.

He nodded. "Are you taking your medication?"

"Yes."

"You haven't forgotten, missed a day?"

I shook my head.

"Not once?"

"Not once."

He knew me so well. I hated medication, yet I took, or had taken, antidepressants, a mood stabilizer, antianxiety benzos, and even, when things got really bad last spring, an antipsychotic to help me sleep. And I'm not psychotic, don't even think that, psychiatrists sometimes go off-label when prescribing—having you take a medicine designed for one thing when it also helps another. It's legal, I checked.

"Is the medication working?" he asked.

"If by 'working' you mean is it making me gain weight, feel like I'm locked in a coffin, completely numb and dead, with my emotions floating around on the outside, then yes."

He smiled. "Yet you have a stomachache and you can't stop crying and you have that slipping feeling."

"Well, yeah."

"So maybe you're breaking through the meds. Why don't I raise the dose on the Zoloft?"

"Really?"

"Yes."

"You know how badly I want to quit them all," I said. "I've been on them over a year. I'm ready."

"You will be, Maia, but not yet. Okay? Remember how sick you got when you went off them too fast?"

How could I forget? Dr. Hendricks, my doctor from Turner, had stuck me on Ativan a few days before my father's wedding to Astrid. I'd started having panic attacks, horrible spells, a feeling of falling through space. Dr. Hendricks told me the prescription would be temporary, just a few weeks, until I stabilized.

I took it for a month but was sick of my jeans feeling too tight. All I wanted to do was eat cereal and peanut butter crackers. The medications gave me a huge appetite and slowed my metabolism. I decided to cut the pills out and stopped the Zoloft and Ativan cold turkey without telling anyone. The first day was okay, but then I started feeling crazy, wanting to claw the walls, manic, in chaos, and generally thinking I might be dying. I wound up in the ER, on IV fluids and some kind of detox medication.

"You were in withdrawal. You could have had seizures," Dr. Bouley said now. "And you were lucky you didn't. You got too far up."

"I'd like to feel up for a change."

"I mean out-of-control up. That's why the crash was so

bad. No matter what, the medication is a safety net. I worry that without it you'll feel unsupported."

"I have you. You support me."

"When I'm not there," he said, his eyes kind. "Can we take our time figuring out the right time for you to go off?"

"I hate them," I said. "I feel fat."

He tilted his head and smiled in that sweetly indulgent you're-the-only-one-who-thinks-you-are way he had.

"Maia?" he prompted.

"I guess," I said, feeling massively unconvinced. I thought of Billy. For a long time I had wanted to really feel, with everything I had, not just the surface stuff that was left after taking meds. I wanted my old happy personality to come through, so he'd notice. But it didn't matter anyway, now that I was leaving.

"Good. Now, this might seem like we're going in the wrong direction, but increasing your dose of Zoloft will keep you home, for now," he said. "Instead of going to Turner. We can add more appointments, too."

"Hmm," I said. "For *now*?"

"If things get worse, Turner is a possibility."

"They'd just medicate me to within an inch of my life. You know hospitals just want us to be zombies so they can control us."

He smiled, waiting for me to relent and come around. I swallowed hard, asking the big question. "Do *you* think I'm crazy for talking to my mom?"

He shook his head. "I sometimes talk to my dad, and he died five years ago."

"Why are you so reasonable when they're not?"

"They're worried. It's natural."

"My father—or should I say *Astrid*—wants to ship me off as soon as possible. They're just so sure all I want to do is sit in the car and off myself."

"I believe you'd tell me if that's what you wanted," he said. "I've always trusted you to let me know if you weren't safe."

Safe was one of those psychiatric hospital words. It meant you were not thinking about suicide or actively planning to commit it. And Dr. Bouley was right: I would tell him. Even if Astrid believed I wouldn't.

When the session was over, he gave me a hug. Maybe that wasn't what most psychiatrists would do, but Dr. Bouley is not just any psychiatrist. Again, a wave of guilt smashed into me. I hugged him extra hard and said a silent good-bye as I left the office.

"I don't have to go," I said to my dad in the waiting room, handing him the prescription. "To Turner."

"Okay, then," my dad said. "I'm glad."

"Astrid won't be."

"Maia," he said, sighing. "You're wrong about her. You couldn't have a better stepmother. She knows I will always put you first, and that's how she wants it to be."

I didn't want to argue with him. How could she have fooled him so completely? How could he have let her?

As soon as I turned my phone back on, it buzzed with texts from Gen and Clarissa, worried about me for leaving school.

I'm fine, I wrote back to both of them. *Just a minor meltdown.*

How can I help? Gen texted back.

I'm seriously definitely okay, but thanks, I wrote back.

Just tell me you're finer than fine, Clarissa texted, a private joke the three of us shared.

LOL, I wrote back to her.

Stay that way! That's an order! Clarissa wrote. She meant well, but she could be bossy.

On the way to the pharmacy, I looked up at the sky—bright blue, filled with big white clouds. One of them was whale-shaped. I felt my heart flip over, knowing it was a sign. The car windows were open, to let in the spring air, and when we stopped at a traffic light I heard an oriole call.

Soon, soon, soon, the bird seemed to say. *You're leaving soon.*

Chapter 3

MAY 20
CRAWFORD, CONNECTICUT

I couldn't get to sleep, so I grabbed my binoculars. Instead of kneeling, my regular ritual, I wrapped myself in a blanket and climbed out the window and onto the roof. I shivered in the night air, making it hard to hold the glasses steady.

There he was, in the window on the far right. He was doing what he always did: looking into the distance. I sometimes imagined that Billy was watching over me the way I did over him. That fantasy made me feel a hundred times better than medication.

But then he raised his hand, pressed it against the windowpane. For a second I thought, *Oh my God, he's waving at me.* Maybe . . . could he see my house? I started to wave back, then stopped myself. He didn't have binoculars; he couldn't see me. He was touching something else—maybe a ghost.

My heart fell again. Where was the hope? Billy would never like me—I was just lying to myself to think he ever could: I climbed back into my room. I knew I'd better be in my bed when Astrid, inevitably, tiptoed in to make sure I was still breathing.

The way she did that reminded me of *checks*. At Turner, they checked you constantly, every two, five, fifteen, or twenty minutes, depending on how at-risk they thought you were. *Checks* were when they looked in on you to make sure you hadn't hurt yourself.

At Turner there was no privacy.

They even read my mother's letters before giving them to me. They'd removed the crimson sealing wax on the envelope fold because it was hard and sharp and if I broke it off I could use it to cut myself. Or I could swallow it.

I was hospitalized for six weeks, so my room situation changed a few times. I started out in a double with Megan, a high school senior from Georgia. She counted the rhythms of her words and made sure every sentence ended on an odd syllable.

"Why do you do that?" I asked.

"It keeps things in good balance," she said.

I counted: seven.

"But wouldn't even numbers be more balanced?" I asked.

"You might think that, but you would be wrong," she said.

"Megan, even numbers are more balanced than odd."

"It can be confusing to people who don't do it themselves."

I counted—ten syllables! "Hey, that was even!" I said.

"Not true, because 'don't' is a contraction and contractions count as two entirely separate words."

She had me.

She was enormously overweight but never ate in front of anyone. I knew she snuck food because I'd hear her chomping away after dark. One night I woke up and smelled something terrible.

"Checks," Allie, my favorite night nurse, said, opening our door, glancing in, closing the door just enough so the hall light didn't keep us awake.

Hadn't Allie smelled that horrible odor? I climbed out of bed and followed the stench to Megan's bureau. I opened the top drawer, and at first all I saw were her T-shirts and sweatpants. Then I lifted them up: Beneath her clothes the drawer was filled with decaying meat she had hoarded from the dining room. There were maggots.

I threw up and started crying. Well, screaming.

The staff came running. One nurse pulled me away from the drawer, and the other roused Megan from sleep.

"Megan, what is this?" Allie asked. She was young but had silver hair in a near–crew cut and always wore a Red Sox shirt under her white coat.

"How dare she look in my drawer?" Megan asked.

"There's rotten food in there!" I said.

"What I do with my food is my business."

I counted—even at a time like this she was sticking to odd syllables. That made me cry harder. I was in a room with a truly crazy person. And the smell was making me gag.

The staff began disinfecting the dresser and I packed because they were moving me that night. As I left, Megan said good-bye.

"I wish you well, but you should never have looked in my drawer," she said.

"It stunk."

"Maia, you've made quite a dangerous mistake," Megan said.

"Megan, there's no threatening other patients," Allie said.

My about-to-be-ex-roommate stepped closer to me. Her eyes glittered, not with tears, but with fury.

"Don't tell me, it can't be possible, you haven't heard the story of Pandora opening the forbidden box?"

I left the room, counted on my fingers, and stepped back in.

"Hey," I said. "That was even. I think you had too many contractions, and you just ended on thirty."

At that Megan began to tremble. A warble came from her mouth that became a shriek. The staff had to restrain her—literally. I'm talking about a straitjacket and the quiet room—the chamber at the end of the hall with soundproofing and a mattress on the floor, no real bed. It wasn't to punish someone, just to protect them—and me, because her words could be considered a threat. A staff member was assigned to sit on a chair in the room with her, to soothe and keep an eye on her.

Megan hadn't said a word after getting out of the quiet room—not to me, not to anyone at the hospital. I worried that she would never speak again, that I had caused it. My doctors at Turner, and Dr. Bouley, after I returned home, said no, her decision not to speak wasn't my fault, that everyone is responsible for their own wellness.

But I didn't believe it. Being so upset at me had caused her to miss—or add—a syllable. I was pretty sure she counted them to keep from really thinking, or from remembering whatever had caused her pain.

Recalling what she'd said about Pandora's box, I wondered what disastrous thing had befallen her, to bring on the monsters.

I wondered if she was still silent.

It made me sad to think about it. And it was weird, but sometimes when I thought of her I found myself counting syllables.

Chapter 4

MAY 21
CRAWFORD, CONNECTICUT

I went to school. I had to go through the motions before reinstating The Plan.

"Good morning, Maia!" Mrs. Berenson, the vice principal, said with a smile so bright you'd swear she'd just won the lottery.

"Hi," I said.

"You know you can come to me with any problems, don't you?" she asked.

"Yes, thank you, Mrs. Berenson," I said, and forced a smile. She stood there in her maroon print dress and black ankle boots, her upswept chestnut-brown hair, huge round horn-rimmed glasses, and coral-pink lipstick, her gaze making me think two things: that half of her felt sorry for me and half of her was judging me for being a mental case.

My father must have spoken to her, because I wasn't in trouble for ducking out of French yesterday. Maybe she knew it was almost the one-year anniversary of my suicide attempt. My nerves were on edge.

"Hey," Gen said, meeting me at my locker. "Are you okay?"

"Fine," I said.

"Finer than fine?" she asked.

"Finer than finest," I said.

She gave me a skeptical look, as if not really believing me. But we laughed anyway—we always did when we said that. It had started when Gen, Clarissa, and I were thirteen, with a TV ad for Valentine's presents from a local jewelry store. *When you really love her, don't stop at finer than fine. Come to Acton Jewelers and give her finer than finest.*

It had cracked us up: the serious announcer, this couple mooning and gazing into each other's eyes, the man putting a gold heart necklace around the woman's throat.

Clarissa hurried over to us.

"Maia, you're killing me," she said, her face red and her eyes angry. "Disappearing and skipping class, barely texting—what were you thinking?"

"Nothing," I said, stunned.

"No kidding! I thought we were your best friends."

"Of course you are, I was just . . ."

"You're always '*just*,'" Clarissa said. "*Just* getting depressed, *just* going to a hospital, *just* ignoring us—as if we don't worry about you! You never even tell us what brings you down."

The way she said it sounded so critical, a slap in the face. I felt myself turning red.

"She's right," Gen said, more quietly. "We want you to open up. Why don't you?"

"I hate talking about it, you guys," I said, trying to keep my voice steady.

"Well, being so mysterious makes you seem like a drama queen," Clarissa said. "And I'm only saying that because I care."

"Drama queen?" I repeated.

"Maia, skipping last period is a little dramatic," Gen said. "You could have told us, and we'd have helped you get through the end of the day."

I couldn't even say anything. These were my best friends, and after all this time they didn't understand. Sometimes I felt more fluent in French than in friendship.

Gen had English class, and Clarissa had history. We hugged, fake and forced. We had uncovered a rift between us, and it hurt. I couldn't get away from them fast enough. At that moment I believed I would be totally cool with not seeing them again.

The day dragged. I thought I'd never make it to study hall, last period. Our class schedule rotated every day.

I knew I had to stay till the bitter end of class; if I ditched out again, Mrs. Berenson would be on the phone so fast.

I walked toward my favorite seat in study hall, in back by the window. I had brought a graphic novel I was dying to read—I love graphic novels, and this one, *The Secret Igloo*, was about two kids who build a house of ice above the Arctic Circle in Norway. They sleep all summer when the sun shines twenty-four hours a day, and stay awake all winter so they can play under the northern lights. But in spite of how much I wanted to read it, I knew I had to study dialogues from my French book. I'd need more proficiency, where I was going.

But I stopped short.

Billy was sitting at the desk next to mine. He wasn't supposed to be here—I knew his schedule. He had history class. His eyes were cast down, but was he watching me as I approached? It felt that way.

Taking my seat, I felt nervous.

"You don't have study hall now," I said.

"I know," he said.

"You're skipping history?"

"You skipped French class yesterday."

"True."

He shrugged, a dark expression in his eyes. "I can't concentrate on history. It's too nice out. I want to be on the water."

The water? I wanted to tell him there was plenty where I was going, but his scowl warned me not to.

I stared at him, remembering last night, how he had touched the window glass. His eyes were green like a creek with glints of gold and gray stones; right now they were shadowed, and made me think of danger. I got lost, trying to think of something to say, the right question to ask. But he looked away, dismissing me.

I wanted to tell him about my plan.

I wanted him to say he'd miss me.

I wanted to tell him I knew what it was like to be in an institution—Turner, my home away from home.

The hospital was in a rambling old mansion, kind of like the Stansfield Home, but made of fieldstone, with a silvery slate roof and bars on the windows. There was a big garden and acres of hilly land covered with sycamores, maples, and an entire pine forest, scored with trails, for when the patients were well enough to go on walks with staff.

Staff. That's what we called the nurses and aides, social workers and art therapists. The psychiatrists were called doctors. I liked Dr. Hendricks. She was about my mother's age, and she didn't just listen—she gave feedback, like Dr. Bouley. I hated going to the other Turner psychiatrists, like Dr. Grant, who just sat there taking notes, never saying a word. I pictured him with an imaginary pipe, just like Freud.

The patients there were mostly teenaged girls, with the occasional boy. I thought of us all as tigers with thorns in our paws. We were beautiful beasts who'd gotten injured by life, by loss or trauma or shock, and if we could just get the splinters out of our paws, we'd be fine.

My thorn was the fact that my mother had left me.

Megan's was Pandora's box.

Turner Institute was full of tears.

I didn't want them anymore.

The bell rang, and Billy walked out. My eyes filled, looking at his back. I hated good-byes more than anything. And he didn't even know this was one. He would get on his bus and I would get on mine.

Au revoir, love of my life . . .

The whole bus ride, wheels turned in my brain. The biggest one: *Don't forget the key.* Not like yesterday.

When I got to the house, Astrid was home, her white Mercedes in the driveway. With her super-human hearing, I knew I'd have to be smart and fast.

I pulled open the big slanted metal doors that led to the cellar. She'd never expect me to enter that way. Then up the basement stairs, down the short hallway past the kitchen, and up one flight to my room. I held my breath, listening.

I heard the fax machine. She was in her office—my mother's whale room—on the phone again. The whirring transmission made it impossible to hear who she was talking to, but I was glad she was distracted.

Today I was ready. Last night I'd hidden the Volvo key on the ledge outside my window. I grabbed it and stuck it into my jeans pocket along with my cell phone.

Then I dove into my closet, rummaged for the duffel bag that I'd already filled with a fleece, my rain slicker, underwear, extra jeans, my diary, bottles of medication, my toothbrush, the packet of my mother's letters, and all the birthday and Christmas money I had.

"Who's there? Maia, is that you?"

I froze. Astrid had finished faxing and making her call, and her vigilance had kicked in. I heard her footsteps on the stairs and quickly locked my bedroom door, just as she began rattling the knob. That lasted exactly three seconds, and then she ran down the hall. I knew what she'd do next: call my father and try to head me off at the pass.

I had to move fast and couldn't risk her grabbing me if I went through the house. I threw my duffel out the window and, just like yesterday, climbed out and shinnied down the pine tree.

Wind blew through the lilacs. They'd just bloomed, and their scent was stronger than perfume. Tiny purple flowers tossed overhead, mixing with the pine needles. I had lived here since birth; my parents had brought me home to this house, and the smell was as familiar to me as anything in my life. I tore through the trees, made it to the garage door, and hauled the door up in one wild motion.

I hadn't started my mother's car in a long time, but it was an indestructible Volvo station wagon and it fired right up. I backed out, my heart beating so fast it could have run the engine. Wheels squealing, I flew out of my driveway, leaving Astrid running after the car, yelling and waving.

My plan was to hit the highway and disappear, but I had a lump in my throat that made me turn right onto Shuttle Meadow Avenue. My phone buzzed in my pocket. I ignored it. I passed my old elementary school and Heckler Pond, where I had learned to ice-skate, and didn't feel an ounce of sentimentality. Leaving home meant leaving home. You had to abandon old things to the past. I was ready.

But Billy.

Martindale Street wound up the steep hill above the pond. Tall trees shaded it, but every so often I'd glance right, and through the branches could see the opposite rise where my house stood.

My phone kept buzzing, the different rhythms that meant that Astrid, and maybe by now my dad, were both calling and texting. I didn't even look.

I pulled into the circular driveway. The massive brick building, Gothic with spires, arched windows on the first floor, and oxidized green copper roof rose before me. This was a different perspective from any I'd ever seen before; I scanned the upper stories, trying to locate Billy's window, but everything looked different, being so close.

A bunch of kids my age were clustered in a play area full of swings, seesaws, picnic tables, and a jungle gym. I saw Mary Porter, Anna Jacoby, and Kevin Hernandez from school. I could ask them where Billy was. I could do that so easily, but I was frozen in the car.

How many times could I say a private good-bye? I had thought yesterday in English class was it, then in study hall today, and now here I was at the Home. I had to see him one last time.

The car running, I gripped the steering wheel hard with my elbows locked, just begging the stars to let him walk by. That's when I spotted him sitting alone under a maple tree, leaning against the wide trunk. And, as if the stars had decided to answer, he looked up and saw me, too. Then my heart had the biggest jump start ever—he leapt up and came toward me. I got out of the car.

"What are you doing here?" he asked.

"I came to say . . ." I said, but I couldn't get the words out.

He looked in the backseat and saw my duffel.

"Where are you going?" he asked.

"Away," I said.

Our eyes burned into each other. I felt heat in my chest, knowing that this *really* was the last time. I wanted to reach over, touch his hand. I hoped he could read my mind and somehow know he was the only person I'd miss, that I'd come here today because he was, ineffably, mine.

"Away where?" he asked.

"To see my mother," I said.

"Can I go with you?" he asked.

I stared at him. Had I heard right? No, I had to be dreaming.

"Will you take me?" he asked.

It was real. This was happening. His eyes were begging me.

"But people will miss you. They'll wonder where you are," I said.

"I live in a group home," he said, gesturing at the building. "They won't wonder for long."

And then he touched me—just one finger on my wristbone— so quickly I would have thought I'd imagined it if it didn't tingle all through my body.

"I can help you," he said.

"Help me?"

"Yeah, you're running away, right? I know how to do that. No one will catch us," he said. He was already hurrying around the car.

I didn't think after that. I climbed into the driver's seat, he got in beside me, and we sped off.

Chapter 5

MAY 21
HUBBARD'S POINT, CONNECTICUT

Barely five minutes away from the Stansfield Home, I was already checking the rearview mirror.

"Is this your car?" Billy asked.

"It was my mother's," I said. "But yes, now it's mine."

"Why didn't she take it with her?" he asked.

"Where she lives she doesn't need one," I said, looking in the rearview again. I pictured Mom in the road-free wilderness at the fjord's edge. "You're shotgun, so you're navigator. Can you pull up a map on your phone?"

"I would," he said, "but I don't have GPS." He held up his cheap, old-fashioned flip phone.

That's right—the state of Connecticut probably didn't provide foster kids with iPhones and unlimited data. I felt like an idiot.

"Here, you can use mine," I said, fumbling in my pocket.

"I'm picking up on the fact that you think they're already following you," he said.

I guess it was obvious, considering I was looking over my shoulder and in the rearview as often as I was keeping my eyes on the road. I tried to act normal with him, but I couldn't get over the fact that he was here. I was driving along, having an actual conversation with Billy Gorman, and it was hard to keep my voice from cracking.

"Yes," I said. "They'll be looking."

"Look," he said. "I know a few things about being followed. My dad . . ." He stopped for a few seconds, as if deciding whether he wanted to tell me this. "My dad was on the run for a few days before they caught him. Evasive measures, that's what he called them, and how he stayed ahead of the cops. Does your dad know you're going to see your mom?"

"Well," I said, "he'll guess it's in my top three destinations."

"What are your other two?"

I thought a minute. "There aren't any."

"If they think you're going north, get off the highway," Billy said. "And head south."

"But that's the wrong direction," I said.

"Sometimes you have to go the opposite way," he said, "to get where you want to go."

"Well, type the address into GPS."

"No. I know the way. Besides, you should turn off your phone."

"Why?"

"They can use it to track you. GPS works both ways. It shows you where you're going, but also shows cops, or your parents, where you are."

My phone was my lifeline: Gen, Clarissa, YouTube, Instagram, Snapchat, Facebook. But Billy was right—that Find My iPhone feature would kill us. My dad had it on his computer, and all he had to do was click "search," and my mobile would appear as a tiny dot, in real time with an exact location, showing him where to find my phone—and me.

I decided The Plan outweighed texts and social media, at least for now, so I took the next highway exit and handed Billy my phone. He turned it off. I thought of what some kids in school said about Billy, that he was the son of a killer and maybe evil was in his genes. How well did I know him? Could I trust him?

My crush easily overpowered the questions, and here I was, taking evasive measures.

"Where are we going?" I asked.

"Go left here. We're heading to the other side of Route 9 south. It's the old back road, not the highway. The state police will be watching for your car, but they can't cover all the two-lanes. My dad was big on that."

"He told you?"

Billy didn't answer.

The narrow road, dappled with shade, followed the Connecticut River. We passed white churches and big old houses. A square granite building, a juvenile detention center—a jail for kids—had bars on the windows, a reminder of Turner. But most of what we saw was beautiful: white horses grazing in a field, a family of deer in a birch grove, kids in a blue convertible, blowing their horn and waving when we passed them.

I began to relax. So did Billy. With only the gear shift between us, I felt crazy-thrilled. Our anxiety drifted out the open windows. He laughed, for no good reason, and so did I. He reached over to jostle my shoulder; involuntarily I reached up and gripped his hand—just for a second.

"We did it," he said. "We got away!"

"Woo-hoo!" I said.

"When I woke up this morning I didn't expect to be on a road trip this afternoon."

"Ha," I said, pleased at how happy he sounded.

"But it's not legit yet," he said. "It won't be till we get snacks. We're gonna need lots of snacks," he explained.

"Should we look for a store?"

"Let's get a few more miles under our tires," he said.

"Then we'll load up," I said.

He nodded. "The other key element," he said, "is music."

He turned on the radio. Ariana Grande came on, but he pressed the SEEK button and stopped at one of the low ninety-point-something numbers, where alternative and jazz stations lived. A saxophone, deep and alluring, played; I glanced over at him.

"This is your music?" I asked.

"Yeah, it's John Coltrane. You don't like jazz?"

"I do," I said, even though I'd hardly heard any. "It's just odd for a high school kid."

"Not for me."

The mystery of Billy continued. I glanced over. "How did you start listening?"

"A trip to New York City," he said, and left it there.

The station played another set and, at the end, the host said the artists had been Thelonious Monk, Chet Baker, and Charlie Parker. "Next up, All Blues."

"Miles Davis, my favorite," Billy said, turning up the volume. I paid extra attention to the soft trumpet and heard passion and desire. I wondered what Billy had been doing in New York that had led him to this music.

Across the river, a sprawling, white-domed nuclear power plant took up acres of land. We passed through small towns with hardware stores and coffee shops, ponds and streams. This was not the land of malls or Walmarts. Forty miles after leaving Crawford, we crossed a wide bridge over the estuary, and we were in Black Hall.

"My family used to go to a beach near here," I said. I recognized familiar landmarks: the boat launch, bait shop, fish store, and ice cream stand. Beyond the river's mouth, Long Island Sound sparkled blue in late-afternoon light.

"This is near where I grew up," Billy said. "Where we lived. Stay on Shore Road. I'll tell you when to turn."

"But shouldn't we keep going?"

"Definitely—this is just a pit stop. I have to get some stuff."

When he gestured, I pulled a right under a train trestle.

An old-fashioned wooden sign said *HUBBARD'S POINT* in carved script. The road wound past a small cemetery filled with oak trees, up hills lined with tiny cottages that all seemed to have colorful shutters with sailboats, anchors, or pine trees cut into the wood.

There was a round boat basin and a sandy parking lot, a crescent beach wrapped around a blue cove of Long Island Sound. Billy inched down in his seat, barely able to see over the dashboard. We passed two women power walking; I figured he didn't want them to see him. He directed me through the parking lot, to the road that ran the length of the beach, dead-ending at a marsh.

"Pull behind this house," he said of the last house on the right. It was small, not at all fancy, two stories with a front porch. There was a FOR SALE sign in the front yard.

I did, tires crunching on a drive made of crushed clam and oyster shells. I felt them sink down, as if the driveway was built on sand. The cottage was pale blue, the paint fading, clearly weathered by salt air and storm breezes. The windows were shuttered. A rusty red truck parked near the marsh was up on blocks, the wheels taken off. The place was deserted.

I parked. The car was completely hidden under a portico built of simple two-by-fours and wide pine slats. I always noticed things like that, because my mother had given me my own tools for my twelfth birthday, helped me build a tree house, shown me how to chop wood. She said someday we'd build our own house on a cove full of whales. We were the Whale Mavens and Construction Crew, after all.

"Who lived here?" I asked. It was obvious no one did now, and my muscles tightened waiting for Billy to say he had, that this was where his mother had been killed. I remembered everyone saying it had happened in the family house.

"My grandparents," he said. "It's their summer place; it's not winterized. But they don't come anymore. My grandmother died right after my mother, and my grandfather moved away and turned into a hermit."

"I thought maybe the house was yours," I said, wondering about the tone in Billy's voice. "You mentioned that you grew up around here."

"Next door," he said, pointing as we got out of the car.

That cottage was almost identical in design. It was missing a few weathered silver shingles. It had white shutters. No, as I looked more closely, they were cream, the color of the inside of a shell. One on the second floor had pulled loose from its hinges and was banging in the wind. I felt cold inside, seeing the place where his mother had been murdered.

Billy reached under a loose board at the back of his grandparents' house. He found a key and unlocked the back door. The house was dark, with arrows of light slanting through the shutters. It smelled musty, like dust, mildew, and sea air had been trapped all winter. Old sheets covered wicker furniture. The walls were natural wood, and there were bookcases on either side of a stone fireplace. The room felt cozy, and I was suddenly so sleepy I wanted to curl up on a sheet-covered sofa—just for a few minutes. I couldn't help yawning.

Billy walked into the kitchen and started rummaging

through drawers. He pulled out some wrenches, a screwdriver, and a handful of something that clanked. Coins? I wondered. A row of ginger jars sat on the counter, and he went straight for the one in the middle. He raised the lid, took out a key ring, and closed it again.

"What are you doing?" I asked.

"We have to ditch your car," he said. "The police will be looking for a Volvo wagon, and they know your license number."

"I can't do that," I said. "There's no other way to get to the boat that will take me to her. And it's far."

"There is a way," Billy said, holding up one large wrench and opening his hand to reveal a bunch of lug nuts. "The truck."

"It doesn't have wheels."

"They're under the house. I can put them on, but we have to wait till dark. The neighbors . . . well, they're nice but nosy. It would turn into a big thing if they saw me here."

"Why, you're allowed, aren't you? It's your grandparents' place."

"It's for sale," he said. "So is our house next door. Well, officially my grandparents own it. They called it 'the Molloy compound.' Like the Kennedy compound, I guess."

"But you're Billy Gorman."

"Gorman's my dad's name."

"Oh, yeah. Right," I said, feeling dumb.

"The Molloys—my mother's family—built these cottages."

"Won't they be yours someday?" I asked. "Or do you have brothers or sisters, cousins?"

"Nope," he said. "The proceeds of the sale are going to Connecticut Victim Services. I'm an only child, and so was my mother."

"These grandparents were her parents?"

He nodded. "They hate my father. And they hate me."

"Because you're his son? You're also your mother's—their daughter."

"It's complicated," he said, his voice sharp.

He turned away. I couldn't understand why their feelings for his father would carry over to him. Why hadn't they tried to take care of him instead of sending him to foster care? Why couldn't the proceeds of selling the beach cottages be used to help him pay for his education, support him so he didn't have to live in the Stansfield Home? It seemed his grandfather was his only relative left, and now he was a hermit. Billy had been abandoned.

"It's dinnertime," he said. "Let's eat."

He went into a small pantry off the kitchen. The shelves were full of canned goods, and he chose a few and carried them to the stove. Ten minutes later he filled our plates with tiny hot dogs, brown bread, and baked beans.

We ate every bite. Outside the sun was setting. Soon it would be dark. We cleaned up. While putting dishes away I kept glancing over at him. His jaw was set, tense, as if he was holding a lot of feelings inside.

"Maia," he said, "I'm gonna go next door. You can wait here if you want. It might be better if you did."

I shook my head. "I'm coming with you."

He stuck the screwdriver in his back pocket. We went out the back door and crossed the narrow strip of beach grass between the cottages. My feet sank, and sand got into my sneakers. The weathered stairs led to a small porch, and I noticed there were several small towers built of beach stones— the largest and widest on the bottom, narrowing to the tiniest stone at the top.

I thought there might be another key hidden here, but instead Billy pulled an empty garbage can close to the house, turned it upside down, and hopped up. He jimmied the screwdriver around the window frame, removed the pane of glass, and reached in to unlock the window. Easing up the sash, he crawled inside.

I felt two ways: nervous that he was so good at breaking into a house and admiration that he knew his way around tools and woodwork. When he opened the back door he grabbed my hand hard and pulled me in fast. I stumbled and fell against him.

"We really can't be in here," he said. "My grandparents' house is one thing, but this is different."

He let go of my hand, but my skin tingled as if electricity had run from his fingers through mine. My heart thumped, and I had to steady myself after crashing into his chest. I was glad the sun had almost set because these windows were not boarded up, and I wouldn't want him to see my cheeks—they felt hot and I knew they were bright red.

He stood still for a minute, looking around the kitchen. I tried to see what he was seeing; even in the fading light the bright colors struck me. A turquoise table, yellow chairs, white curtains with red ball fringe. A light fixture hanging over the table by a chain; the shade was stained glass, a mosaic of jewel colors in the shape of dragonflies. There were more stone towers, smaller than the ones on the porch, on the windowsill over the sink. Someone who loved her family had decorated this kitchen.

"What are these?" I asked, pointing at the stones.

"They're called cairns," he said. "My mom and I always picked up stones on the beach and built them."

I walked over to the refrigerator. On the wall next to it were five framed drawings obviously made by a child: a house, a family of three, a boat, a bridge, and a big fluffy dog. Each was signed *Billy*, and an adult had penciled in dates. The most recent was ten years ago, when Billy would have been about six. There were also framed snapshots of Billy at different ages: skating at Rockefeller Center, in front of dinosaur bones at the American Museum of Natural History, in Central Park by that big fountain with the angel.

"New York City?" I asked.

"She loved Manhattan," he said. "It was her favorite place."

I thought about that. While my mother loved whales and wild nature, his mother had loved the city.

"How about you?" I asked.

"We had good times there," he said, his gaze lingering on the photos. In one, in front of the Statue of Liberty, Billy and a little golden-haired girl waved at the camera. They were about seven, and grinning. In another photo, taken outside the Village Vanguard, they were teenagers.

"A jazz club," he said, noticing my curiosity.

"It looks cool," I said. But my interest was really about the girl—she was totally chic in skinny jeans and a black leather jacket, big square glasses, straight yellow hair, and red lipstick. "She's pretty," I said. "Does she live in New York?"

"No," he said coldly, shutting down any more questions.

He headed toward the stairs, and I followed him, but we stopped short at the foot. There were scraps of yellow tape, the kind police use at crime scenes, still attached to the wall. Billy pushed aside a braided rug, and I gasped. People had cleaned it up, but there was a big white splotch on the dark fir floor.

Billy took my hand again and walked me around the spot—I had the feeling it wasn't to help me, but to protect the area itself. The shiver that ran down my spine told me it was where his mother had died.

"Were you here?" I asked.

"I was," he said. "And this is my first time in the house since that day. Since I found her, right there."

"Why . . . why did you want to come back?"

"Because this was our house," he said. "It's our home. And she . . . there was nothing I could do to help her."

He stared down for a long time. Then he shook his head as if dislodging memories or a scene he'd rather forget.

"We've got to get my money," he said. "If the police didn't find my hiding place."

We stepped over the stain and went upstairs. It felt strange going into his bedroom; it looked so normal, with posters of racing sailboats, a desk, and bookcases filled with the Harry Potter books, *The Golden Compass*, *Artemis Fowl*, *The Book Thief*, *Looking for Alaska*, *Eragon*. I'd read them all, too.

There was a poster of the New York Public Library, and tacked to it a snapshot of Billy, his mother, and that same little blond girl standing next to one of the lions on the wide front steps.

"They're named, you know," he said.

"Who?"

"The lions. Patience and Fortitude. My friend and I called each other after them. She was Pat and I was Fort."

"Where is she now?"

"It doesn't matter," Billy said. His voice didn't invite further questions.

A billow of fine orange cloth hung over his bed like a canopy.

"Is that . . ." I began.

"A spinnaker," he said. "It's a kind of sail, made for light air. It was on my grandfather's boat."

I nodded. "We sailed, too," I said.

"We were happy on boats," he said, touching the spinnaker, making it flutter. Then he climbed onto his bed and reached onto the ledge above the window. He felt along the top, caught hold of a piece of fishing line. He grinned, pulling up a leather pouch hidden in the wall. "Score," he said.

"Looks like a lot," I said, admiring the thickness of the pouch.

"Yeah," he said. "I saved up."

"Birthday money?" I asked, thinking of my meager wallet.

"I had a paper route starting when I was eight, and then I worked on the beach crew, raking seaweed and painting the benches along the boardwalk. And my grandfather paid me to help with his lobster business. I hauled pots all summer, scraped barnacles off them in winter. I'd catch fish for bait."

He sat on his bed and gestured for me to sit beside him. I did and the springs creaked beneath us and I could barely catch my breath. I stared at his hands. They looked strong. I wanted to put my palm against his to compare the size. Or maybe I just wanted to touch his hand.

He counted out two hundred and seventy-six dollars and gave me half.

"In case we get split up," he said.

"We won't," I said.

"You don't know," he said. "You can plan to stick together as tight as you want, but people lose each other when they least expect it. Whenever my mother and I got on the train to New York, she made me stick a twenty-dollar bill in my shoe. You have to plan for emergencies."

"Okay," I said. It made my heart race to have him confide

in me this way, share his money with me, as if we were really in this together.

He filled a canvas bag with clothes, a big manila envelope, a flashlight and extra batteries, and then we headed to the stairs. He looked around as if wondering if he'd ever come back to this house again. When we got to the big white blotch, he stopped. I knew without asking that it had been made by bleach, or strong cleaning fluid, that it had burned his mother's blood out of the floor, from where she'd landed when his father had pushed her.

He crouched down, put his hand palm-down on the floor. He sat that way for a long minute. When he lifted his hand, he kissed his fingers. The sight of him doing that made my eyes sting with tears. I had the feeling of intruding, and I turned.

When we walked out of the house, it was dark. We worked fast. If Billy was impressed by how I could lift the truck's heavy wheels off the pallets where they'd been stored, by how I knew how to use the jack, crank the truck—its body lacy with rust—up off its blocks, by the way I knew how to use a wrench, how to fasten the lug nuts quickly and in the dark, in the tiniest sliver of light from the streetlamp on the dead-end street, he didn't show it. My mother had taught me to lengthen my grip on the wrench for more purchase, to tighten the nuts with one, two, three strong pulls. I knew my way around tools.

It took over an hour, but we did it, we got all four wheels on the truck. The battery was dead so we used my mother's car for a jump. The engine fired right up. Billy went back into his grandparents' house to grab the rest of the canned food. I took the time to drive my mother's car back under the portico, to hide it from anyone passing by.

The car still smelled like her, a combination of the leather seats, her lemon-sage shampoo, and paper: the books she read, the notebooks she filled with observations and drawings of whales.

Instead of feeling sad or on the edge of depression, thinking I might never see her car again, I felt elated. For the first time since she'd left us, left me, I was on my way to her. And I was going there with Billy.

I got out of the car just as he came outside, carrying bags of food and supplies. He stuck them behind the seat with everything he'd brought from his house. I noticed the manila envelope sticking out of his canvas bag.

"What's that?" I asked.

"My birth certificate, some pictures, a couple of cards from my mom."

We climbed into the truck and drove away from the houses. He didn't go past the boat basin this time; he took a different road and idled in front of a cottage with lights blazing and the blue glow of a television.

His gaze was hard and steady. He'd said he didn't want anyone to see us, but stopping out here felt so defiant, as if daring the people inside to come out and see us. If they did, our trip would be over before it started. He was gripping the steering wheel so tightly, his wrist felt taut like wire when I touched it, to remind him we had to get back on the road.

"We should leave," I said. "Before anyone sees us."

He didn't reply and he didn't take his gaze off the house. There was a streetlight overhead, and I saw his eyes glinting— bright with sadness or anger or both, I wasn't sure.

"Who lives there?" I asked.

He was silent another minute. "No one," he said. I had a really strange feeling—it was the way he stared with such intensity. I wanted to press him, to find out who was in that house. But the look in his eyes let me know I shouldn't, so I kept my questions inside.

Then we drove away.

Chapter 6

MAY 22
MYSTIC, CONNECTICUT

I woke up suddenly, out of the deepest sleep ever, with Billy's head on my shoulder.

OMG, OMG, this is real, not a dream.

I remembered that we'd fallen asleep on our own sides of the truck, sitting up and leaning away from each other against the doors. Now I was wedged into the corner, and Billy was dead weight against my left side.

We had parked in a shipyard in the seaport town of Mystic, to catch some sleep before really getting on the road. Now the sun was rising, just peeking over the boat sheds. I hardly moved, partly not wanting to wake Billy and partly because I couldn't—I was trapped. My left arm had pins and needles, but I didn't stir; I wanted this to go on forever.

I'd been sleeping next to Billy. Our shared body heat felt like a furnace, keeping us warm in the chilly dawn air. I shook my head to clear the cobwebs away—he was so close, right here with me; he'd found his way onto my shoulder. I couldn't believe it. I flexed my numb hand a little.

"Hey," he said, waking up, but not opening his eyes. "You tickled me."

"I'm sorry," I said. "I couldn't feel my fingers."

"I forgive you." He stretched, moving to his side of the seat. I wanted him to come back, warm me up again. But he opened the truck door. "Breakfast," he said.

He bent down to pull his wallet out from under the front seat.

My heart was pumping so hard. I took the chance to quickly palm my pills when he wasn't looking. I gulped them down. They nearly choked me, but I couldn't take the chance of waiting till we found breakfast and a glass of water. One thing was for sure, I'd never let Billy know I was on medication.

We had a long way to go on this trip, and I knew we had to make our money last, but my stomach was growling. We followed the smell of coffee to a silver diner a half block away. The early shift of boatyard workers had jammed the booths, but we found two stools at the counter and ordered bacon and eggs. I had rye toast, he had white, and we both had coffee.

"Okay, why did we come to Mystic?" he asked. "You started telling me last night."

"I have to figure out exactly where my mother is," I said.

He nearly dropped his fork. "I thought you knew."

"In a general way," I said. "She always sent photos, and I know she lives on a fjord, so once we get there, I'll recognize the exact spot. But I write to her at a post office box in Tadoussac. Not an actual address. It's a big area."

"Where's this big area?"

"Canada," I said. "Across the Saint Lawrence River from Maine, a couple of hours east of Quebec City."

"Maia, I don't have a passport."

"I think you only need a license. Or any government ID."

"You *think*?"

I nodded. "I thought I was going alone," I said. "And I always carry my passport in my backpack, just in case I hear from her and she wants me. I didn't plan on you coming."

"Well, I've got my license and birth certificate," he said, frowning. "I guess I could go with you as far as the border. And if I can't get across . . ."

"You'll get in," I said with more assurance than I felt.

We finished breakfast and walked along the water toward the Seaport. Kids were waiting for the school bus. They stared at us, and I realized how out of place we looked, walking in the opposite direction. Sun glinted on the Mystic River. The tall dark masts of the ship *Charles W. Morgan* looked stark against the blue sky. I felt nervous and paused on the stone-and-pebble-strewn path.

Crouching down, I found the largest, flattest stone and placed it on the wall that ran along the river. Billy leaned down beside me and balanced the next biggest stone on top of mine. Without saying a word, we kept doing that till we had a cairn. We grinned at each other, left our tower where it stood, and kept walking.

It seemed ironic, my mother loving whales so much but working part-time as a researcher here at the Seaport. She'd been a specialist on the *Morgan*—a hundred-and-six-foot-long ship built for whaling in 1841. She had raised me to love whales, from my earliest days, and the first time she took me belowdecks and showed me the tryworks, large cast-iron pots set into the furnace to render the blubber of the whales they hunted, I cried.

"Why did they kill the whales?" I asked.

"Back then they converted their fat into whale oil," she said. "And it was used to light people's houses, streetlamps, whole cities."

It made me sick; I swear I could smell the dying whales, and hear them crying, and I threw up on her shoes. She didn't get mad. She just hugged me.

"My sensitive girl," she said, rocking me back and forth. "My fellow Cetacean Maven." Sometimes she said "cetacean" instead of whale—it was their scientific name, from the clade *Cetacea*.

I remembered that moment as I led Billy down the paths of the reconstructed nineteenth-century maritime village. The houses and buildings were real, and old. They'd been transported from all over, set down here to attract tourists and school kids. When the Seaport opened, the "town" would come alive with people dressed in costumes as blacksmiths, riggers, coopers, and sailmakers.

I pulled my phone from my pocket. I hesitated—what could it hurt, turning it on for just a minute, to take a couple of photos? It was so early, my father and Astrid wouldn't be awake yet.

"Hey," I said to Billy. He turned to look, and I snapped a shot—his wide mouth half-open, hair falling in his eyes, ship masts behind him.

"You gotta turn that off," he said.

"One more," I said. I raised the phone, but he took it from me. His arm came around my shoulders, and he extended it, took a selfie. I couldn't believe it. When he handed me the phone and I saw us smiling on the screen, it took everything I had to not post it to Instagram. All I wanted was for everyone to know I was with him. Instead, I just tucked my phone back into my pocket.

I'd assumed we couldn't get into the Seaport before the gates opened, but Charlie the security guard recognized me and waved.

"Hey, Maia!" he said, walking over. "Look at you, all grown up. What are you doin' here? Taking a walk down memory lane?"

"Sort of," I said, my mouth dry. I was relieved to know the word hadn't spread to Charlie to be on the lookout for me. Maybe my dad figured the Seaport was too much in my past and that I'd be heading somewhere more pertinent to the future.

"Don'tcha have school?"

"Not today," I said.

"Ah, okay. You decided to bring your friend here, show him around?" he asked, sizing up Billy.

"Yes. He's never seen whaling ships," I said.

"Well," Charlie said. "Why don't you wait in the ticket office till we open up? We'll let you in no charge, of course.

But you can't be wandering around before the full staff is here. I'd letcha, but rules, you know."

"Charlie," I said, my heart pounding so hard I thought it would burst. "Could we wait in the Seamen's Library instead? That was my favorite spot when I was little. I loved all the books."

He squinted, deciding. "Sure," he said. "Busy yourself in there. A good place to wait till opening time."

"Thank you," Billy and I said at the same time.

Charlie glanced at his watch, then led us to the little one-room yellow building. The sign above the door said SEAMEN'S FRIEND SOCIETY READING ROOM. My fingers twitched, wanting to grab the exact volume that would tell me what I wanted to know. He unlocked the door with a master key.

"Now you stay put here," he said. "I want to know where to, uh, find you, when we open. That's about an hour from now, so you just make yourselves at home. Don't go wandering around!"

I nodded, and Charlie left us. I looked at the long Shaker bench where I'd sat with my mom as she'd shown me her favorite books and told me the facts and discoveries she was making in her research. I looked at the narrow cupboard that held the library of volumes Peary had taken on his North Pole expedition.

"You better get what you need, fast," Billy said, standing just inside the door, gazing out.

"Why?" I asked, suddenly wanting to stay for hours, sinking into the comfort of memory and the feel of my mother's presence.

"Because ol' Charlie is a good actor," Billy said. "He's on his cell phone right now, calling someone about us. Or maybe someone called him. Did you turn off the phone after you took the photo?"

I fumbled in my pocket—I hadn't. "Oh, no," I said.

"They're tracking you," Billy said. "Charlie's still talking—okay, now he's heading over here. He's hurrying, Maia. He's got his hand up like a stop sign."

I barely thought. I went straight for the small green book with flaking gold leaf on the cover, jammed it into my waistband, and lurched after Billy out the door.

"You kids stay right there!" Charlie yelled. "Don't move, Maia. I've got orders to keep you here."

Billy grabbed my hand and we started running in the opposite direction from where we'd parked the truck. We zigzagged through backyards and side streets, staying as close as possible to buildings and hedges, finally reversing course and making our way along a seawall to the shipyard.

"More evasive measures?" I asked, out of breath.

"My father taught me at least one thing worth knowing," Billy said.

By the time we climbed into the truck, we saw two police cars speeding past, toward the Seaport. I'd thought Charlie had been on the phone with my dad, but now it was even more serious. If they knew I'd stolen *Beluga and Humpback Whales of Saguenay Fjord*, the classic book written by Laurent Cartier in 1898, I'd be in even more trouble than for running away. The book was valuable—to me, it was priceless.

"They'll be looking for the Volvo," I said, giving Billy an admiring smile.

"Yeah," he said. "Till they figure out you're with me, we'll have a good head start. Even then they might not know about the truck."

I ducked down, and Billy drove the opposite way from where we wanted to go, avoiding the Seaport. We got stuck at the drawbridge for ten incredibly nerve-racking minutes, but then we rumbled through town and onto I-95.

"Which way now?" I asked. "Basically north, but we still need a map. You said that yourself."

Billy shot me a stern glance across the seat. "Why did you have to take that book? Couldn't you just have looked up what you needed?"

I turned my face away, feeling stung.

"There wasn't time," I said. I couldn't tell him the truth: I wanted the book. My mother had held it in her hands. She had lovingly turned the pages, pointing out intricate line drawings of marine mammals, of the fjord's soaring cliffs, and shown me the pages about the exact spot we'd build our cabin, for the Whale Mavens and Construction Crew. This was our own personal guide to life.

"My father was a thief," Billy said. "He did a lot of other bad things, before he hurt my mother. He ripped people off, took what wasn't his. I don't like people who do that."

"What about you, taking this truck?" I asked. "Are you so perfect?"

"The truck's mine," he said.

"No, you told me your grandparents were selling the houses, not giving you anything," I said.

"Before all that happened," Billy said, "my grandfather told me the truck belonged to me. He taught me to drive in it, when I was just thirteen, three years before I got my license. We'd catch lobsters together, take them to the market, and he'd let me drive home on back roads. He said it was mine, and he never got the chance to take it back."

"Oh," I said.

"My grandfather was more of a father to me than my dad. I don't want to be anything like my dad, and I don't want to be with someone who is."

"I'm not like that," I said. I wasn't. I'd thought Billy understood the desperation I felt, the way I'd do almost anything to get to my mother.

"Yeah, whatever," he said harshly.

"I'm not!"

"What people do matters way more than what they say," he said.

"Why'd you run away with me if I'm so horrible?" I snapped.

He just drove, not answering me. I squirmed in my seat, clutching the book. I didn't care what Billy said—I was glad I'd taken it. This was my mission, not his. He didn't understand a thing.

"Give me your phone," he said, after about ten silent minutes.

"Why?"

"Because your dad used it to find you once. You want to get to your mother, don't you?"

"Of course," I said. I pulled the phone from my pocket and stared at it.

Again, a long wait before he spoke.

"Everything matters," he said. "Every detail. I didn't pay attention before. I missed everything. If I'd been watching, really listening, I would have known something terrible was about to happen."

"To your mother?"

"Yes." He paused. "I can't," he said, an edge of ice in his voice. "I can't let bad things happen. To anyone. When I see something bad I have to stop it. From now on, that's how it has to be. You can't steal again, Maia. It's for your own good— you're not going to feel right if you do it."

"I won't."

"And if you don't want your father to find you . . ."

My emotions felt like fire. I heard a dial click; he was trying to turn on the radio.

"I forgot," he said. "It doesn't work."

I didn't care. All I really wanted to hear was the sound of his voice. I wanted him to say more about protecting people. About protecting me.

I rolled down the truck window, and as we drove north through the countryside, past farms and low green hills, I threw my phone out the window. And even though Billy's phone didn't have GPS, he threw his out, too.

Chapter 7

MAY 22
PROVIDENCE, RHODE ISLAND

he time has come," Billy said, about ten miles after we'd ditched our phones.

"For what?"

"The most key part of any road trip. I said it before."

"Music? But the radio doesn't work."

"Food! Lunch and snacks!"

I smiled. There's nothing like a quest for junk food to clear the air. We saw road signs for Providence and veered off, toward the east. From a distance I spotted a couple of downtown towers, some church steeples, and a hill covered with redbrick houses that looked rosy in the sunlight.

"Hey, the Superman Building!" Billy said, pointing. And he was right—the tallest building stepped upward into the sky, the stories diminishing in size, all the way to the two-story turret. It was straight out of a movie.

"Can you leap it in a single bound?" I asked.

"Just watch me," he said, laughing.

But we angled up the hill, past Brown University's stately wrought-iron gates, and parked on Thayer Street. We were in a very college-y-looking neighborhood. Students in denim jackets and sleek sneakers walked by in twos and threes and singly, backpacks over their shoulders.

Billy and I strolled down the street, jostling our way through the college kids. I wanted to go into every shop—the Brown Bookstore; a shop that sold gauzy white peasant shirts, tie-dye tees, and Indian print skirts; Urban Outfitters; a little boutique called Zuzu's Petals. The old-fashioned-looking art deco Avon Cinema was showing a movie called *Miles Ahead*.

"Hey, a movie about Miles Davis!" I said, spotting the poster.

"No way," Billy said.

"Should we see it?" I asked.

"No, have you forgotten? We have something way more important to do."

"Drive to Canada?"

"Food, Maia," he said, bumping me with his shoulder. "Stay focused!"

We had a little wrestling match right there on the sidewalk, shoving each other, and I laughed, my heart bubbling over as students circled around us.

We stopped into the Provvie Mart and loaded a basket with Cape Cod Chips, gummy bears, Hershey's kisses, cheese doodles, and a six-pack of Sprite. At the last minute I asked the clerk for a disposable camera. Billy rolled his eyes, but he didn't object.

That photo of us on my iPhone was haunting me. If I couldn't have that one, I'd make sure we took others.

I saw Billy counting his money after we left the cash register.

"Are we doing okay?" I asked as I ripped the yellow foil wrapping off the camera.

"Yeah, as long as we're careful, just buy necessities." He lifted the bag of snacks. "Which these are." I snapped a shot, caught his grin.

We left Providence and drove an hour before stopping for fuel. Filling the tank was a huge wake-up call. The gauge didn't work, and we'd been lucky we hadn't run out. It cost fifty-three dollars, a chunk of Billy's money, to fill it with diesel. He checked the oil, added a quart, and bought a Road Atlas for the United States and Canada, for a grand total of seventy dollars and thirty-six cents.

"That's sobering," I said.

"This thing eats fuel," he said, patting the dashboard. "But it will get us there."

I opened the atlas. Everyone I knew relied on GPS and had trouble reading an actual map. Not me. Thanks to my mother obsessively teaching me navigation, I knew how.

Billy and I drove on. We avoided I-95 and aimed for the back roads that would take us in a big circle around Boston, along the New Hampshire coast into Maine, and up to the Canadian border.

"Since they know about Mystic," Billy said, "they probably figure you're on the way to see your mother. They'll call her, right?"

"My parents aren't exactly on speaking terms," I said.

"But if you're involved, they'll make an exception. To take care of you," he said.

"My mother is hard to find," I said. "She's on boats a lot. And she lives so far up the fjord, in the boondocks, there's no reception. She doesn't even have a cell phone. We write each other letters."

"But she has email, right? To stay in touch with other researchers or whatever?"

"Yeah," I said. "She does." It was a sore point, but I wasn't about to say anything. I used to email her all the time, and she never answered.

"The mavens write on stationery and use stamps and sealing wax," Mom had said. And that's how it was: She'd sent me a brass seal imprinted with a spouting whale and sticks of special wax made in Paris from ground limestone, pine resin, lacquer, and carmine-colored dye made from cochineal—the bright red shells and wings from a certain insect in Peru.

"So your father will email her," Billy said. "To tell her to expect you. And they'll be watching for you along the way."

"She'll be glad to see me when I get there," I said. "She'll understand how I can't go back to my father's." And I thought of what she'd written in the last letter I'd received before leaving: *Someday you will visit and hear it, too.* Ahh, the elusive *it.* I couldn't wait.

"Why can't you go back?" he asked. "Your parents obviously take care of you."

"They're not my parents," I said. "They're my father and stepmother."

Thinking about it gave me a basketball-size lump in my chest. My father had been lost and numb after my mother had left. We both had been, like survivors who'd fallen from a sinking ship into icy, arctic waters.

While Billy drove, I pulled my mother's last letter from my backpack and started to read.

> *I've been out in the boat, listening on hydrophones, and as much as I love humpbacks, I find our local beluga song to be the most beautiful sound in the world. Do you know they are endangered, fewer than nine hundred of these beautiful, rare, snow-white whales? We have to hope for babies this year. The species could disappear. When I hear their song I feel hope.*
>
> *Someday you will visit and hear it, too . . .*

I wanted that. I wanted to hear it, too.

When Mom was young—just a little older than me—she'd gone to Connecticut College in the old whaling port of New London. My dad had been at the Coast Guard Academy, and they got married right after graduation. For a while they'd shared a dream maritime life. She was at grad school in Woods

Hole, he was stationed in Menemsha, and they lived on Martha's Vineyard. She was so cool—she commuted to classes in her own boat, no matter what weather. It must have been so romantic.

Eventually they had me. I'd thought we were happy. For a long time, I guess we were. Then my dad inherited his father's boring insurance business in Crawford, and Mom got the job in Mystic. She spent time commuting and working and researching when Dad thought she should be with us, and life was all downhill from there.

She'd left a note on my pillow the day she left. I could recite it if Billy had asked. I could tell him about how she'd said she was dying inside, that she'd stop breathing if she couldn't escape suburbia and go live with the whales, how leaving me would leave a hole in her heart until she saw me again.

Someday you will visit and hear it, too.

"You'll always be pure magic to her," my dad said after she left, trying to reassure me of her love. "Why do you think she named you Maia?"

Maia was a star in the Taurus cluster. The name came from Greek mythology. So did those of the other sisters in the Pleiades, my mother's favorite constellation. She used to remind me that Maia was a spectral blue giant, the fourth brightest star in all of Taurus. She said she'd known my name as soon as she'd seen my deep-blue eyes.

"Where are we on the map?" Billy asked, rousing me from my thoughts.

"Here," I said, leaning into him and pointing at a road

slightly northeast of Boston. We jounced over a pothole, and he put his arm around me to steady me. It took me by surprise, and I bit my lip. He held on for a minute. Then he reached into the bag for a handful of gummy bears. He popped one into my mouth, and we both laughed.

We drove through an old industrial river town filled with abandoned factory buildings, with smokestacks, broken windows, and weed-choked asphalt parking lots. It reminded me of Crawford. My grandfather had had a booming insurance business; by the time my dad stepped in, half the customers had moved away. My mother had said the city was stultifying. Maybe those customers thought so, too.

Suddenly I looked at Billy. He'd lived at the beach, right on the salt water of Long Island Sound.

"What was it like when you moved to Crawford?" I asked. "Was it stultifying?"

He laughed. "That sounds weird," he said.

"Why?"

"It's kind of a guidance counselor word."

"Well, tell me anyway. Was it?"

"The Home was," he said. "So many rules, and sharing a room with a bunch of guys. No running on the beach, no sailing. I missed all that."

"What about Crawford itself?"

"I didn't belong there. I knew I never would." His eyes looked hard again, the way they had last night, when we'd stopped in front of that cottage with the blue TV light inside.

"Can I ask you something?" I asked.

"Sure," he said. "Go for it."

"Whose house was that?"

He glanced over quickly, surprise in his face. He frowned, as if I were way out-of-bounds. I noticed how his brown hair slanted across his green eyes, and I couldn't help myself—I reached over to brush it back.

"How can you even see the road with your hair in your eyes?" I asked, to cover my embarrassment.

"What house?" he asked as if he hadn't felt my hand on his forehead.

"The one you stopped in front of, when we were leaving Hubbard's Point."

"Huh," he said. "The question most people want to ask is, 'Why did your father kill your mother?' And, 'Do you hate his guts?'"

His voice sounded flat but charged, cold as a sheet of metal. I heard freezing rage just beneath the surface. I was afraid the anger would break through his control, flow toward me.

"I wasn't going to ask that," I said.

"Because you don't want to know?" he asked.

"Only if you want to tell me," I said.

"I don't hate his guts," Billy said.

"Okay," I said.

"You know why my grandfather hates me, though?" he asked. "Do you wonder how I know so much about back roads and avoiding the police?"

"How?" I asked, my mouth suddenly so dry I could barely speak. A chill ran down my spine.

"Because I helped my dad get away," Billy said.

There had been stories in the paper. I knew he had been detained, questioned after his father's capture. But hearing him say the words, admit what he'd done, shocked me to the core.

I turned to look out the side window, anywhere but at him, as he drove us north on roads where my father would never think to look, in a rusty old truck no police would be watching for. I saw a sign for the route that went by Turner Institute, but I didn't say anything. I wondered if I really knew anything about the boy I'd fallen madly in love with.

And I couldn't help noticing he still hadn't told me whose house it had been.

Chapter 8

MAY 23
MIDDLE OF NOWHERE, MASSACHUSETTS

That night we slept in the truck again, but this time Billy's head didn't wind up on my shoulder. There was tension in the air from our conversation and the ensuing silence, so we stayed as far across the cab from each other as possible.

We'd pulled over behind a shed, in a junkyard in a small Massachusetts town near the New Hampshire border. We blended right in with the other rusty trucks and cars.

I couldn't sleep. The air was cold and knifed through my hoodie. Neon lights from a nearby shopping center glared. There were lots of spooky sounds, rattletraps creaking and settling, a crane's magnet swinging on a cable. I imagined criminals creeping around. A dog barked all night from inside the office, and I swore I heard his fangs clicking. Turner Institute was fewer than twenty miles away. And I couldn't stop hearing Billy say he'd helped his father escape.

I must have drifted off, because the next thing I knew, I

woke up with my arms around myself, shivering. The sky was turning lavender, the color just before dawn that made the stars shine brighter than ever. And I was alone. The dog was snarling and growling. I looked around, afraid to leave the truck but worried that something had happened to Billy. I made myself get out.

"Hey," he said, hurrying over.

"Where were you?" I asked.

"Getting breakfast," he said, holding up two plastic-wrapped cranberry muffins. "There were vending machines at the gas station next door."

In the glow of the sky and the neon lights, I saw that in his other hand he held a dark object with wires trailing from it.

"What's that?"

"A radio. I took it out of that Plymouth over there."

"I thought you said you didn't steal."

"This is a salvage yard. Everything here is destined for the crusher, to turn into little squares of metal and sold for scrap. Besides, I'll replace it."

"How?" But the dog was howling now, throwing its weight against the office door. "We should get out of here before the owner comes. That dog wants us out, too . . ."

"There's a sign on the door—it doesn't open until eight. Let me just do this."

It took two seconds for him to pop the old radio out. He leaned under the dashboard, poking around with pliers and a screwdriver. I held the flashlight so he could see. His head leaned against my left knee, and his right arm was wrapped around my calf as he worked in the tight space. I was too nervous, watching the entrance, but the heat of his arm felt good after the chill of the night, and in about a thousand other ways.

"Do you know how to splice wires?" he asked.

"Totally," I said. My mother had shown me; the skill was an important part of seamanship, in case of emergency repairs offshore.

"Can you do these last two while I throw the old radio into the Plymouth?"

"I thought you said it was just salvage," I said, crouching down beside him in the impossibly tiny space under the dash, our faces an inch apart.

"They do it by weight," he said. "That's how, if I put this one back, it isn't stealing."

I nodded and stared at the tangle of wires. I saw the two unconnected pieces and twisted the bare copper ends together. We needed electrical tape to make it safe, and when Billy returned he had a sticky old piece he'd gotten from the Plymouth. He wound it around the splice.

I remembered my camera and grabbed it just in time to snap a photo of Billy at work. He turned at the click, gave me an exaggerated smile.

"Cheese," he said belatedly, but then I snapped again.

He turned the ignition, and the truck chugged and chugged, not wanting to start. He gave it another few seconds and tried it again. The battery whirred as if wanting to die, but it finally caught and sputtered. I couldn't wait for him to turn the heat on.

We pulled out, no heat and no radio yet, letting the battery charge. The sun had come up enough for us to leave the headlights off. I shivered as we drove in silence along the town's main strip. Fast-food restaurants and a silver-top diner were just opening, but we made do with our muffins and what was left of our snacks from the Provvie Mart.

When Billy finally turned on the radio, it worked. We turned to each other and smiled.

"You're in charge," he said. "Find us something good."

The radio was old-school AM-FM. We caught a college station; I tuned it the best I could, and "Flume" by Bon Iver came on.

"We're in business," I said, and Billy nodded.

We drove out of Massachusetts, along the eighteen-mile coastline of New Hampshire. As soon as we crossed the Route 1 bridge over the Piscataqua River into Kittery, Maine, I rolled down my window and let fresh salt wind blow through the cab.

"Ocean alert," I said.

"Yeah?" he asked.

"The Atlantic's just a couple of miles down the road."

"Should we stop?" he asked. "Or keep going?"

I skimmed the atlas. Tadoussac, the fjord, and the elusive cabin were at least two days away if we stuck to back roads. I squirmed in my seat. He saw.

"Is your back killing you?" he asked.

"A little," I said. "Is yours?"

"Totally." He patted the truck's dash. "This baby is fine for around Black Hall, but all the way to Canada? The shocks are shot, springs are poking through the seat. Can't you feel them?"

"That's what this is?" I asked, readjusting to avoid a sharp coil coming through the vinyl.

"We should have traded her in for one of the junkyard heaps."

"Bite your tongue!" I said. "She's our girl. She needs encouragement."

"And we need a walk on the beach. Let's look for one."

"Okay," I said. "Besides, the longer we take to get to Tadoussac, the more they might start looking somewhere else."

"Good thinking," he said. "So, now . . ."

"Beach time," I said.

He grinned, and we angled down to the coast road along wide Atlantic bays, some craggy rock cliffs, a classic white lighthouse, and finally, the perfect sandy strand. We found a parking spot on the road. One side was lined with tiny shops, restaurants, and a motel; the other was nothing but a long, broad, silver beach with crashing waves. Billy and I kicked off our shoes and walked down toward the blue water.

It was low tide, and the air smelled of seaweed and marine life. There were channeled whelks, clumps of dried sargassum weed, and driftwood. Billy picked up shells as we walked along. Stones rattled in the waves, left behind on the hard sand, flat and smooth and perfect.

"Hey," Billy said, having the same idea I did. This time he

placed the first stone. Then my turn. We sat next to each other on the sand, building tiny towers all around us until we were surrounded by cairns. I felt as if we were in a magic castle. Some of the stones glinted with quartz and silver-black mica, like crystal-and-black diamonds.

I kept my eyes on the ocean, hoping to see a spout, a whale passing by. A seal's head popped up, and I pointed. Billy saw just before it disappeared into the waves again.

"There are lobsters out there, too," Billy said. "I can hear them."

"Yes, lobsters love to sing," I said, kidding along with him.

"I'm serious," he said. "My grandfather used to tell me I had an ear for them. I'd tell him where to sink his pots, and when we pulled them up the next day, they'd be filled with keepers."

"Keepers?"

"Legal size, no egg-bearing females. Something happened in Long Island Sound, though. Lobsters got rare three summers ago. We talked about moving to Maine. He'd never have left Connecticut, but this was his dream."

He stared out to sea, every so often glancing over at me. I physically felt his gaze, a combination of prickles and warmth on my skin. The tide was coming in, each wave crashing closer to us until we felt the foamy white spindrift splashing our feet.

"We can't let it wash away our cairns," I said, starting to move one.

"It's okay," he said, grabbing my wrist. "We make them,

and whatever happens is fine. It doesn't matter if the waves knock them down. We'll just make more."

"I want to remember these," I said, taking a photo with my handy disposable Kodak.

"Gimme that," he said, and backed up, aiming the camera. It felt weird, cool, and wonderful to think he wanted to take my picture.

A wave whooshed up just as the shutter clicked. The water smashed into us and toppled the first tower. The tide yanked at our feet, swirling around our knees. I tottered on one leg, nearly falling in. Billy's arms shot around me, pulling me out, and I pretended to drag him into the waves. We hovered together, our faces practically touching. I felt his lips brush my forehead. Then he laughed, giving me a little shove as we stumbled back onto the hard sand.

I studied the breakers as they advanced, receded, came closer again, just so he couldn't see my eyes, read my emotions.

We stayed till all the cairns washed away and my heart stopped pounding. We kept laughing, and I wasn't even sure why. I kept watching for my mother's whales, and I knew Billy was listening for his grandfather's lobsters. He cupped his hand to his ear.

"There's another," he said.

"What's this one saying?" I asked.

"Oh, it's a secret," he said, giving me the most tantalizingly adorable smile, a glint in his green eyes that made my cheeks feel hot.

The minute we started walking again, he bent down and came up with a sand dollar. I thought he was going to stick it in his pocket with the shells he'd collected, but he didn't. He held the sand dollar carefully, pressing it into my hand so we could hold it together. He stared into my eyes, and his gaze didn't waver.

"Thank you," he said.

"For what?"

"Letting me come with you. Getting me out of there. I was dying in that place."

"Seeing where you grew up, I can imagine why," I said.

"We're only sophomores," he said. "I was going to be stuck there until I was eighteen, two more years. I couldn't have done it. And I'm never going back."

"I don't want to go back, either," I said.

"This is our pact," he said.

He took his hand away, and I held the sand dollar. It was small, no bigger than a quarter, pure white, incredibly fragile. I bent my head to look at the flower shape in the center. I didn't want him to keep watching my face, to see what I was feeling.

I closed my eyes. He was taller than me and must have lowered his head because I could feel his warm breath on the top of my head. Our closeness was even more intense than when we'd played in the waves. My legs turned to jelly, barely holding me up.

"Promise me," he said. "That we won't go back. No matter what."

"I promise," I whispered. "No matter what."

I looked up then. He tilted down so our foreheads touched; he stared into my face another minute, and I got lost in the golden green of his eyes, waiting for something more.

The moment ended. Billy walked away. I stayed in the spot where we'd stood a few seconds more. He could have put his arms around me. I could have tipped my head back. I closed my eyes to feel what hadn't happened. Walking back toward the truck, my mind spun with all my confused desire and possibly the strongest wish I'd ever had, for my first kiss. From Billy.

Big secret: I'd never been kissed before. But that was going to change on this road trip. Billy wanted to kiss me, didn't he? It had almost happened, right? Or maybe it hadn't. Maybe it was only in my own mind.

I held the sand dollar in my hand. It meant something. It symbolized our pact not to return home, never to go back, but it felt like something more. I just didn't know what.

Chapter 9

MAY 23
THE COAST OF MAINE

We drove along the beautiful shore, spiky with pine trees and glistening with rock ledges sloping into the blue sea. One alt radio station faded out with Fleet Foxes, and another college station came in with Radiohead. Every so often they played a song I really liked and I'd sing low, almost under my breath.

"Don't keep it to yourself," he said.

"You might miss the lobsters if I do," I said, to avoid having to sing in front of him.

"I've heard enough from them for now. I'd rather hear you," he said, giving me the same feeling of liquid bones I'd had on the beach.

So I sang, and with every song I got a little surer of myself. My father liked classical music, but my mother had loved driving with the radio on or her iPod plugged in, and we'd sing and harmonize together.

Number one on her playlist was Dar Williams, so I practically jumped out of my seat when our favorite Dar song, "Mercy of the Fallen," came on. I sang it right out, no reservations about Billy hearing me, feeling my mother's harmony, and knowing the fact that it had come on the radio was such a good sign.

Not long after the song ended, my stomach growled, and Billy's did almost at the same time. I laughed, embarrassed. Our snacks were gone. We'd gotten back on Route 1, and up ahead was a big white building with a carved green lobster on its sign.

"This is living dangerously," he said. "The next fill-up is going to take a lot of money, but here we are in Maine, and here's a lobster pound. Should we do it?"

"Definitely," I said, already tasting the melted butter.

We ordered at the counter. Instead of getting really expensive shore dinners, we got hot lobster rolls. I picked up a tourist brochure on the counter and we headed outside to a picnic table. We drank lemonade and took turns reading fun facts about the town out loud until they called our number.

The rolls were toasted buns filled with claw and tail meat soaked in butter and lemon. They came with fries. I'd never had a more delicious meal. The day had warmed up after our cold night, and it felt great sitting outside in the late-afternoon sun.

Billy went inside to get us coffees. A yellow school bus went by, and my heart skidded slightly—this was our third day on the road, and we'd just promised not to go back. Was there a high school near my mother's cabin? Did I really care?

That's when I noticed: I did feel a little guilty about missing school. About making my dad worry. If there was a way to contact him and not have him find me, I'd do it. But the other thing I noticed, and it was huge: I didn't feel depressed. Not at all. I had all these emotions, up and down, really soaring, a little dip here and there. But they passed instead of sticking to me like Velcro moods.

It felt weird not to have my cell phone. Not just because I was dying to take a million pictures and post them all, or because I wanted to text my friends, but because of my dad. There was a pay phone at the far end of the parking lot.

"I have to call my father," I said when Billy came back.

Billy lowered the cardboard coffee cup from his mouth to the table.

"I thought we promised," he said.

"We did," I said. "I won't tell him where we are, but I have to let him know I'm okay."

Billy shook his head. "He'll see the number on caller ID and figure it out from the area code. And we're miles from any highway where he might think to look. We'd be giving up on our trip, Maia. He'd call the local police and they'd be here in two minutes."

"You can block numbers," I said. "Clarissa showed me how, and we did it all the time, tricking each other for fun, pretending to be other people. You just use star sixty-seven."

"Not from pay phones," he said. "My father told me when he was trying to get away."

"Seriously?" I said.

"Yeah," he said. I wanted to hear more about that, but Billy had walked back into the lobster pound. He returned with a local tourism map.

"We'll find the library," he said. "And you can email him. Email can't be traced the same way. He won't know where you sent it from."

It was nearly five o'clock. I located the town library on the tiny map. We didn't know what time it closed, so we quickly drove about a mile through the most postcard-perfect town I have ever seen: white churches with tall spires at either end of Main Street, ancient oak trees with spreading branches that were just starting to leaf in, and restored old houses that reminded me of Mystic. I wondered if they had belonged to sea captains and shipbuilders.

We parked on the street outside a small stone library with curving granite steps and two white Doric columns flanking the sign: THE ELIZA HEWITT MEMORIAL LIBRARY. The library looked so small and old-fashioned, I doubted there would be computers, but as soon as we walked in we saw a special room, walled off by glass, with three computer stations. The room was empty except for two girls who were about our age.

Seeing them reminded me of how much I missed Clarissa and Gen. I couldn't wait to check for emails from them. But I wasn't ready to write my father. What would I say? I needed a few minutes to think about that, so I wandered away from Billy, into the stacks. Books surrounded me and felt so familiar and comforting. I took one randomly off the shelf: *Eye of the Albatross* by Carl Safina. I paged through and read about

Amelia, one particular bird he studied. I read how adult albatrosses fly up to 25,000 miles across open ocean to feed their
chicks.

Feed their chicks.

Even albatrosses cared that much about their children. My
thoughts started swirling, and I thought of my mother and had
to sit down, cross-legged, on the floor. The library tilted, and
my heart ached so much I couldn't catch my breath. But if my
time at Turner taught me nothing else, it was how to *ize*: ratio-
nalize, compartmentalize, internalize.

But I'm not a chick, I told myself. It was ridiculous to expect
my mother to feed me anymore. *I'm a grown girl. We're
the Whale Mavens and Construction Crew, independent
women, YEAH.*

"Hello," said a voice. I glanced up, and it was a librarian
with an armful of books to reshelve. She had short sleeves and
I caught sight of two tattoos: an anchor inside her left forearm
and *Expecto Patronum,* from Harry Potter, inside the other.
"Are you finding what you need?"

"Oh, yes," I said, scrambling to get up. Maybe this library
didn't allow sitting on the floor. I held up the book.

"Ah, Amelia," she said. "Everyone loves her. That book
has been the basis of more book reports than I can count." She
was both cool and smart, just like Ms. Rhilinger, my favorite
librarian at home.

After she walked off, I glanced around for Billy but
couldn't find him. I headed into the computer room. Amelia
the albatross was still haunting me, in spite of my ability to

ize. Would my mother fly 25,000 miles to feed me? Probably when I was just hatched, I told myself. Definitely then.

I took some deep breaths to stop hyperventilating. That worked perfectly. Now I shoved my neediness, my dumb baby-chick-ness, down into the compartment where it belonged, and I started thinking of my responsibilities.

I sat down at the wide oak library table, where the computers were. The two girls there were hunched over books, papers spread around them. I thought of the school assignments I was missing. I had chosen a good topic for English, the literature of whales, wanting my class to know that *Moby-Dick* was far from the only book to read on the subject.

"Hey," the girl on the right said quietly, giving me a very intense stare. She had super-short black hair tapered sharply against her neck. Her bangs were cut in a straight line above her thinly plucked eyebrows, one of which was pierced with a stud. She wore a plain white T-shirt and long silver necklaces layered over one another.

"Hey," I said.

"You're new blood," she said.

"Are you a vampire?" I asked, laughing nervously.

"No," said the girl next to her. She was really skinny and had long, pure white hair, obviously bleached, a bunch of earrings in one ear, and she wore a red fleece jacket that said ALL-MAINE ORCHESTRA on the front. "Just that this is a small town and we know everyone."

"I'm only visiting," I said.

"Passing through?" White T-shirt Girl asked.

"Uh," I said.

"Don't invade her privacy," Red Fleece Girl said.

"I'm Darrah, by the way," White T-shirt Girl said.

"Cleo," Red Fleece Girl said.

I hesitated and decided to use my middle name, my parents' tribute to Rachel Carson, the greatest environmentalist ever. "I'm Rachel," I said.

"Huh," Darrah said, squinting a smile at me.

"What grade are you in?" Cleo asked.

"Tenth," I said. "How about you?"

"That's complicated," Darrah said. "Not for me, but for our dear Cleo. I'm a junior. And . . . you want to tell or should I, my love?" she asked Cleo.

"You," Cleo said.

"Well, we're together," Darrah told me with a smile. "As in in love."

"That's great," I said. "Why is your grade complicated?"

"Long story," Cleo said.

Since I had one of those of my own, I knew to leave it alone. I logged into my email and saw that I had fifty-seven new messages. I glanced through them. As usual, most were from Gen and Clarissa. I wanted to sit there and DM with them for hours—there was so much to say. It killed me to hide my online status, but I knew if I started I might never get off the computer.

There were lots of other emails from my dad, and—of course—Astrid. I took just enough time to open the one I'd sent myself, and smiled to see the selfie of Billy and me in Mystic.

Then I closed that email, opened a new message box, and started typing.

> *Dear Dad,*
> *I am sorry for leaving without telling you. I know*
> *you must be worried, but please don't be. I am fine,*
> *I haven't hurt myself, and I promise I won't. I took*
> *the car, but I'm sure you figured that out already. I*
> *am fine. Do not blame Billy.*
>
> *Love,*
> *Maia*

"Are you checking in with home?" Darrah asked me.

I nodded, not wanting to go into it.

"They're super worried about you," Darrah said, and I froze.

"We spotted you and Billy as soon as you walked in," Cleo said.

My blood stopped in my veins. How did they know his name?

"Don't take it the wrong way, and we totally understand," Cleo said. "I'd give a fake name, too, Maia."

"Oh, no, oh, no," I said, jumping up, nearly knocking my chair over, looking frantically around the library, outside the computer room's window, for Billy. I had to tell him, we had to leave.

Darrah reached across the table, grabbed my arm, gave it a firm shake. "You're safe with us. We should have told you we recognized you right away, but we didn't want to spook you. You should know you're on the news."

"Like, everywhere," Cleo said.

My teeth were clenched, and I could barely speak.

"What are they saying?" I finally asked.

"They don't know what happened to you. They're worried you might have done something to hurt yourself. And they think Billy's bad news."

"No," I said. "He's wonderful."

Cleo nodded. "You two are together, right? Like, you're not his prisoner?"

"No!"

"Didn't think so," Darrah said. "I know a couple when I see one. Comes from being with Cleo. There's love electricity or there's not."

Love electricity? Between Billy and me? I knew it was sizzling inside me, and I wanted to ask them if they saw it going both ways, but this wasn't the time to obsess over my crush.

Darrah and Cleo seemed nice, but would they report us the second we left? I itched to get away.

"They don't know where we're going, or how we're getting around?" I asked.

"They said you're driving the family Volvo," Cleo said.

"I've got to find Billy," I said, backing toward the door.

"Look, you're here—maybe you should read the news stories online? Go ahead," Darrah said.

"It's okay," Cleo said, giving me an encouraging smile.

I sat back down, went to Facebook, scanned the news feed—it was all about us, Billy and me. My friends' posts were filled with news stories from the *Hartford Courant* and the New London *Day*, video clips from Channel 30, a rehash of Billy's father's murder trial, a statement from the Stansfield Home: *William Gorman is part of the Stansfield family. We thank the Connecticut State Police and all who are working so hard to bring him home, and we won't rest until he returns to us.*

My timeline was also full of personal pleas from kids in our class.

From Jenna Bridges: *Maia & Billy, if you're reading this, we love you and want you back home!*

From Cathy Alfonso: *We miss you—that's all I can say. If only you knew how much, you'd come back right now.*

From Peter Barowski: *Dude, where'd you go? We're thinking of you. Seriously. Call someone.*

From Lisa Brown: *Prayers for our classmates, please!*

Gen posted a photo of us in gymnastics class, standing side by side on the balance beam. *Maia, you're my heart. I need you home—don't do this to us, we're all so scared. Hurry back.*

Clarissa's photo showed me, her, and Gen last Halloween, when we'd all gone to the school dance as witches. We'd sprinkled glitter on our black hats, painted our faces green, and wiggled our fingers toward the camera as if casting spells. *If I could perform magic right now I'd bring you home safe and sound,* she'd written. *I'd make sure you were okay. Please be okay, Maia. Please please please.*

I brushed away tears and couldn't take any more Facebook. I closed the window and glanced back at my email, ready to log out. But then I saw this unfamiliar address:

Beluga.GS@QuebecEast.com

And I knew. My mother.

She NEVER emailed me. All our communication was by letter. I drew in a sharp breath and held it. I couldn't let it out or breathe right.

> *Dear Maia,*
> *Wherever you are, wherever the tides have taken you, know I love you. I am with you.*
>
> *Use your strength, your tools. Be my strong daughter. You are an invincible woman. Feel me with you, Maia. Remember you are named for one of the brightest stars in the sky, and use the constellations—including your own—to guide you.*
>
> *Right now I am watching a beluga mother and calf, and I know they will share the sea forever, whether together or miles apart. The mother is*

teaching the calf lessons that will save her life,
keep her safe from predators, guide her to the
richest feeding grounds. Mother and child whales
can hear each other's songs hundreds of miles
away from each other. That is science, not poetry.

Follow your instincts; they will never fail you.
Our communication is complex, like whales, and
it carries far and forever. Never forget that.

I love you,
Mom

I stared at the email and this time I couldn't hold back my tears. I printed it out. And I thought of that albatross and her chick, the beluga and her calf, my mother and me.

"Hey," Darrah said, snapping me back to reality. "Do you need a safe place to stay and hide out for a while?"

"All I know is we have to get on the road," I said, rising to my feet. "Right now."

"There's an abandoned inn," Darrah continued as if I hadn't spoken. "It belonged to my great-aunt and -uncle, a total wreck. The roof leaked and part of the third floor caved in after a blizzard last winter. The heat and electricity have been turned off, but you could chill there, get some rest."

"Where is it?" I asked.

"It's actually pretty far away, over a hundred miles—in

Canada, in New Brunswick," Darrah said. "And you don't want to get there after dark, it's too hard to find, so you might have to save it till tomorrow. It was a fishing lodge, but my relatives got old, and the fishermen found other places to go. It's abandoned now. But it's cool. Cleo and I have stayed there. Here, I'll give you directions."

I hesitated, unsure of what to say. Darrah started scribbling in her notebook, filling nearly half a page.

The glass door opened, and Billy walked in. He cleared his throat, a signal we should leave.

"This is Darrah and Cleo," I said.

"Hi," he said, looking nervous.

"We're on your side," Darrah said.

"Our side?" he asked, startled.

"They know," I said. "The word is out. You should see Facebook, our friends . . ."

"We have to take off," Billy said, grabbing my hand.

"They won't tell," I said at the same time Darrah said, "We won't tell."

"No offense, but we don't know you," he said.

"Trust issues much?" Darrah asked.

"Yeah, actually," he said, turning red.

"They have a place we can hide out," I said quickly, before Billy could bolt.

Billy frowned, looking both angry and worried. "Thanks anyway," he said.

"Look, the inn is hidden," Darrah said. "Save it for

tomorrow, it's way into the woods. Here—directions, and our phone numbers." She tore the page out of her notebook and thrust it at Billy. He read it.

"Birch trees?" he asked.

"You'll know them when you see them," Darrah said.

"C'mon, let's go," he said to me.

He was being rude, and I shot him a look as I left a dime on the printer for my copy.

Outside, the sun had gone behind the trees. It stayed light past seven thirty this far into May, but it was getting late and the shadows were long.

Darrah and Cleo walked us to the truck. Aware of Billy's impatience, I turned away from him to face them.

"Hey," Cleo said. She had been quiet up until now. "You asked why I wasn't sure what grade I was in. I missed a little school."

"Like Billy and I are doing now," I said.

She nodded. "Yeah," she said.

"Our parents didn't approve of us being gay," Darrah said. "They took a very Romeo-and-Juliet approach and tried to separate us by moving Cleo in with her grandmother, way up in potato country."

"Aroostook County," Cleo said with an exaggerated shiver. "I'm the least farming-type person you can imagine, and being so far from Darrah, I kind of lost my mind."

"*Kind* of?" Darrah asked. "You did lose it."

I waited for more: a girl who had lost her mind? Kids who'd

had mental illness had an instant shorthand language. It felt as if they knew about my depression, that I was a kindred spirit. Billy stood right there, listening.

"Anyone who hasn't lost her mind at least once is just boring," I said.

"Did you have to go to a hospital?" Cleo asked me.

"Oh, yes. Six weeks, locked in."

"My kind of girl!" Cleo said. She reached over to link pinkie fingers with me, like a secret, ex-mental-patient handshake.

"Are you better now?" I asked.

"Much, thanks to the wonders of medication. And you?"

"Antidepressants-R-Us," I said.

Everyone but Billy laughed, but I was surprised to see a certain look of recognition on his face. What did that mean?

Cleo kissed the back of Darrah's hand. "Before they sent me to the clinic, Darrah and I ran away to the lodge. It's a hideaway, in the backwoods on a river, and no one will find you."

"You need a refuge. Being on the run is exhausting," Darrah said.

"Yeah," I said. But honestly, it hadn't been. I felt guilty, because obviously people were worried about Billy and me, but it felt thrilling to be with him, on our way to my mother's fjord.

"We'd better go," Billy said.

Cleo, Darrah, and I gave each other a long hug. They stood in the library parking lot waving good-bye to us, and I waved back. I glanced over at Billy, figuring he would have his eyes on the road as we pulled out of the parking lot.

But he'd stopped to let a row of cars go by, turned toward me. His eyes were steady, not even blinking.

"Do you still have the sand dollar?" he asked.

"Of course," I said, taking it out of the glove compartment, where I had carefully placed it, wrapped in tissue.

"Don't forget our promise," he said.

"I won't," I said. "But why did you have to be so rude to them?"

He leaned across the truck seat. For a second I thought he was going to put his arms around me, but all he did was stare hard into my eyes.

"Because you trusted them too quickly. What if they tell?"

"They won't."

"You don't know that, Maia." He paused. "You told them more about yourself than you've told me."

"You know almost everything!"

"The hospital? Medication?"

I felt rattled. He was right; I hadn't talked to him about it. "Maybe I didn't want you to think less of me."

"As if I would. It's just a lesson."

"What are you talking about?"

"You're not the only one. I was on it, too, for a while."

"Medication?" I had no idea—I was shocked, even though it made perfect sense.

"Yeah. It was all part of going into foster care. It was supposed to help 'ease the transition.' It sort of took away the sharp edges. I don't know, it's hard to figure out."

"I had no idea. I haven't seen you take them, the whole trip."

"I don't anymore. The doctor took me off, once I got used to Stansfield. But see?"

"See what?"

"When it comes right down to it, you don't trust me. It's not your fault. You're just like everyone else. No one should believe in anyone."

"Billy," I said, shocked by the tone of his voice. Hurt shot through me, from the top of my head down to my toes. He exhaled, sounding exasperated, speeding us down the town's main road.

A few miles later, when the streetlamps thinned out and the sky turned darker, I glanced over at him. I wanted to say I believed in him, he could count on me. We could count on each other. But his silence made it clear he wasn't in the mood to hear anything.

I reached for the radio dial and tuned it away from the alt station till I found jazz. A mournful trumpet played. I was pretty sure it was Miles Davis. But it didn't seem as if Billy cared or even heard.

He just drove.

Chapter 10

MAY 23
GRAYSON, MAINE

W e have to change our plan," Billy said after a long time.

"Which part?"

"Pretty much all of it. If our pictures are on the news and even people up here recognize us, we have to be more careful. Let me see the atlas, okay?"

He pulled over and turned on the cab light. We examined the map of Maine, places where the state line intersected the Canadian border. If we kept going straight, east along the coast, we would hit less populated territory.

"Where's the best place to cross?" he asked. "We have to look for big green patches on the map, woods, where there aren't towns or too many roads."

"This part looks pretty rural," I said, my finger trailing along the red line of the St. Croix River, hugging the eastern-most part of southern Maine, separating it from New

Brunswick. There was nothing but green on that part of the map, wide-open space with no one to spot us.

"It would be so much faster to head this way," he said, pointing at Quebec, the province where Tadoussac and Saguenay Fjord were located, due north from where we were. "But we'd hit Bangor and too many other towns. Let's keep driving along the coast for now, then toward the spot you picked out."

"Darrah did say Calais would be good," I said.

"Maia . . ." he said.

"What's your problem?" I asked.

"People betray you," Billy said, pulling back onto the road and driving ahead. "They can look nice, and act like friends, then stab you in the back."

"You have to trust your instincts," I said. "How else can you make friends, let people into your life?"

"Instincts can lie," he said.

He still sounded angry. I pictured him the way I knew him from school and from looking up the hill—mysterious, full of secrets, but, well, adorable. Right now his expression was hostile, as if everything he'd been through was finally coming to the surface, directed straight at me. He looked tough, a different person, as if he'd turned from Dr. Jekyll into Mr. Hyde.

"I'm sorry I didn't tell you much about that part of my life," I began. But he cut me off.

"You know that house you asked about?" he said.

"The one you parked in front of?"

"My girlfriend lives there," he said. "Helen."

I couldn't speak. Of course he had people in his past: I knew that. But the way he said her name with such intensity gave me a pit in my stomach. And he'd called her "my girl-friend." Present tense.

"I loved her since first grade," he said. "We grew up on the beach together, rode the school bus all those years. When my grandfather taught me to fish for lobsters, he taught her, too."

I pictured them at Hubbard's Point, at the beach, out on the water.

"Through middle school and freshman year—all that time. My mom loved her, treated her like a daughter. They were practically best friends. We'd take the ferry to Block Island, or head into New York to hear jazz or just walk around, and Helen always came."

Helen was the blond girl in the photos on their kitchen wall, in Billy's room.

"And her parents were like my parents. Her dad took me surfing at Misquamicut. He gave me a board for my fifteenth birthday. Helen and I got wetsuits, and we surfed all year, even on New Year's Day. She was my girl."

Those words stung worse than anything. *She was my girl.* I stayed silent on my side of the truck, looking out the window.

He drove without speaking for so long, I thought that was all he was going to say, and I couldn't bring myself to ask more.

But twenty minutes later, driving through the dark with the latest college radio station crackling in and out, here in the middle of nowhere, I couldn't stand not knowing.

"What happened?" I asked.

"My father happened," Billy said. "He came back after being away from us for so long. And when he needed to run, he took me along." He paused.

"Took you?" I asked, not getting it. "You mean kidnapped you?"

"I wouldn't put it that way."

"You went with him? After what he did?" I pictured that bleached stain on the floor.

"He's my dad," Billy said. "I didn't really have a choice. We threw out our cell phones, ditched police all along the way. He had a scanner, and he could always figure out where they'd be waiting. He showed me exactly how to hide, how to cover my tracks. But I never wanted to be like him, be that person."

"You're not him," I said.

"Helen thinks I am."

"How could she? Doesn't she . . ."—I hesitated because it felt so weird to say the word in front of him—"um, love you, too?"

"She said she did. We both felt that way since seventh grade. I already told you, she was Pat and I was Fort. Patience and Fortitude. We had that for each other, we were each other's lions. We were going to be together."

"You mean married?" I said, my stomach tightening.

"I thought so. Down the road. So that's what I mean by

you can't trust people. I would have trusted her with anything. With *everything*. She broke every promise we ever made."

"How?"

"I called her from the road, with my dad, and she turned me in. I told her where we were, and she told the cops. They found us and arrested my dad that day."

I stared at him.

"And they arrested me, too," he said. "That's what you don't know about me. I didn't just *end up* at Stansfield. I wasn't just a poor orphan. That jail we passed on the way to Hubbard's Point? I was there. They held me for a week, trying to figure out who killed my mom, him or me—they actually thought I might have done it, or else why would I have run? My lawyer said my father forced me to go with him, that I was just a kid and couldn't say no. He basically said I was kidnapped."

"But you weren't," I said.

Billy took a deep, ragged breath. "At first, well, he told me I had to go with him. But like I said, he's my dad. I could have gotten away sooner than I did. My lawyer wouldn't let me say that."

"He was your advocate," I said. "That's what lawyers do." I thought of how I'd been appointed a lawyer of my own, a guardian ad litem, during the divorce, after I'd told everyone I wanted to live with my mother. I'd wanted her to get custody. It just hadn't worked out that way.

"My lawyer said stuff like 'Stockholm syndrome,' that my dad brainwashed me into helping him, stuff that got him even more years in prison," Billy said, his eyes on the road. "Because he took me across state lines, that was an interstate kidnapping charge. But that's not what happened—I just . . . went with him."

I stayed very still while he talked.

"They were my parents, I loved both of them. He pled guilty—I think so there wouldn't be a trial, so I wouldn't have to testify against him. He took twenty-five-years-to-life. He's not getting out before he dies."

My mind spun. What should I say to that? He deserved it if he killed Billy's mom. "But he did it, right?" I asked.

"Yeah. I was up in my room and heard the crash." He stared hard at an oncoming car, as if the image of what had happened was too hard to picture, as if he wanted to burn it away in the car's high beams. "I ran downstairs, and there she was. Broken on the floor, you saw the spot."

I nodded, picturing the horrible white blotch again.

"I keep thinking, if I'd paid attention I could have saved her," he said.

"How, Billy?" I asked, as gently as possible. "If he'd really wanted to do it?"

"The prosecutor said it had to do with money. He was always broke, and he drank, and he kept leaving us. My mother worked hard to support us."

"What did she do?"

"Teacher's assistant. She didn't make much, and my grandparents helped. They weren't rich, either. The prosecutor said my dad wanted her 'inheritance.' As if it were more than an old lobster boat and a couple of cottages they could barely afford to pay taxes on. The prosecutor said my dad made it look like an accident so he'd inherit the house and the money my grandparents had put in trust for her and me."

"That's terrible," I said.

"I wanted to believe they'd had a fight, and it got out of control. And if I'd been awake, I could have stopped it . . ." He trailed off, shaking his head. "But the prosecutor said my dad waited for me to be asleep. And did it then, so I couldn't help her."

I pictured that beautiful place Billy had lived—the bright colors in the kitchen, the view of the beach, his grandparents right next door, the Molloy compound. He got torn away from all that. "Then you went to Stansfield."

"Yeah. No one wanted me—who would? My grandparents hated me by that time, and Helen . . ." He shook his head. "I actually thought her parents might take me in, let me live with them. We were that close, practically family. But the last time I called, she wouldn't come to the phone. Her father answered and told me never to call again."

"But why? They know you, the way you really are."

"Everything changed," he said. "You'll see. That happens in life. You're going along, everything's great, and then it collapses. The person you trust most turns into your enemy. Even people in love betray each other."

"You can trust me," I said.

"We hardly know each other, if you think about it. Let's drop it."

I was shaking. I had to wrap my arms around myself, just

to keep my insides from flying apart. I felt shocked, devastated. I could feel the hostile energy pouring off him, a force field that kept me away.

We passed through small coastal towns with long stretches in between them. A sign loomed in our headlights: GRAYSON. The atlas said we were almost to the Canadian border, but we were both on edge and too tired to keep going. Billy drove toward a beam of light that pierced the sky.

The town of East Grayson was just ahead. When we got close, we saw its red-and-white-striped lighthouse on a granite ledge at the edge of the ocean. Billy parked the truck out of sight from the road, close to a stand of pine trees that seemed to grow straight down into the sea.

He left me in the truck and walked, then ran, to the edge of the rocks. The ocean was turbulent, the sea spray so strong it seemed to wrap him in a cloud. He leaned out, looking down. Seeing him this way reminded me of kids I'd met at Turner, of ways they'd talked about wanting to end their lives. I got out of the truck and tore over to Billy, slipping as I ran, skinning my knee and tearing my jeans, then lunged and grabbed his hand.

"Don't," I said.

He must have seen the panic in my eyes. "I'm not going to jump," he said.

"Then what are you doing?"

"Listening to the lobsters, what else?" he asked, his lips turning up in that enigmatic half smile of his. But he sounded sarcastic.

He glanced down at my leg.

"You're bleeding," he said.

"It's no big deal," I said.

"We should clean it off," he said.

I kept thinking of how he'd said we barely knew each other.

"I'm fine," I said sharply.

The rocks were slippery under our feet, from the wild waves and a fine film of black seaweed. We headed toward the lighthouse. It had a cottage attached to it, but all the windows were dark. I knew that lighthouses were automated now, run by machines and computers, that it was too expensive to pay for lightkeepers to live there.

The beam made the sea glimmer and illuminated our path. Billy tried the door in the striped tower. Someone had left it unlocked. We walked inside and the space was narrow and round. A cabinet with a big red cross was attached to the wall. Billy reached in and pulled out a first-aid kit.

He eased me down onto the bottom rung of a spiral staircase. There was hardly any light, just enough to see him pouring some hydrogen peroxide on a gauze bandage.

"This might hurt," he said.

"Okay," I said. It stung like crazy, but I wouldn't let him see. He gently pushed aside the torn edges of the hole in my jeans, swabbed away dirt and blood from my scraped knee, rubbed on ointment, and covered it with a bandage.

He glanced upstairs, toward the flashing light.

"Should we check it out?" he asked. "Nothing could be as nice as last night, sleeping in a junkyard."

"I guess," I said. After what he'd said earlier I couldn't even fake sounding happy; I couldn't kid around. My knee was really sore and stiff, but I limped up the circular stairs for what felt like ten stories, just ahead of Billy. At one point I felt his hand on my back, giving me a little push up.

At the very top, we stood inside the light room. The rotating Fresnel lens looked like magic, beautiful beyond belief, as if made by a wizard and not by humans. Rows of prism crystals formed a six-foot-high cylinder, throwing rainbows onto the dark ceiling and sending a beam into the sea, to protect mariners.

The lens produced white light every fifteen seconds, and I knew from sailing that it was called an *occulting flash*. That seemed appropriate because this place felt like a zone of enchantment. And I needed some enchantment, because inside I was completely torn up.

Billy stepped close to me. I felt stiff, unable to get the bitterness he'd shown me out of my mind. What had I done to deserve his attitude?

We were almost touching. He put his hand under my chin, tilted my face up. A thin beam of light fell between us. I heard him breathing. He bent toward me, his lips half an inch away from mine, holding me so hard I felt his ribs pressing into me, and I thought my head would explode. But I was so hurt and mad, and this wasn't how I'd dreamed a first kiss should be, so without even thinking, I gave him a shove.

We both stepped away so quickly, his eyes flashed pain. Shards of light spilled from the lens, glittering all around us.

I half wanted to start over, have him kiss me for real, but I felt totally dazed about the whole night. I tried to think of something to say, but he turned away and took his sweater off.

"We'd better get some sleep," he said. He put his sweater on the floor, gestured at it.

"What?" I asked, feeling more confused than ever.

"Our pillow," he said. He lay down, facing away from me. I settled beside him. Our heads were nearly touching on his sweater, but our backs were to each other. Even with a foot of space between us, I felt heat from his body.

Outside, the ocean crashed against the rocks and a bell buoy clanged. The lighthouse made creaking noises. My body was stiff, and my skinned knee ached, but that was nothing compared to how I felt inside: hurt and misunderstood, the worst turmoil in the world. Maybe I should never have let Billy come along in the first place. Real life was disturbingly different from the fantasy of staring up the hill through binoculars, keeping watch from a distance, having a crush.

"Maia?" he asked after a while.

"Yes?"

"Good night," he said.

I waited a minute before answering.

"Good night," I said back.

A long time later I fell asleep to the sounds of the waves and Billy breathing beside me.

Chapter 11

MAY 24
U.S.-CANADIAN BORDER
CALAIS-NEW BRUNSWICK

Just before dawn we woke up next to each other. Awkward. The lighthouse floor was cold, and the sea air was colder. I shivered and was sure my lips were blue. It was still dark, a very faint gold loom on the eastern horizon hinting that the sun would eventually rise above the ocean.

We eased apart and Billy gave me a hand to pull me up. We felt our way down the pitch-black circular stairs.

Outside there was dew on the grass, a low layer of mist on the ocean. The waves crashed against the rocks, white spume flying up like a geyser near the spot where we had stood last night.

"I'm sorry," Billy said. "For what I said last night. And for lumping you in with Helen."

"I'm not like her," I said.

"I know," he said. "I really know that. I wouldn't have told you about her, about everything, if I didn't trust you."

"Thank you," I said. "I'm sorry, too."

"You don't have to be. You didn't do anything."

This was our fourth day on the road. In some ways it felt like forever, and in others it seemed we'd just left.

A coiled hose lay beside the lighthouse. We hadn't had showers since leaving, so we decided to take turns. Billy walked away so I could go first. I was so nervous and shy at the idea of taking off my clothes while he was nearby, I kept glancing at the spot where he'd disappeared. Then I turned on the hose and took the fastest shower I ever had, gasping at the ice-cold water. When I was done, I ducked behind the truck to dry off with the T-shirt I'd been wearing and change into clean clothes. I heard Billy turn on the hose and whoop from the shock, and I couldn't help laughing. What a relief—we were clean, we'd spent the night in a striped lighthouse, we weren't mad at each other anymore, and the blue-black waves glittered in the light's beam.

And I'd had an almost–first kiss.

When Billy was done washing up, he came over to me. We smiled and gave each other a little nod at the fact that we were basically twins in fresh T-shirts and jeans. Billy looked around, scanning the sea wall.

"One thing we have to do before we leave," he said. As soon as I saw the ground covered with stones tossed up by the sea, I knew. We walked over together, began collecting the best rocks. They were mostly blue-gray, and I compared them in my mind to the sand-colored ones at Hubbard's Point and the rusty-green ones on the beach.

"We're leaving a trail of cairns," I said.

"We are," he said.

It felt like a continuation of our sand dollar pact: a promise that we were in this together. We made the tallest tower so far, an homage to the lighthouse and celebration of the fact that we were so close to Canada.

Once we got in the truck I realized that, for the first time since we'd left, I'd forgotten to take my medication. Our luggage was jammed just behind the seat. I could have reached into my duffel, palmed my pills, and secretly popped them into my mouth just as I'd been doing all along.

In spite of our talk, of opening up to each other, I still felt too embarrassed to have Billy see me do it.

Then I had a brilliant idea: Why take them at all? The more I thought about it, the better it sounded. A list of reasons why I shouldn't continue to take the meds formed in my mind:

1) The slipping feeling—it was gone.

2) Being with Billy.

3) Our almost kiss.

4) The cairns and sand dollar.

5) Most of all: I felt happy. I was going to see my mom.

I scanned myself and realized I felt better than ever: more alert, awake, and alive. Taking antidepressants made me feel contained, as if I had plastic wrap on my emotions. They stopped me from getting the terrible lows, but they also blocked the soaring highs.

I closed my eyes and thought of last night, the lighthouse lens sending sparkles around the tower room, the feeling of heat pouring off Billy, his lips so close to mine. The moment had been so intense, but what would it have felt like if I hadn't been dulled by meds?

That was it, decision made. Day one, pill-free!

"Today, the border," Billy said as we started driving again. "I know we said we'd try for one of those remote spots on the map, but now I want us to go through customs here, the right way, officially."

"Here?" I asked, looking at the atlas. The Canadian border was just a couple miles away and the International Bridge would have taken us to Campobello Island, which I knew had been the summer home of Franklin Delano and Eleanor Roosevelt.

"No, up to Calais."

Where Darrah had said. The girl who couldn't be trusted; I hid a smile.

As we drove an hour north, I started wondering what would happen when we faced the customs agent. Would Billy and I be on a list? Did the Canadian authorities get the same bulletins as the U.S.?

We passed the Calais Free Library. It was a gorgeous yellow brick building with a turret and a spire, and a brownstone block above the arched doorway that read PUBLIC LIBRARY 1892. I felt a twinge, thinking my dad might have responded to my email. I wondered if there'd be any clue about where they were looking for us.

The border came up fast. One minute we were on the open road, next we saw a sign: FERRY POINT BORDER CROSSING. We joined the line. It was surprisingly long for so early in the morning, and I guessed the cars and trucks were full of people going to work, making deliveries. The sun was still below the buildings. The big clock on the station read 5:30 a.m.

Now that we were actually at the customs post, my heart raced so fast I thought I might pass out: I was positive as soon as the authorities looked at my passport they would stop us.

"Billy, we can't," I said, flooded with fear and adrenaline.

"We have to," he said. "Talking about my father last night—I don't want to do it his way, illegal and sneaky."

"But our pact, to never go back." I held up the sand dollar.

The car ahead of us moved along; there were two big trucks ahead of us, and we were number five in line. I craned my neck out the window to see ahead. The Canadian officer looked about my dad's age, with graying sandy hair, aviator glasses, and a badge stuck to his jacket.

"Think about it, Billy," I said, pulling my head back into the cab. "It will all be over. If we cross here they'll catch us and send us home."

The next car inched ahead, and Billy decided. He backed the truck slightly, and then made a slow U-turn out of the line. I looked over my shoulder, to see if the officials would chase us. But they didn't. They seemed intent on inspecting a fish truck.

"You're right," he said. "I promised I'd get you there."

He reached for my hand. We locked fingers and squeezed.

It lasted only a second, but it made me feel we were really together, pulling for each other in a new way.

I pored over the atlas page that showed the way north. As the sun rose higher we drove along paved roads as far as we could, through woods, past farmhouses and pastures, with glimpses of a wide stream on our right. We came to a dirt fire road heading due east. It had a metal gate across the entrance. I looked at Billy.

"If we go that way we'll be in Canada," I said.

"It's locked and chained," he said. "It's private property."

"There's no one around," I said. "We can cross here, and no one will know."

I could see him weighing the options in his mind. Then he nodded.

"You're right," he said. We both got out of the cab. He climbed into the truck bed, opened the toolbox, and found the bolt cutters. The chain was wrapped around a rusty post and through a big padlock on the gate's latch. I held the chain while Billy cut it. It slid to the ground like a dead thing.

"We could leave money for it," I said.

"Yeah," he said.

We got back into the truck and drove through. He stopped, got out of the truck again, and did his best to wrap the chain around the fence post, tucking a ten-dollar bill from our dwindling funds through the lock's shank.

We drove down the rutted road and didn't say anything for a long time. I thought of his father and how he didn't want to be like him. We'd just broken through a locked gate and become trespassers; I swallowed hard. We crossed a narrow stone bridge, over the rushing stream into Canada, and I tried to tell myself it was worth it.

The fire road ran through a pine forest. Sunlight penetrated the branches and needles and speckled the truck. We emerged onto a paved road. Luckily there wasn't another chained gate. Eventually we crossed a covered bridge over the Saint John River and were in Hartland, New Brunswick.

I spotted the Canadian flag, a bright red maple leaf on a white background, and knew we had made it. We were getting low on fuel. We passed a station where the prices were in Canadian dollars, and fuel came in liters, not gallons.

"Okay, we don't have the right money," he said.

"Maybe they'll take American."

"That'll make us stand out," he said.

"Billy, we have Connecticut license plates."

"They might not look if we pay in Canadian dollars."

We drove toward town looking for a bank. Before we came to one, we saw a sprawling and turreted Gothic brick building surrounded by a sharp and pointy black wrought-iron fence and a big sign:

THE BEAUNE FOUNDATION KINSHIP HOME

School buses were parked out front and children were filing out the door, down the wide granite steps, onto the buses.

"They're everywhere," Billy said.

"They?" I asked.

"Group homes. And kids to fill them."

The sight of the home seemed to darken his mood. We drove on, and finally found a bank. Billy went inside and changed our money. Tim Hortons, a brightly lit donut shop, was next door. After Billy was done at the bank, he and I went inside. I got a booth for us while Billy ordered at the counter.

He came back with two coffees and two glazed donuts. He was still quiet, and had barely said a word since the fire road.

The coffee was hot and bracing, and it gave me a jolt.

"Are you upset about seeing those kids?" I asked.

He shrugged, sipping his coffee.

"Or is it because we cut the chain?" I asked.

"On the road with my dad," Billy said, "he showed me how to get around everything. We broke into a house for food, and he stole stuff to sell. He never thought about the people who lived there—all he cared about was that there weren't cars in the driveway. That showed they probably weren't home so we could get in and out without, as he put it, 'having to restrain someone.' He never thought they would miss what he took, or have to spend money to fix the window we broke."

"Restrain?" I asked.

"Yeah," he said. "He said it like it was no big deal, but all I did was pray no one would be there."

"What we did was different. It was just a chain," I said, trying to convince myself. "And you left ten dollars."

"The money isn't the only point," he said.

"Still, you did something to pay for it," I said.

"You know what happened at that house, where my father broke the window?"

"What?"

"There was a cat inside. It was yellow. It scooted away from us when we walked in; we'd scared it. While my dad was stealing clocks and silver and whatever else he could stuff into a pillowcase, I tried to find the cat, to pet it and let it know everything would be okay. There were cat toys all over, a bowl of food in the kitchen. Those people loved that cat."

My stomach clenched, waiting for the next part.

"It jumped out the broken window," he said, "and ran away. I didn't know if it was an indoor cat, if it was used to being outside. I ran after it, to bring it home, and my father stopped me, yelled that we had to escape. Then he laughed. He called me 'a little jerk' for caring about the cat."

I thought of how awful it must have been for Billy, in shock about his mother, and being dragged along with someone like that.

"What happened to the cat?" I asked.

"I don't know," he said. "We drove off and I didn't see it again. I don't know if it ever made it home. When you do something wrong, you start a whole chain reaction. It's not just the one thing. It's everything that happens next."

We finished our coffee; I left half of my donut. I'd been so hungry from not eating last night, but now I'd lost my appetite. I felt uneasy, wondering what we'd unleashed by unlocking that gate.

We went back to the gas station, and Billy pumped the tank full of diesel and replaced a quart and a half of oil. He handed me the rest of our cash to count—the pile looked dangerously small. And then—

Billy turned the key, and the engine made a sputtering sound. It didn't whine like a dead battery; it sounded more serious.

"Not good," Billy said, getting out again.

The gas station guys rallied around—they had a small repair shop out back—and I watched Billy and them with their heads under the hood, tugging on wires.

"Do you mind if I find the library?" I asked.

"No, go ahead," Billy said, his head still buried in the engine.

I walked through town. The river was brown with spring mud, logs, and branches pushed downstream by melting ice. Even if Billy had been here I knew he wouldn't hear any lobsters in the fresh water. I meandered around until I found the Dr. Walter Chestnut Public Library.

It was the coolest old place: fieldstone with graceful curved windows, a sweeping staircase, and a clock tower. It felt familiar. That's the thing about libraries: no matter where they are, they feel like home. I said hello to the red-haired librarian wearing round black-rimmed glasses, then went straight to the computers.

Since fixing the truck would take a while, and I had plenty of time, I knew this was the perfect opportunity to DM with Gen and Clarissa. I told myself that if I didn't tell them where I was, they wouldn't feel bad about not telling their parents.

As soon as I logged into my email, I saw the subject heading:

FROM DAD.

I'd expected that. I'd answer him, then start messaging my friends.

I read my dad's email:

> *Dear Maia,*
> *You don't know how relieved I was to hear from you. I was so afraid you had hurt yourself.*
>
> *We found your mother's car at Hubbard's Point. The Coast Guard, including some old buddies of mine, searched the area—they dragged the shallows around the beach, looking for you—for your body. It was the worst day of my life, sweetheart.*
>
> *The only reason we found the car at all was because of Helen Lessard, an old friend of William Gorman. If not for Helen, we wouldn't have found the car at all. She warned us what kind of boy William is. Of course I knew what the newspapers said when he first entered your school, your class. But the papers made him sound like a victim.*
>
> *Helen says he went willingly with his father, a fugitive, and helped him hide from the police. She told us that he had money hidden, and that the two of you might have taken the train to New York City, a place he knows well.*

*I have another theory and assume you are somehow
heading to see your mother. I called her, and it took
forever, because she is deliberately un-findable and
can only be reached by satellite phone. She left us—
it was her choice. I don't mean to hurt you, but I
think you've figured this out for yourself by now.*

*She said she has not heard from you. I don't know
whether to believe her or not. Whatever your
wishes about her—they won't come true. I am
afraid for you, if you get your hopes up. She is not
capable of giving you what you need.*

*Nothing, no one in life, is more important to me
than you. No matter what you think about Astrid,
she knows that you come first, and she wouldn't
have it any other way. She really cares and wants
you to come home. Maia, this is hard to say, but
she has been more there for you than your own
mother.*

Just tell me where you are. I'll be right there.

*Love,
Dad*

I stared at my father's email for a long time. I cringed to
think of the pain he must have felt, watching the police and

Coast Guard dragging the bay at Hubbard's Point. Waiting for them to find my body.

But his words about my mother stung most. Had he forgotten that Mom had left us to save her own life? She'd been dying in the suburbs and didn't HAVE a choice. I totally got that. Astrid could never begin to comprehend how whales and fjords and climbing onto the roof in the snow were more important than a white Mercedes and cashmere.

I reread what Dad had written about "William." Of course Helen would say bad things about Billy—she was against him now. My dad didn't understand any of it.

It made me feel sad, but also defiant and powerful. Dad had no idea I was in love, that I had stopped taking my medication to feel again—to be alive, to be real, not encased in chemicals. I could do this on my own. It wasn't like the last time I went off meds, when I was still depressed. I felt great now.

And obviously Dad and Astrid didn't know we'd taken the rusty red truck.

Finally I hit the REPLY button, confronted the blank screen, and wrote:

> *Dear Dad,*
> *You asked me to email and tell you I'm safe.*
> *I am. Please don't worry.*
>
> *Love,*
> *Maia*

*P.S. Billy is wonderful. Don't listen to anyone who
says he's not.*

That was all I could manage for the moment. And some-how, after that, I didn't feel like messaging anyone, not even my best friends.

When I got back to the garage, Billy was still working on the truck. The distributor was shot, and so were the points. The garage owner told him he could pick through used parts. I pitched in, and it took us a while to find what we needed. As our repairs began to work, a little at a time—one wire connected, then another, a distributor cap, although really old and oily, that fit—I could tell he was in a much better mood. We were saving a ton of money, fixing the truck ourselves.

Just as we finished, the sky filled with clouds and it started to shower, then pour. He glanced at me and his eyes bright-ened. Our hands were covered with grease, our heads under the hood. The metal clanged, pelted by rain.

Billy stepped out from under and looked up. He stuck out his tongue to taste the raindrops.

"Try it," he said.

So I did. I tilted my head back and opened my mouth. The drops tickled my lips. It made me laugh, and Billy, too. I felt as if we were six years old with nothing to worry about.

"You know what we need?" he asked. "Ice cream."

"I'm ready," I said.

We went into the restroom and washed the oil off our hands with the grittiest soap I've ever felt. It smelled like oranges and made my skin burn. But by the time we thanked the garage owner and drove away, we were clean.

The Black Cat ice cream stand was a mile out of town; the guys at the garage had given us directions. Small and white, it had red shutters with cat silhouettes cut into them, a red awning with black polka dots, and a small line of people at the open window. Billy got a cup of chocolate and I had raspberry swirl. The rain had stopped, but the picnic tables were still wet, so we stood under the overhang. The clouds were breaking up, blue sky gleaming in the spaces between them.

Without asking me, Billy reached out a spoonful of his ice cream toward my mouth, and I tasted it. It was delicious. Then I gave him a bite of mine.

"How much do you think we saved, fixing the truck ourselves?" he asked.

"I have no idea," I said.

He kept eating his ice cream, seeming to add things up in his head. "The parts would have been fifty, sixty dollars. And labor could have been, I don't know, another fifty?"

"That's a lot," I said.

"I was thinking, with some of the money we didn't spend on the truck, we could buy extra ice cream."

"I'm pretty full now," I said. "And if we get it for later, won't it melt?"

"It's not for us," he said. "I want to give it to the kids at that place we saw this morning, the Kinship Home."

I loved the idea. He went to the window, and I saw him peeling a few bills off our shrinking wad of cash. Then he gestured me over, and we walked away laden with three half-gallon tubs—vanilla, chocolate chip, and raspberry swirl—and a bag full of wooden spoons.

We'd spent so much time fixing the truck, the afternoon had flown by, and school buses were already returning to the Home as we parked in the driveway. We got out of the truck and stood there with our bag of ice cream. The kids had started walking inside, but when they saw us, they first hesitated, then came closer. There were about twenty, ranging in age from very young—kindergarteners, first graders—to teens, about the same age as Billy and me.

Even before they reached us, Billy was pulling the lids off. The ice cream had softened a bit, and a few drips ran down the side of the cardboard tubs.

"Wait, shouldn't we give it to the administrators, or whatever you call them?" I asked Billy. "For them to serve after dinner?"

"Nope," Billy said. "These guys need a treat that's just for them. From someone who actually cares." He looked up, beckoning everyone to come forward, and he started passing out wooden spoons.

"What's this?" one boy asked, staring at the open tubs. He looked like the oldest, with long dark hair and tattoos on his arms. He had a black eye half-swollen shut, and he squinted with suspicion out of his other eye.

"Ice cream," Billy said, an edge of sarcasm in his voice.

"What do we have to do for it?" a tall black boy about our age asked. He stepped forward, in front of the other kids, as if protecting them.

"Nothing," Billy said.

"What if you poisoned it?" a girl asked. She looked to be a few years younger than me, and in spite of her freckles and braided red hair, her turquoise plaid shirt and cool-looking torn leggings, she sounded tough.

"We're not supposed to take food from strangers," a younger girl said, standing close to what had to be her sister— she had the same freckles, same russet-colored hair.

"I'm not a stranger," Billy said. "I'm one of you."

"What do you mean, 'one of us'?" the tattooed boy said, looking ready to fight. "We don't know you."

"Yeah, you do," Billy said.

"He lived in a place like this," I said.

"A place like this?" the older red-haired girl asked.

"A group home," Billy said. "Foster care. The Stansfield Home in Connecticut."

The two older boys still looked suspicious, but the younger kids couldn't hold back. They grabbed their flat wooden spoons and dug into the ice cream. The red-haired girls hung back for a minute, then both went for the chocolate chip.

"Why'd you get this for us?" the tattooed boy asked, finally grabbing a spoon.

"Because I know what it's like," Billy said. "The same food on the same days of the week, none of it good, mystery meat and watery pasta, and it's spring, and everyone should have ice cream."

"Old Whistler's going to love this; we left him out of our treat," a black girl who must have been eleven said, laughing. She wore a pink hoodie and faded jeans, and she pushed a young boy I thought must be her brother right to the front of the pack.

"Who's Old Whistler?" I asked her.

"He's on duty today," the girl said. "He's probably watching TV in his room right now. He can't be bothered to wait for the little kids getting off the bus, but he whistles for us whenever he wants us to do something."

"Just like we're dogs," her little brother said.

"Well, you're not, and the ice cream isn't for him," Billy said. "It's for you."

"Thanks, man," the tattooed kid said.

"No problem," Billy said. "What happened to your eye?"

"A fight at school," he said. "I guess you'd say I'm a problem."

"Aren't we all?" Billy said.

"It looks like you're doing okay."

"Trying," Billy said.

"Yeah," the boy said.

They shook hands. The ice cream tubs were emptying quickly, and Old Whistler hadn't even looked out the window by the time Billy and I drove away. Our hands were sticky. I couldn't stop smiling.

"Well, we may have to get jobs to pay for the rest of the trip," Billy said. "We're not totally broke yet, but that put a huge dent into what we have left."

"It was worth it."

"You sure?"

I nodded. "Oh, yeah. I mean, you must wish someone had done something like that for you at Stansfield."

Billy thought for a second then nodded. "Yeah. They take 'care' of us, but it stops there. No one treats us as if we're special, as if we stand out or really matter in the long run. We're just a bunch of kids on state aid."

"You're more than that," I said.

We stopped at a red light.

"I feel that right now," Billy said. He turned to me, touching my cheek. "For the first time in . . . a while."

My skin tingled because I wondered if he was about to kiss me. I thought of the night before. My eyelids fluttered closed, waiting and hoping that he'd do it again, for real this time.

"We'll have to work if we want more ice cream," he said, breaking the spell. The light changed and he drove on.

"Or lobster rolls," I said, hiding the fact that I was disappointed the moment had passed.

"We're going to have to find another place to sleep tonight." He shot me a smiling glance. "And last night will be hard to beat."

Chapter 12

MAY 24
WILDERNESS
NEW BRUNSWICK, CANADA

I told Billy about my dad's email and what Helen had told him. Billy was silent about that. But now that we knew my dad was onto us, at least suspecting we were heading toward my mother, we had to be even more careful. The fastest way to get to her would be to jump on the highway and zoom north.

Instead, we stuck with Plan A and found the rugged back-way logging trail Darrah had told us about—the one that led to her family's abandoned inn—that would eventually take us to the Saint Lawrence River.

The trail was much rougher than the fire road, barely wide enough for the truck, and led through the most remote and mosquito-ridden area I'd ever been in. According to the atlas, there wouldn't be any stores or lobster rolls or Tim Hortons. Not even a gas station. There were a few fishing and hunting lodges, and a couple of campgrounds, and that was all.

We bumped along, over ruts so deep Billy had to hold the wheel with both hands and wrangle the truck to keep us from tilting into a ditch. We slapped at mosquitoes that had made their way into the car. We went through a deep mudhole, and it took the four-wheel drive to get us out. Clouds scudded through the sky, making the air feel heavy, as if it wanted to thunderstorm. The late afternoon turned muggy, and even though we were up in Canada, it felt as hot and still as midsummer.

Rolling down the windows brought a welcome breeze but also a major flock of buzzing insects: the mosquitoes were joined by green flies and gigantic winged creatures that seemed more mythical than real.

Aside from the insects, here are a few other things we saw:

- Ten, yes, TEN moose, including a mother and calf
- Too many bald eagles to count
- Two men fishing in a boat on a wide lake
- A woman fly-fishing at a narrow stream
- Darkening clouds and spitting raindrops
- A red fox
- A boy and a girl hiking with enormous backpacks

"Should we give them a ride?" I asked as we drove past and we all waved at each other.

"Um, serial killers," Billy said.

"Of course. All serial killers have Merlin stickers on their backpacks."

"They did?"

"Well, she did," I said.

Billy kept driving, and I have to admit, it was just as well: I didn't really want to share the ride with anyone but him. I realized I was waiting for him to take a hand off the wheel and put his arm around me. I wanted him to pull over so we could take a break from driving, and my mind was going crazy remembering the almost kiss and imagining what might happen on this dark, romantic back road on our way to an old abandoned inn.

"Okay, we'll pick them up if you want to," Billy suddenly said.

"You sure?"

"Yeah. I guess I'm trying to learn from you and, um, trust a little more," he said.

I had to smile at that. We pulled over on the side of the road and waited for them to jog over.

"Hey," the boy said, adjusting his backpack. "Thanks for stopping."

"Want a ride?" Billy asked. "Escape the mosquitoes?"

"More like stinging helicopters," the girl said, slapping her wrist.

"Well, you have a choice," Billy said. "Sit in the back, where they'll get you anyway, or crowd inside with us. No air-conditioning, though, so they're coming in the open windows."

"Inside," the girl said, meeting my eyes. "If you don't mind."

"I don't," I said, a less-than-half-truth. She was tall and

beautiful with long blond hair—that unfortunately reminded me of Helen—and bug bites all over her neck and arms. The boy was just as tall, and handsome, with dark brown skin; his curly hair poked out from beneath a red cap. They dropped their packs into the truck bed and climbed in. We were squeezed so tightly together, I was practically sitting on Billy's lap.

We introduced ourselves. The boy's name was Richard Faguais and the girl was Morgane Beaudoin. They were students at a private school in Fredericton, doing their senior science project on gray tree frogs in western New Brunswick.

"How about you guys?" Morgane asked. "What brings you from the States to our boonies?"

"We're doing a sophomore project on road trips," Billy said. I glanced at him, surprised at how quickly he lied.

"Seriously?" Morgane asked. "So cool!"

"He's kidding," I said. "Sort of. We're from Connecticut, heading up to the Saint Lawrence River. To, um, see whales."

"That's awesome," Richard said.

"There's massive feeding action right now," Morgane said. "My family vacations there, and we've seen it. Whales are so freaking intuitive and clairvoyant, and they love the Saint Lawrence—a few bodies of water merge up there, and it gets all churned up, and you get this incredible gathering of whales to feed, especially in June—before summer—and September, immediately after. They sing to each other; they're the selkies of the marine mammal world." She shivered and smiled, as if getting a creepy thrill from it.

Whales? *Freaking intuitive and clairvoyant? Selkies of the marine mammal world?*

She was too cool for words, sleek and confident, and she made me feel insecure. Girls like her always did.

"Where are you heading?" Billy asked them. "We don't want to take you too far if you'll be missing great frogs."

"Well, we just left Langley's Pond, and we're heading to the Granville Reserve, right here," Richard said, showing me the map on his phone. He pointed at the next destination, at least twenty-five miles north. "We thought we'd have to camp along the way, but we might make it driving with you. Seriously, thanks."

"Seriously," Morgane echoed. "To tell you the truth, we are on a discouraging quest. It's sad. The gray tree frog is uncommon in New Brunswick. For a long time it seemed they only existed in a certain marsh near Fredericton. But that is being developed, and they are on the way to disappearing there."

I glanced over at her, softening toward her slightly. She was mourning something gone, or on the way out. I understood that. The sun glowed orange, inching down into dusk.

Billy reached for the radio and spun the dial, but catching a station out here was a dream that would never come true. Morgane pulled out her iPhone and set it on the dashboard. She put on a playlist, and we listened to Mumford & Sons and didn't talk for a while.

We stayed on the dirt road, and we alternated between keeping the windows open and getting chewed alive by mosquitoes and closing them and wilting in the sauna of our sweat. In the distance, thunder rumbled and every so often the sky lit up with a quick, bright flash of heat lightning.

Although we hadn't yet come to the Granville Reserve, everything looked like a nature sanctuary to me: pine groves, oak groves, bogs, marshes, and the uneven, dusty road heading due north. I reached into my bag and pulled out the green book from Mystic. We were actually in Canada, getting closer to my mother. Holding the book made everything feel even more real. I wanted to turn on the overhead light and dive in, but I felt it would have seemed rude to read in front of these strangers.

The sun had gone below the tree line. It was almost evening, the light fading. Darrah had said we should get to the cabin before dark. Night creatures started calling: whip-poor-wills, owls, and . . .

"Hear them?" Morgane asked.

"Tree frogs?" I asked.

"Yep, our guys or their close cousins. They have such a spiritual sound, don't they? We should probably get out here."

"No, it's too dark," I said, worried to leave them even though I wasn't crazy about her and she'd said whales were clairvoyant and frogs were spiritual.

"They're nocturnal—this is the best time. Besides, we have our tents," Richard said. He had an accent I couldn't quite place, but it was beautiful, melodic, and I wanted to hear him talk more.

"Are you French?" I asked him. I was suddenly eager to practice my French; it was one of the few things I realized I missed about school.

"I was born in Haiti," Richard said. "But I was adopted and came to this country when I was ten."

"That must have been a big change," I said.

"Yes," he said. "Quebec City, where my parents live, is very cold compared to Port-au-Prince. It's not much warmer here, at least in winter."

"You don't live with your parents?" Billy asked.

"I go home on vacations and some weekends," Richard said. "But I'm at boarding school, the same as Morgane. École Sainte-Anne is very good, and it's helped with getting into a good college."

"Are you from far away, too?" Billy asked Morgane.

"No, I've always lived in this province. New Brunswick is my family's home, so I get to see my family much more often than Richard and our other classmates do."

I half listened to her but found myself wondering what had happened to Richard at age ten that he had to leave Haiti and come to Canada. As we kept driving along, the sound of the tree frogs got louder, and Morgane and Richard leaned out the window to hear them better.

"Hey," Billy said to me, a couple of miles later. "Check that out."

"What?"

"Birches!" he said, pointing at a grove of trees with thin white trunks.

He pulled Darrah's note from his jeans pocket and handed it to me. It was too dark to see in natural light, so he turned on the overhead cab light. I read:

North on ENDLESS dirt road past beaver pond, eagles in dead oak tree, then look for granite pump house and lots of white birch trees. Take a right straight through the birches and brambles. Go half mile to the most gorgeous lake you have ever seen and find haunted house. Well, I mean family inn. The sign says Aurora Inn. Key is under stone flowerpot. How imaginative, right? Sleep in turret room but be careful of rotted-out floor. You will thank me later!

Peering into the birches, I spotted the pump house and sign.

"We're here," I said.

"Hey, if you want to get out here, it's fine," Billy said, leaning around me to talk to Morgane and Richard. "But someone told us about an old family place, an inn on a lake. It's down that road. We'll probably cook some food and spend the night. Come if you want."

"Sure, as long as there are frogs," Morgane said.

"They're really loud," Richard said, his head out the window. "A good sign they are here, nearby."

The road narrowed, then practically disappeared into the overgrown brush. We felt branches swishing and smashing against the truck doors, and they nearly obscured the way ahead. The thicket enclosed us, but then the road widened slightly and we entered a clearing. At the far end was a tall, dark, imposing, and ramshackle Victorian house. Behind it, a lake shimmered in twilight and the chorus of tree frogs seemed louder than ever.

"The Aurora Inn," Richard said, reading the faded sign.

"I've heard of this place," Morgane said, gazing up at the ornate gingerbread work around the wide front porch. "I'm pretty sure my great-aunt used to come here."

We piled out of the truck, and Billy grabbed a flashlight from the glove compartment. The wind direction had changed, and not one mosquito struck between the truck and the time we'd walked to the front porch. The steps creaked. I tried to be surreptitious as Billy, Richard, and Morgane stood in the side yard—actually a field of tall grass leading to the vast lake, surrounded by pine and birch trees—and fumbled under the stone flowerpot on the top step to find the brass key.

I stuck it in the old, rusty lock and opened the door. Last light slanted through tall windows, and Billy turned on his flashlight. The interior screamed *fishing lodge*. The dead-fish trophies were the first clue. There were deceased trout all over the walls. Rainbow trout, brown trout, speckled trout, and brook trout, all stuck on wooden boards with names of the fishermen and the day of the catch engraved on brass plates.

Cobwebs stretched from the ceiling beams to the white-sheet-covered furniture. I had a quick memory of Billy's grandparents' cottage, as humble as this was grand, but the chairs similarly protected. A single couch by the fireplace had been uncovered. I wondered if Darrah and Cleo had sat there when this had been their hideaway. On the table beside the couch was a matchbox and a tall candle in a tarnished brass holder. I lit the candle and carried it around the room to light others on the mantel, sideboard, and top of the bookcase.

Richard and Morgane were exploring outside so Billy carried in a couple of our bags, including the cans from his grandparents' cottage. I knew I should help, but I was slightly frozen. Something deep inside was giving me twinges. It couldn't be going off the medication—I'd only missed a day's worth so far. I sat on the uncovered sofa and had the weirdest feeling.

What was I doing here, in this spooky inn? A swoon of doubt and depression came over me. I wanted to grab Billy and tell him we should leave. Suddenly the trip was closing in on me. I wanted to get to my mother.

Before I could move, Richard came in carrying some dry logs and a bundle of kindling.

"There's a wood stack out back," he said as he placed the logs by the wide stone hearth. "It's odd. This inn looks perfect inside, and they had all those logs ready for fires, and what happened? Everyone just left."

"My friend said people found other places to go," I said.

"Like Haiti," Richard said with a smile.

We piled twigs in the fireplace and built a pyramid of three logs on top. I jiggled the iron handle to check the damper. Richard knelt on the hearth and peered up into the chimney to make sure the flue was open. He found a jar of dry matches on the mantel and lit the kindling. The fire began to crackle.

"You're good at building a fire," I said.

"It was one of the first things I learned when I came to

Canada," he said. "My parents had a woodstove, and I liked to sit by it. Anything to get warm."

He crouched by the fire, stirring the logs with an iron poker, and I watched and listened to him. He moved with quiet grace, economy of movement. I loved the way his voice lilted.

I leaned forward, to feel the heat of the flames, just as Billy walked in from the kitchen. He frowned, and I realized it looked as if I had moved closer to Richard. The idea that he might be slightly jealous zinged through me.

Then Morgane came through the door with a flourish.

"Oh, yes," she said. "Definitely."

"Definitely what?" I asked.

She began to pace the room, head turning from side to side as if searching for something she'd lost. Tall and thin, she was built almost like a boy, but that long blond hair flowed like gold, swishing all around. Her dark brown eyes held steady and serious. She wore a white T-shirt that hugged her incredibly thin body but stopped just above her bug-bitten hip bones, jutting out over slouchy jeans. I knew I could never feel as cool, dress as cool, or be as cool as her.

"She's here," Morgane said.

"Who?" Billy asked.

"Morgane sees spirits," Richard said. "The dead, who haven't been released from this world."

I gave him a look of pure skepticism, but at the same time I felt a chill in my chest. What spirits, what dead? It had to be a joke, or a game. I shook off the sensation and carried one of the candles to light my way into the kitchen.

The counters were polished wood, the stove the biggest I'd ever seen, and there must have been a hundred cupboards. I eventually found pans, plates, and utensils, and wiped the dust from them. Billy came in and opened a can of vegetable beef soup, dumped the contents into a copper pot, and stirred.

"What were you and Richard talking about?" he asked.

I gave him a quick glance. He *was* jealous! "Just the fire," I said.

"That's a fascinating subject," he said dryly.

I couldn't hold back a smile.

I set out plates on the round oak table by the fire, folding cloth napkins, loving the idea that Darrah and Cleo had eaten here. The fire crackled as a log exploded. Sparks shot into the chimney like fireworks, drifted down, and fizzled out. The four of us sat down and devoured the entire pot of soup, a can of brown bread, and a box of cranberry-nut bars.

"You brought this food with you?" Richard asked.

"Yes. I'd make a good survivalist, hiding out forever," Billy said. I glanced over, knowing he was referring to lessons learned from his father.

"So," Morgane said, leaning forward on her elbows. "Tell us the real story, please. Why are two kids from Connecticut traveling the back roads of N.B. with the key to this magical place?"

"You're right, there's always a real story behind the story," Billy said.

He and I sat beside each other. I gazed at his face, his freckles showing even in the firelight, his hair burnished reddish-brown, and his eyes more beautifully green-gold than ever.

"Yes?" Morgane asked.

"Yes," Billy said. "We're running away."

"Why are you on the run?" Morgane asked, smiling. "Are you in trouble? Desperate young criminals?"

"Well, one of us is," Billy said. "Sort of."

Morgane squinted at him, fully engaged and wanting to hear more. I had the strangest feeling that she knew more than she was letting on.

"Tell me more," she said, leaning in.

"Nothing," I said interrupting. "There's nothing to tell."

"*Why* did you run away? Kids our age don't just leave unless there's a good reason."

Billy hesitated, and I could feel him weighing his words. *Don't tell the truth,* I willed him. But he didn't get the message.

"Because Maia has somewhere to go. And I'm over the group home I've been living in for way too long. I guess you could say we're on a mission together."

"Ooh, a mission," Morgane said. "But still, there's more. I can feel it. It's coming through me, something about you being in a group home. Why were you there?"

"She can be a little blunt," Richard said.

"I got sent to foster care after my parents . . . well, I couldn't live with them anymore. My father did something . . . bad. And I helped him afterward."

"What did he do?" Richard asked.

"He killed someone. And I'm the killer's son," Billy said, and I felt him wanting to shock them with his statement and defiant tone of voice. But the strange thing was, he wasn't looking at them: He was staring straight at me, as if he wanted to see my reaction.

"Who did he kill?" Richard asked.

"Yes, tell us," Morgane said.

"I'm going to leave it at that."

"You tell us you're the killer's son, that's too provocative. It's unfair to just drop it," Morgane said. "What did you do to help him?"

"I didn't stop him from getting away. And I went with him."

I stood, started clearing plates. Billy took them from me so I could carry the candle and illuminate our way into the kitchen.

"You didn't seem like you just now," I said to him. "Why were you like that?"

"It builds up," he said. "I always acted like a jerk at the Home when I felt someone getting too close."

"Morgane was getting too close?" I asked.

He didn't respond, just clattered the dishes into the sink. Then he turned his back on me and returned to the living room. I felt confused and hurt by his sudden change. His anger seemed directed at me, and I couldn't understand why.

When I returned to the living room, Morgane was walking slowly in a circle, looking up at the ceiling, flickering with shadows from the firelight and all the candle flames.

"Hello, Aurelia," she said in a low, trembling voice.

"Aurelia?" Billy asked.

"My great-aunt," she said. "I sense her now."

"What do you mean?" I asked, following her stare up to the vaulted ceiling where spiderwebs glittered and an old chandelier caught the candlelight and threw prisms onto the dark oak floor.

"My great-aunt was clairvoyant, and I inherited that from her. And I believe she's here to help you and Billy."

Clairvoyant whales, spiritual frogs, and now a long-lost great-aunt here to help Billy and me? She sounded totally bogus. But an unwelcome eerie feeling went through me. Richard watched her, caught in a spell. Morgane stood still, staring as if she were seeing her great-aunt's ghost.

Outside, the tree frogs had let up, with only an occasional peep and croak, drowned out now by the sound of crickets and the snapping of firewood.

"You're getting weird again," Richard said.

"Yes," Morgane said, giving him a warm glance.

"Isn't that an insult?" Billy asked.

Morgane laughed. "Haven't you ever read *The Scottish Play*?"

"You're don't have to call it that here," Richard told her. "It's bad luck to say '*Macbeth*' in a theater, but you're in an old inn."

"You're right. In *Macbeth*, Shakespeare called them the weird sisters, but they were witches," Morgane said. "They had powers, second sight . . ."

"And you're a witch?" I asked.

"She says she is," Richard said.

"Of all people, you should know," Morgane said to him. "Haiti is a true center of magic, of *Vodou*."

"My mother—my birth mother—didn't believe in black magic. She told us to stay away from it," Richard said.

"Well, this is good magic; it's not my fault I was born this way. It runs in our family, and I'm named for Morgane le Fay."

"Who?" Billy asked.

"Enchantress from King Arthur," she said, just throwing it out as if it was simultaneously no big deal and incredibly impressive. "My great-aunt is standing right there." She pointed at a spot beneath the chandelier.

Billy was silent for a minute. He stood up and walked over. I watched him pass his hand through the air as if trying to touch a ghost.

"Can you talk to her?" he asked.

"Yes."

"And other spirits, too?"

"If they want to be contacted," Morgane said. "Should we have a séance?"

"I don't think so," I said.

"Yeah," Billy said. "We should."

Morgane pulled a notebook from her backpack and ripped out a few pages. She wrote the alphabet, large letters on each page.

"A homemade Ouija board," Richard said. "She should probably carry a real one wherever she goes. It's bizarre. We're both planning to be science majors at McGill in the fall, but she's really into the magic-spirit world."

"Bite your tongue, not scientific!" Morgane said. "You know there's proof. I've spoken to both your parents, Richard."

He didn't respond but sat very still, staring into the fire.

"Proof of what?" Billy asked.

"The next life. And that spirits return to us," Morgane said. "Just because you can't see gravity, does it mean it doesn't exist? Does it make sense that you can plant a dry, old bulb in October and have a daffodil sprout the next spring?"

"It's not the same," I said. "And by the way, whales aren't clairvoyant."

"They speak. They communicate very clearly," she said. "And they see what we cannot." She drifted into the kitchen, moving as if working herself into a trance. Eventually she came back with a dusty wineglass.

"This will have to do for a planchette," she said. "The Ouija board pointer."

We sat on the floor around the pages of letters. The fire was dying down, the red coals throwing shadows on the walls and everyone's faces. Billy seemed fixated on the alphabet.

"Okay," Morgane said. "I will talk to Aurelia first. She will guide us forward. Richard, please write down the letters as they come. Billy—is there someone special you hope to talk to?"

"My m—" he began.

"Will Aurelia really answer?" I asked quickly, cutting Billy off, not wanting to give Morgane any clues.

"Let's see." Morgane turned the wineglass upside down, then placed her fingertips on the base. She closed her eyes, arched her back, then straightened her spine. She licked her lips with the tip of her pink tongue.

"Spirit," she said, her voice deepening an octave. *Lame and stagy*, I thought, looking around to see if Billy and Richard agreed. But they both had their eyes glued to her.

"Are you Great-Aunt Aurelia?" Morgane asked.

The wineglass spelled *YES.* Stunner!

"I love you, the whole family misses you," Morgane said. "Is there anything you can tell me that I should know?"

It took forever for ol' Aurelia, aka Morgane, to spell out *YOUR GIFT IS GREAT. DO NOT SQUANDER THE POWER AND HONOUR.*

"Nice touch, the 'u' in honor," I said.

"That's how it's spelled in Canada," Richard said, and my shoulders instantly flew up to my ears. I felt stupid.

"Shhh," Morgane said. "No conversation." Then, "Thank you, Great-Aunt Aurelia. I do not want to take too much of your time . . ."

TIME DOES NOT MATTER IN MY REALM.

"Of course not," Morgane said. "My new friend would like to contact a spirit. Can you tell us if one is near, has sensed his desire for contact?"

Here it comes, I thought, and it did: She'd caught that *m.*

I SENSE TWO MOTHERS.

"Two mothers?" Morgane asked. I could tell she was genuinely surprised, and that made me sit up straighter.

ONE FROM MY WORLD AND ONE FROM YOURS.

Morgane opened her eyes. She reached for Billy's hands, one after the other, and directed him to place them on the wineglass's base. Then, to my shock, she reached for mine. "We'll do this together," she said. "You ask the questions. Keep your fingertips very lightly on the glass."

"But my mother's alive," I said. Then my heart skipped—

what if she wasn't? What if something had happened to her since she wrote that last email?

"Maia, she clearly said one of them is from our world," Morgane said gently.

"How do you know she's not talking about you or Richard? About one of *your* mothers?"

"Because Aurelia is staring at you."

I kept my fingertips on the base of the wineglass. What could my mother say to me? Even if ghosts could talk through mediums, how could my mother, alive—I had to believe she was—get through?

"Who wants to go first?" Morgane asked.

Billy and I exchanged glances and he nodded at me.

"I have to," I said. "Is my mother . . . in your world or ours?"

The planchette moved slowly at first, then darted to each letter:

YOURS.

"So she's not here?"

NO.

"Then how can you speak to her?"

SPIRITS CAN READ HEARTS.

My fingers started trembling so hard, the planchette veered left, right, up, down.

I felt Morgane's hand on my wrist. "Breathe deeply," she said with true kindness and gentleness in her voice. "This can upset those who've never done it before. Why don't you take your fingers off for now and let Billy ask his questions. We can return to you later."

Almost reluctantly I let my hands drift away from the glass, dropped them to my sides. I found my gaze darting to the place where Morgane had said Aurelia stood. *There's no way this is real*, I told myself.

"Okay," Billy said. "I feel dumb doing this."

"Your mother is in the room," Morgane said. "I doubt she would want you to feel dumb. Close your eyes. Talk to her."

"Okay," Billy said, squirming. "Uh, Mom?"

HELLO MY DARLING.

Billy hesitated, then cleared his throat. "Um, that doesn't sound like you, Mom. *'Darling'*?"

I AM NOT USED TO SPEAKING IN THIS REALM. FORGIVE ME.

"Okay."

"Ask her some questions," Morgane urged. "She has come to answer whatever you want to know."

Billy nodded. He opened his eyes for a second, glanced around at all of us. I tried to keep my expression from communicating what a crock I thought—hoped—this was.

"Mom," Billy said. "Did you know Dad meant to . . ." His voice got gravelly and he had to stop. He coughed, covering up the fact that he couldn't talk. Suddenly my heart was pierced; no matter whether this was real or not, Billy was gripped with intensity. "Mom, were you scared?"

YES.

"Could it have been an accident?"

NO. HE HAD A PLAN.

"What did he plan to do?" he asked sharply. No movement

for a whole minute, and I thought it would all stop right there, but the glass inched forward, then sped around the letters.

KILL ME.

"He pled guilty, but that was to protect me. I can't believe . . ." Billy said.

"You can't contradict the spirit," Morgane said quietly. "This is as traumatic for her as it is for you."

Billy raised his hands from the glass's base and bowed his head. Then his fingertips touched the glass again.

"I'm sorry, Mom," he whispered.

YOU DID NOTHING WRONG, BILLY. KNOW THAT. I LEAVE YOU NOW WITH MY LOVE FOREVER.

My mouth dropped open. I wanted to hold Billy, to reassure him somehow, to say this was probably a horrible charade. But he kept looking down, his face hidden. I wanted to say that maybe his questions had given Morgane the clue for the "spirit's" answers. But he wouldn't look at me. The hurt I'd felt in the kitchen deepened.

"Would you like to try again?" Morgane asked me.

I shook my head no.

Morgane stood. She walked over to the spot where she said Aurelia stood, and Morgane seemed to listen.

"Yes, Aunt," she said and seemed to listen again. "I understand and will ask her."

"Ask me what?"

"Are you an only child?"

"Yes," I said. Morgane nodded, as if that meant something to her. She turned back to Aurelia.

"Thank you, dear aunt, and farewell for now. All love and peace to you."

I stared at Morgane. I felt torn up inside but didn't want to give her the satisfaction of asking any questions.

"Maia, Aurelia said that because your mother is in her body and not a spirit, she could not transmit direct questions. But she read her heart, and these are the words that came up: *missing, waiting, child,* and *song*."

"She's waiting for me?" I asked, my voice tight.

"I can only assume. The word *child* seemed to indicate she holds you strongly and forever in her heart, and that she treasures the maternal bond."

"She does," I whispered. "She always said her leaving had nothing to do with me . . ."

Waiting. My mother was waiting for me.

Suddenly my emotions overtook me. Communicating with ghosts and hearts, Billy's coldness—all of it felt like too much. I stood up, and my legs quivering, I grabbed the flashlight Billy had brought in from the truck. I walked across the room, up the stairs with their fancy, tooled wooden banister. I felt like an apparition myself.

I swept the flashlight around and saw that the second floor was full of bedrooms. One was a three-room suite with an ornate marble fireplace, a big brass bed, and a curved window overlooking the dark lake. There were tiny rooms, too, with single beds and tiny dressers. I wandered through them, feeling unsteady.

The beam lit a narrow path, and I found a back staircase,

steeper than the front one, with no light whatsoever. Instead of a handrail there was a heavy, rough rope that seemed to be strung through metal fittings along the right-hand wall, and I used it to guide myself up another flight.

The third floor was the turret—a round room with windows looking in every direction. Not one wall was straight, and they rose to a pointed tower overhead. Darrah was right—there were creaky and broken floorboards. Starlight came through the glass, and I stepped carefully over to the bed and clicked off the flashlight.

Missing, waiting, child, song. I was exhausted and lay down in the total dark on the ancient mattress, the collapsing bed. Springs creaked as I turned over, lay on my side. The iron had so thoroughly rusted out, the frame had broken in the middle, and the mattress sagged into a deep V.

I closed my eyes. It was almost as if Aurelia had read my heart, too. I had yearned for my mother all these years. The wait was nearly at an end.

When I was depressed, I missed my mother so badly I thought I would dissolve. That my body was too weak to contain the unbearable longing I felt for her. One major symptom of my depression had been staying in bed. There were days I couldn't make myself get up, when my father, or the staff at Turner, had had to literally lift me out from under the blankets.

People suffered with love, but they also rose with it—it might take time, and come when you least expected, but it could lift you up to a place you never thought you'd be. That's what I was on my way to, and Billy was taking me there. I turned my head to look toward the window and thought of how far he and I had come, how he'd promised he'd take me to my mother, and how that promise was coming true.

"Hey."

At the sound of Billy's voice, I turned my head to look. The room was so dark, but I could make him out. He was standing in the doorway to the turret.

"Hey," I said.

"Are you okay?" he asked. He sounded gentle again, not hostile. But my throat still ached from how hurt I'd felt. I didn't answer.

"The frog people went . . . back out to search for frogs," he said, still standing in the doorway. "They have their nets and flashlights out."

"I thought maybe you'd keep talking to your mother," I said. "Through Morgane."

"Did you think I believed that?"

"You didn't?" I asked.

"I wanted to," he said. "But the minute I heard 'darling' I knew it was fake. My mother never would have said that."

"Why did you keep it up?"

"I wanted to see how far Morgane would go," he said.

"She went pretty far."

"Yeah," he said. "And it got me for a minute, hearing 'kill me.' I knew that was Morgane, not my mother, but it still punched me in the stomach. I was really mad at myself for asking real questions. Like if he meant to do it. I mean, I'd given Morgane enough clues when we were talking before. That's how she kept up the con."

"You seemed so into it."

"I wasn't."

"And you seemed mad at me."

He shook his head. "I meant what I said. I act like a jerk when people go there. I'm sorry if I gave you the idea it was you."

His apology washed over me. But I still felt confused by his rapid change of moods.

Outside the frogs peeped. It started to rain. I heard it tapping the roof, softly at first, then hard and steady. Somewhere in the dark room I heard a leak, a drip-drip-drip coming through a hole in the old roof. It soothed me. I closed my eyes.

I heard Billy open a closet door. He rummaged inside, and then I felt him tuck a quilt over me. His hands lingered on my shoulders for just a second, and I tensed up. Then he settled down on the other side of the bed, on top of the cover. We lay there, facing away from each other, and my heart was racing. So were my thoughts, but I didn't say anything out loud, and a long time later, I drifted into sleep.

Chapter 13

MAY 25
NEW BRUNSWICK, CANADA

It was still dark when I woke up. Both the rain and the tree frogs had stopped. I looked for Billy next to me, but his side of the bed was empty. The room was empty. I got up from the broken bed and felt my way down the pitch-black stairs.

The fire had died down during the night, and the living room was chilly. Billy stood at the fireplace, stirring the last coals with the poker, making sure they were out. We watched to make sure there were no sparks. We ate a few granola bars, then carried our duffel bags and the rest of the food onto the porch and closed the door behind us.

We loaded the truck. I figured Morgane and Richard were still sleeping, but then I heard feet crunching twigs and dried leaves. Richard's voice was low, and so was Morgane's. They walked over to the truck holding nets and specimen jars.

"We stayed up all night and were rewarded," Richard said, holding up one of the jars. The water looked murky, and there were squiggly little things swimming around. "Quite a few tadpoles to study. So many, in fact, we thought we might spend the day here. Would that be cool?"

"We don't need to go back into the house," Morgane said.

"Sure," I said.

Richard and Morgane went to the house to get their stuff. I waited till they returned to the truck to return the key to its hiding spot.

"Maia," Morgane said as I walked closer. "I hope you're okay. I know how crazy it can all seem. It seemed that way to me, the first time I saw my mother speak to a spirit. I thought she was insane. But over the years the gift has come to me, and I know it's true."

I thought I saw genuine concern in her brown eyes.

"I think you're very special," Morgane said. "Aurelia has never done that before, carried a message from a living person. But you heard the message."

"Yes," I said. *Missing, waiting, child, song.*

"Hold on to the four words if times get hard," Morgane said, hugging me tight.

I choked up, the words running through my mind. I wondered if she had any idea what they meant to me.

We all said good-bye. Billy pulled out of the driveway and left Morgane and Richard standing in the clearing, alone with the frogs and the ghosts.

We drove for miles. The day's first silver light reflected in the lake and lit our way. Morgane's words about my mother rang in my ears.

"You honestly didn't believe that was real?" I asked.

"No," he said.

Billy drove along in silence. These days together had shown me he had several variations of being quiet. Sometimes he was right there, totally present, but just not saying anything. Other times he was intensely engaged, like a person playing chess, focused on the next move.

But there was a third way, like now, when he zoomed out and saw the whole picture, when he was wiser than any sixteen-year-old kid had any right to be. Maybe it was because of what he'd been through, who he'd lost.

"You have to be careful, Maia," he said finally. "Morgane was cruel to trick you that way."

"Trick me?"

"Those four words could mean anything."

"I know what they mean," I said. "Exactly what they say."

"Except Morgane pulled them out of thin air. You're making them fit the situation with your mother, but think about it. Anyone could apply them to their own lives."

"No," I said, anger building in my chest. "She feels them for me. I know it."

"Look," he said. "That was bull, what happened back there. My mother's dead, and there's no way she can talk to me. And there's no way to know what your mother is thinking now."

"Thinking *now*?"

"Yeah. As opposed to before she left. That's impossible. All you can count on is that she loved you then, loves you still. Let that be enough. She had her reasons for running out, but it wasn't you. No one could ever want to leave you, Maia. But you can't be sure she doesn't want her own life, doesn't want you to stay away. You have to be prepared for that."

"Well, I'm not. She wants me," I said. I felt burning fury and stared out the window, anywhere but at him.

He could have softened his words, said something to make me feel better. But he didn't. I knew that wasn't his way—he was defiantly unsentimental, and he didn't trust anyone. He drove in silence, still on the predawn dark logging road.

I matched his silence. There was nothing I wanted to say to him. We were back in range of radio stations, and I found one that played singer-songwriters. The very first song that came on was Gillian Welch singing "Revelator" and I took it as a sign: My mother's name was Gillian, too.

As mad as I was at Billy, I couldn't shake one thing he'd said: *No one could ever want to leave you, Maia.*

Had he meant my mother?

Or had he meant himself? I thought of our almost kiss.

The miles went by, and I had to hold on as tight as I could to the seat. Inside, my heart was jumping around, I was veering back and forth between feeling mad, feeling hurt, and hoping that I meant something to him.

Another song came on and the radio guy said it was "Wagon Wheel" by Old Crow Medicine Show. Billy glanced at me to see if I knew it. I didn't, but it sounded happy, full of guitars and fiddles.

He pulled over, shifted the truck into park, turned up the radio, and opened the door.

"Come on," he said.

I hesitated. My bad mood kept me from moving. But the way he stood by the open door, and the look in his eyes, made me get out. We stood in a glade of pine trees, with brown needles underfoot, the music surrounding us. Billy gave me his hand, I took it, and suddenly we were dancing. The sun was just coming up, a line of red beneath gray clouds. It was a fast song, but our dance was slow. I felt Billy's hand on the small of my back, his breath on my cheek. The song played.

Rock me mama like a wagon wheel, rock me mama anyway you feel . . .

My heart thumped in my chest, and I felt his beating against mine. The song ended, another began, and we kept dancing for another minute.

What would he think if he'd known it was my first dance? What did I think?

He let me go, and we both climbed into the truck.

"That's better," he said.

"Yeah," I said.

"You're not mad anymore?"

I shook my head, still feeling, just lightly, the pressure of his hand on my back. We stared at each other. I wanted to say something, but the words caught in my throat. It seemed he had something to say, too, but we sat there quietly, our unspoken words swirling in the air above our heads.

After a minute he shifted into drive, but he kept his foot on the brake. It seemed he didn't want to leave this spot. I didn't, either. But once we started moving, it was okay.

When we got to the end of the logging road, he gave me one long, last glance. Then he hit the gas and we merged onto a blacktop with actual lines in the middle and signs for Edmundston and Rivière-du-Loup.

A thin drizzle turned into thick fog. Trucks barreled past, kicking up mud and spray. Now a Celtic singer came on singing in a high, sweet voice about a maiden down in the sunken garden, about the boy who'd left her there. I turned my head so Billy wouldn't see me smile. I felt bad for the girl who'd been left, but I'd just danced with Billy, at dawn under the pines.

After a while I reached for the small green book and opened it again. I had been so eager to start on it, but right now all I could think about was dancing with Billy and how I wanted the feeling to last forever. I forced myself to concentrate and take notes on what we would need to find my mother.

We were getting close now. I smelled the Saint Lawrence River before I saw it: a mixture of salt and fresh water, exhaust from the stacks of passing ships, and, I was positive, krill breath from the spouts of whales. Billy could hear lobsters, and I turned down the radio because I was positive I was hearing the songs of whales.

We pulled up to the dock in Rivière-du-Loup, where we'd catch the ferry for Saint-Siméon, just about fifty miles from Tadoussac. From there it was straight up the fjord to my mother's cabin. A few big commercial trucks were idling in the parking lot, waiting to board. The first boat wouldn't leave for a few hours, so Billy inched down behind the steering wheel to get comfortable. We'd gotten up so early, and the emotions of the drive had tired us out.

My eyelids started getting heavy. Billy slept at his end of the seat. The morning chill intensified in the fog, but I felt warm inside. I curled up against the door, drifting in and out of light sleep and deep dreams of a boy and a girl slow dancing, then dreaming together at the edge of the water.

Chapter 14

MAY 25
RIVIÈRE-DU-LOUP/SAINT-SIMÉON FERRY

I was glad I'd stopped taking the meds. I felt good. No hint of depression. In fact, after our dance, I felt almost high. All I wanted was to cross the Saint Lawrence River and get to the north side. I know it was strange, but I felt I could fly us there.

The day—or at least its first moments—started out so well. I was full of excitement as we woke up in the ferryboat parking lot in Rivière-du-Loup. Fog hung low over the wide and salty water, but you could tell the sun was trying to burn through. Billy stretched.

"Did you catch a nap?" he asked, looking over at me.

"I did. How about you?"

"Definitely. Ready for anything now," he said.

We smiled at each other, and I was surprised I didn't feel shy or awkward after our dance. Maybe it was all the days we'd been together, the fact that I was starting to feel I knew him better than anyone else did. Better than Helen.

The first departure was at eight a.m. We were at the head of the line. As soon as the office opened, we went inside to buy our tickets.

"Bonjour," the woman behind the counter said. We were in Quebec province, the French-speaking part of Canada.

"Bonjour," I said, happy to practice the language.

"Do you speak English?" Billy asked.

"Bien sûr," the woman said, smiling at us. "Yes."

"We'd like to buy tickets," Billy said.

"How many passengers?" she asked. I loved her accent; it was different from Richard's but somehow the same.

"Two," Billy said.

"Vehicle or on foot?"

"Vehicle," he said. "A truck."

"There is a surcharge for a truck," she said.

"It's just a pickup," he said.

"De tout façon," she said.

"What?" he asked.

" 'In any case,' " I translated.

"Désolée, but pickup or not, it's still a truck," the woman said. "Forty-five dollars for the vehicle, sixteen-dollar surcharge for the truck, and twenty-four dollars each passenger. That's one hundred and nine dollars total."

"Thanks," Billy said. He grabbed my arm, pulled me out of line.

"What's wrong?" I asked.

"We don't have it," he said. "We're down to fifty-five dollars."

"No!" I said. Our truck was right there, perfectly positioned in the very front of the loading zone, the big white ferryboat waiting for us to drive aboard.

"I shouldn't have bought the ice cream," Billy said.

"Don't say that. I'm glad you did. But what can we do now, to get across?"

We walked over to the ferry. The stern doors opened, and the largest trucks started rumbling aboard. Some were eighteen-wheelers, several with raucous refrigerator units pumping frost into the air. A few had fish painted on the side, probably going to pick up the catch in the Gulf of Saint Lawrence. With a pang I noticed that one was emblazoned with dancing lobsters, and I remembered our good time in Maine.

A long line of vehicles—cars and smaller trucks—had formed behind ours, and I realized we were going to lose our spot. Billy handed me the keys, and I reluctantly moved the truck to a parking lot off to the side.

I got out to wait, feeling helpless as I watched the other vehicles starting to drive on board. Billy stood across the lot, talking to a guy in a khaki uniform. The guy was a little older than college age, very trim with a crew cut and a neatly trimmed beard. He stood absolutely straight, his expression impassive as he listened to Billy.

A minute later, Billy ran over to a lobster truck just before it drove aboard the ferry. The driver rolled down the window, and Billy started talking, gesturing, half turning to point at me. Next thing I knew he was running toward me, calling out as he approached.

"Remember saying 'will work for lobster rolls'?" Billy said. "Well, this is our chance. The mate on the ferry told me that the fishing trucks sometimes hire day workers, and the lobster guy said his company on the other side needs pickers, whatever they are. We can do that for a day or so and earn enough money to get to your mother."

"But we still don't have money for the ferry tickets."

"We do, Maia. We have enough for passenger fare, but we'll have to leave our truck."

"The truck?" I asked, almost too stunned to notice he'd said "our." It had been our transportation, our home. I loved our truck.

"We don't have a choice," he said. "I'll ask inside if we can leave it here in the lot, and we can come back for it when we have the money."

"I don't want to leave it," I said, touching its hood.

"Maia," he said. "We have to hurry."

The ferry hands had almost finished loading the hold with vehicles and cargo. Billy ran inside the office to buy the tickets, and I gathered our stuff from the truck. I had the green book, my most important belonging—even if wasn't, officially, mine. Billy hurried back, and we grabbed our duffel bags. We locked the canned food in the toolbox.

It was so hard to leave our sanctuary on four wheels.

The truck had driven me away from being forced into the

hospital and now had taken me to the edge of the river, the last thing that separated me from my mother. And it had let me sit close to Billy for all these days and miles. It had played the music that had led to our dance.

"Thank you, truck," I said. I touched the hood again. It was still warm from being driven.

"C'mon," Billy said. He tugged my hand, and I finally tore myself away. We bolted onto the ferry as fast as we could, just as the whistle sounded.

"Are we sitting with the lobster guy?" I asked.

"No," Billy said. "We can ride across on deck, alone together, then meet up with him when we dock."

I loved the way that sounded: Billy and me, alone together. It was how we had gotten this far on our almost-impossible journey. We gave the deckhand our tickets, walked through the exhaust-smelling hold, and climbed some steep metal stairs to the top deck.

We sat as far forward as possible. Maybe because of the fog and a slight chill in the air, everyone else had gone into the cabin and we were the only people on deck. We sat right next to each other on the white bench along the rail, covering our ears as the horn blasted again. The ship's engine roared in reverse. Looking down we saw the churn of water around the steel hull, and then a white wake foaming in a trail behind us as the ferry steamed ahead.

The wind blew our hair back. It felt damp, salty, and wonderful. I opened my mouth to taste the sea. The fog kept me from seeing across to the far shore, but I knew cliffs were rising in the distance, that they marked the long and narrow fjord that would lead us to my mother.

The time had come. I opened the green book, *Beluga and Humpback Whales of Saguenay Fjord*. I turned the pages tenderly, remembering how my mother had first shown it to me. It was a reprint, not as rare and valuable as the first edition from 1898, but still old. It was by Laurent Cartier, a descendant of Jacques Cartier, the Frenchman who had claimed Canada for France and mapped this area of Eastern Quebec. Laurent loved whales, pure and simple.

Pre-Billy, Laurent used to be my crush. Yes, a long-dead guy. He seemed so dashing and cool, exploring the region not to rule it, but because he was obsessed with whales. The little green book was full of his field notes, descriptions of belugas like, "O, they are spry as butterflies and playful as children, their hides as smooth and iridescent as Carrara marble in the finest homes in Paris. These creatures are wonders of nature and inspire me, a non-poet, to pray for the talent to praise them in verse."

I used to love picturing Laurent on his knees in his ship's cabin, praying to God to make him a poet.

"What's that?" Billy asked, leaning close.

"The book," I said. "My stolen property. I promise to return it!"

"I know you will."

Aha, more trust.

"For now, it makes me feel . . . so happy. We're about to see whales!"

"Read me something," Billy said.

"Okay." I thumbed through the pages. It was hard to choose from the many perfect sections. "Here's one. 'This June day crackles with the promise of whales. When we first arrived in April, winter's ice choked the fjord, but now the cold, clear water is a magnifying glass into the deep. We approach the summer solstice and the longest day of the year. In last night's dying light I saw tantalizing shadows alongside the ship, heard the joyful exhalations of a pair of humpbacks just off the starboard bow, as if the beasts were enjoying our companionship as much as we were theirs.'" I looked up at Billy. "Isn't that wonderful?" I asked. "I can't stand how wonderful it is!"

"Well, it makes me excited to see 'the beasts,'" Billy said.

I blushed, because he couldn't possibly feel what I did: that even though the words didn't rhyme, Laurent had found a way to write poetry. His prose was nothing but.

The book was full of old hand-drawn maps; I spotted the tiny, almost invisible pencil dot and pointed at it.

"My mother made that," I said. "When I was about six, sitting in her office."

"Why did she mark that spot?" he asked.

"She was using the book to plan a future expedition with other whale researchers, and she showed me the best place to find and listen to beluga and humpback whales." I could see her now—barely touching the page with the delicate, retractable, engraved gold Cross pencil my father had given her when she'd completed her master's degree.

"You're not supposed to mark up books," Billy said.

"I know," I said. "But she did it so lightly. She said it was our secret, no one else would see it." She'd said it was for Whale Mavens only, showing me the spot she and I would go one day.

"See," I said to Billy, tracing the map with my finger. "She's all the way up here on the eastern edge of the Saguenay Fjord, this little section."

"There's no town," Billy said.

"That's true. You have to hike to it; there are no roads, no way for a car to get in."

Laurent had written: *The fjord is a sixty-mile scar in the earth, gouged by glaciers advancing downstream, leaving striations in the rock, during the Ice Age. The cliffs soar five hundred feet above the water, high and sheer, grooved by glacial movement as if by claws of a giant, and travelled by few Europeans, intrepid souls, trappers who brave the sheer trails down to the water's edge.*

"We'll have to get to one of those paths by boat," I said.

"What boat?" Billy asked.

"We'll figure that out." I grinned. "Like we've figured everything out on the trip so far."

"Will there be snacks on the boat?" he asked.

"Oh, yeah," I said.

"Cool, then," he said. Our stomachs were growling, and the smell of hot dogs and popcorn wafted out of the ferry's cabin. We just didn't have the funds for delicious seagoing junk food, so to keep from caving in from starvation we kept scanning the book.

These pages about the rock formations, the sunrise and sunset light reflected off the cliffs, the wild blueberries, and the incredible numbers of whales showing up to feed used to make me love Laurent even more. But now they only made me tingle for Billy, the idea that I'd be seeing all this for the first time with him, that this was *our* magical expedition. Our arms touched as we hunched over the book, and I totally forgot to be hungry.

The ferry chugged along. The last mist fizzled in the sun, the breaking light turning the river blue instead of gray, and the contours of the far shore came into view. I felt so happy, so excited to be within sight of that land. Glancing at Billy, expecting him to be taking in the nature around us, I felt startled to see him watching me.

"What?" I asked.

He shook his head, as if not sure what to say, but he didn't take his eyes off me.

"You're staring," I said.

"Yep."

"Why?" I asked, my cheeks feeling flushed.

"This is good," he said.

"That we're on the boat?" I asked.

"All of it," he said, still watching me as if, somehow, there was more to see in my eyes than in the scenery.

"All," I said, his words, and the way he'd said them, shimmering in my mind.

He nodded, slouched down in his seat with his arms folded across his chest, and kept looking at me. I finally turned my head, because it was too much for me to handle. If he could have seen my face he'd have known I was smiling.

We got to the other side with my skin electric from Billy's strange gaze, from him saying "all of it," as if that included me. We didn't spot any whales—maybe because I was too wrapped up in Billy to watch for them.

The ferry docked, bumping back and forth between the pilings, and the vehicles began to drive off. The lobster truck rattled over the ferry's metal ramp, and the driver waited for us at the far end of the parking lot. I hesitated, dragging my feet as we walked over. What would my father say, knowing that I was even considering getting into a truck with a stranger? My mother was dauntless, but he was a professional worrier.

"My dad would kill me for this," I told Billy. "He'd think we were about to be kidnapped. Disappeared forever."

"We could change our minds, not do this," Billy said.

I hesitated. My dad's warnings buzzed in my head. Being so depressed, I'd been protected—and I'd stayed small in my life. I'd kept myself, or allowed others to keep me, from spreading my wings, taking risks, courting surprise. Now I thought of how I wanted to be, jumping into life with all I had, and I knew what I had to do.

"No," I said. "We've got to."

I swallowed hard as we approached the lobster truck. The driver leaned across the seat to open the door for us.

"Sorry, the latch sticks," he said with a French accent as we climbed into the cab. He wore dark glasses with white frames, his skin was red-brown, and he had a friendly smile with a gap between his front teeth just like mine. But was the smile fake, just to lure us in?

"No problem," Billy said. He slid in before me, and I knew he'd done that to keep himself between the driver and me, just in case.

"I'm George," the driver said.

"Billy and Maia," Billy said.

"You're not from around here?"

"The States."

"The States are a big place."

"Connecticut," I said.

"Yeah, that's where I went lobster fishing with my grandfather," Billy said.

"Ah, good! My *grand-père* taught me the lobster business," George said. "How's the catch down there?"

"Kind of bad in recent years," Billy said.

"Well, we switched to snow crabs a few years back," George said. "More demand, better fishery."

"But there are lobsters on your truck," I said.

George laughed. "My aunt painted them on the panels a long time ago. We didn't want to hurt her feelings by redoing them."

That made me like him, and I felt a little more secure.

"So are you loaded up with snow crabs?" Billy asked.

"Nope," George said. "I just made a delivery to the other side. I'm going home empty to fill up again. That's how it works, back and forth."

"So, if the truck is empty . . ." Billy began. "Where are we going? And what kind of work will we do?"

"Depends on what stage of the operation you're most needed," George said. "It could be you'll be picking the crabs out of the bins, putting 'em on the conveyor. Or we might ask you to remove the meat from the shells. You'll help us process the crabs, get 'em ready for market. One thing for sure, we work hard and move fast. Are you ready for that?"

"Definitely," Billy said.

"Where's the plant?" I asked.

"Past Tadoussac," he said, and just hearing the name gave me the best jolt—it was where my mother got her mail, the town closest to her cabin on the cliff.

Driving east, I felt my excitement building. I felt Mom's presence so strongly, it was almost as if she were in the truck with us. George had the radio on, tuned to a Quebec pop station. All the music was in French, and even that seemed enchanting. I mentally translated as many lyrics as I could. This was learning in action, better than any French class could be.

The truck boarded another ferry, but not just ANY ferry: this one across the Saguenay! The voyage was short, just ten minutes, but looking left I saw all the way up the amazing, fantastic, magnificent fjord—the land of Laurent Cartier! I was *here*. I could barely hold myself together.

The cliffs rose on either side, disappearing into a point on the northern horizon—the fjord extended that far, way beyond what I could see. In the bright sunshine I could almost imagine seeing mirror-sharp light glinting on windows atop the western cliff—could that be my mother's cabin?

"This is it," I said to Billy.

"The fjord?" he asked. "The one?"

"Yes, we're so close!" I had a brainstorm. "What if we just paid George the money we have left, get out at the dock, and find her?"

"Yeah, we could," Billy said.

"Wait, what's that you're saying?" George asked.

"Well, Maia's mother lives here. We'd like to pay you for the ride and get out."

George was silent. He didn't exactly frown, but he looked troubled.

"Hmm," he said. "Shoot."

"Why, what's wrong?" Billy asked.

"I called my brother after you and I talked in Rivière-du-Loup," he said. "We're shorthanded at the plant this time of year. The crab season is just starting up again, and many of our workers are out fishing. We were kind of counting on you helping. We pay real good."

Billy shook his head. "Sorry, but this is really important to Maia."

"Okay," George said, shrugging.

The small ferry pulled closer to Tadoussac. There were docks, whale-watching boats, churches, and an enormous white hotel with a bright red roof. I would know it anywhere. Over the years I had scoured websites and pored through guidebooks, history books, photo books of this area. The Hotel Tadoussac was always featured.

"Hey," Billy said to me. "How are we going to get in touch with your mom?"

"We'll call," I began. But she didn't have a phone. "We'll make our way up the fjord. We'll use Laurent's book and know the spot when we see it."

"That's pretty much wilderness," George said. "You got a boat?"

"No, but we'll find someone to give us a ride."

Both George and Billy were silent, and as my words hung in the air I heard how unlikely that was. We didn't know anyone here. After paying George, we'd be flat broke. I could hang around the post office waiting for Mom to pick up her mail, but how long would that take?

"Email!" I said. "I can email her from the library."

"Why don't you just call or email her from your mobiles?" George asked.

Billy and I exchanged a look. We weren't about to tell George about the evasive measures that had led to us tossing our phones.

"It's complicated on her end," I said. "Besides, uh, Billy and I both lost our cell phones." Billy raised his eyebrows, as if that was the lamest thing I could have said, which it was.

"You can use mine," George said, handing me his smartphone.

"You sure?" I asked.

"For you to contact your mother? Of course."

I hesitated, but then I took it eagerly.

The ferry eased into the slip, sloshing between the big wooden pilings at the Tadoussac dock. Holding George's phone, I went online and signed into my email account.

During that one moment at the Eliza Hewitt Memorial Library in Maine, I had memorized my mother's email address: Beluga.GS@QuebecEast.com. I typed it in, then wrote my message:

> *MOM! I am here! On the ferry pulling into*
> *Tadoussac. Could you email me back, like*
> *immediately? It's a slight emergency. I'll explain*
> *as soon as you write me.*
>
> *The most love there is,*
>
> *Maia*

I sent it.

Less than a second later the email bounced back with a message:

Undeliverable/Recipient not recognized

"No," I said out loud.

Billy leaned over to see the screen.

Had I gotten her address wrong? I scrolled back through my received mail till I found hers. My thumbs flew over the keyboard, retyping my message in the reply window, then hitting SEND.

Undeliverable/Recipient not recognized

I can't lie; I wanted to die. Had Mom changed her email address, deleted her account, knowing I had run away and had no other way to contact her?

George was gunning the engine, impatient to leave, but I had to check one more thing. I looked more slowly through my unread mail and yes—my heart raced to see that there was one more message from her. I opened it and read:

> *Dearest Maia,*
> *Your dad has emailed me again (and again and again) and so has the lovely Astrid. The emails are quite blaming, and hurtful. Maybe they don't mean it that way—they are worried about you. But they don't know you the way I do. They don't understand how resourceful you are, and how independent. I am shutting this email down for now. Hearing from them serves no point.*
>
> *You still have my address—the real address. Write me a letter as soon as you get this and let me know how and where you are. Clearly you are on a quest. Don't forget to rely on those instincts.*
>
> *Mom*

I sighed with relief, still shaking: Yes, letters were how she and I stayed in touch. That hadn't changed, and she wasn't hiding from me. I handed the phone back to George and started to open the truck door.

"Maia." Billy grabbed my wrist, talking quietly. "I read what she wrote."

"She knows I'm on a quest," I said. "She must know that means I'm on my way to her."

"Okay," Billy said, sounding dubious.

"And we're here," I said. "We've arrived."

"But not quite," he said. "We still have to get up the fjord, and George is right—we don't have a boat or the money to charter one."

"You could still work for us," George said, eavesdropping. "Just a day or two, and you'll make enough for what you need. I told you, we pay good."

My heart cracked. We were so close. I knew if we got out of the truck we could walk into town and find the post office. We could hang out there until she came.

But when would she check her mail? How long would Billy and I have to wait?

"Let's go to work, Maia," Billy said. "Earn enough to charter the boat. Then we'll come back."

"I'll deliver you here myself," George said. "I make this trip three times a week."

Shutting that truck door and watching Tadoussac slip by as we drove past the town might have been the hardest thing I'd ever done. Tears stung my eyes as I stared over my shoulder, watching the cliffs of Saguenay disappear as we picked up speed, heading east.

Chapter 15

MAY 25
TADOUSSAC-MITSHISHU

George had said the plant was east of Tadoussac, but after the second hour of driving, when distance between villages began to seem endless, I got nervous again. How *far* east? We didn't know him at all. He could be taking us anywhere—in fact, that's just what he was doing.

He kept making and receiving calls on his phone, but he spoke French so fast I could barely pick up any words. Sometimes he laughed sometimes he sounded impatient once he sounded tender, as if he was talking to his wife or a child. I held on to that and told myself he had a family, he wouldn't be the type to hurt us. But my good old reliable stomach began to ache, as if it knew something I didn't.

Billy shifted in his seat. He was in the middle, with the hump under his feet, and his legs were on my side of the truck. I tried to keep mine as close to the door as possible, but then

I'd have to change position, too, and after a while our feet got tangled. He didn't try to separate them.

I stared at his feet. He wore black high-top Chucks, the white toe scuffed and no longer white. I was wearing my favorite old topsiders, pretty decrepit at this point. My feet looked small next to his. We were entwined at the ankles. I tried to pull one foot away, thinking he'd like more space, but he trapped it between his, foot wrestling instead of arm wrestling. It became a game, our way of amusing ourselves to the point where we started laughing and couldn't stop.

Our shoulders were bumping, too. He leaned against me, and I pressed into him. I glanced over, saw his green eyes flashing, his wide mouth in a devilish smile. He started up our foot-wrestling match again just as George turned on the blinker and rumbled off the main route. We passed a sign:

MITSHISHU

INNU FIRST NATIONS RESERVE

"Mitshishu . . ." Billy said out loud.

"It means 'eagle,'" George said. "And our people are Innu. That word means 'human being.' Nature gives us our lives. It is our religion."

The truck bounced down a narrow road and we wound up in the most beautiful parking lot I've ever seen. It was right at the edge of a wide blue bay. Five small fishing boats lined the dock, and a rock island rose out of the water in the distance.

Seagulls were madly swooping and calling, and I saw why: The boats were unloading huge blue tubs of gigantic, long-legged crabs scrambling to get out.

Beside the dock was a big rectangular building. The sign, painted with the same dancing lobsters as on the truck, said CLAUDE ET FILS PÊCHERIE. A crowd of workers wearing blue paper gowns and caps came out to line up and cheer the catch. The fishermen bowed and pumped their fists into the air.

"This was a very good day," George said. "There will be a lot of work, so I'm very glad you're here."

He led us into the freezing-cold plant, gave us the same blue paper outfits to wear, along with blue paper slippers to go over our shoes and plastic gloves. The paper rustled when we moved.

It felt as if we were in the middle of nowhere, but the equipment was so high-tech and the crabs so huge we could have been in a futuristic movie about crustaceans taking over the earth. Giant stainless-steel conveyor belts curved through the space, which echoed with the noise of engines, compressors, and plastic bins being shifted, with crabs clicking their long claws.

"We are the best, cleanest, most pristine fish-processing plant in Canada," George said proudly. "Everyone who works here is family. Most of us are actually related, but the ones who aren't are family anyway."

"That's really cool," Billy said. I glanced at him, the boy without a family.

"Our tribe used to be known as 'Montagnais.' But that is French, and years ago we went back to our aboriginal name."

"Is this your reservation?" Billy asked.

"We call it a reserve in Canada, but yes. It is our community. We don't usually bring outsiders to work here, but our catch is so plentiful we need extra hands and you need money. Let me introduce you."

George took us around and we met everyone, about twenty people. His father, Claude, worked on the processing line along with his mother, Marie; his twin sisters, Nathalie and Jeanine; his younger brother, Marc; and several cousins who were or weren't actually related by blood. It didn't matter. In spite of the fact that George had said they didn't usually invite non-Innu to work here, I felt completely welcomed.

Billy and I jumped right into our jobs. We stood side by side at the tail end of the line. By the time the crabs got to us they'd been steamed, their legs separated from the carapaces, and it was our job to crack the bright red shells and extract the meat. We had to do it as perfectly as possible, not leave any hard bits of shell or cartilage, and at first it was okay—even good—because I was so close to Billy, and he was helping me.

"It's not exactly like lobster, but close enough," he said, showing me exactly where to crack the shell, remove the glistening crabmeat in one perfect chunk instead of shreds, how to place it on the conveyor belt that would take it to the canning station.

"There, that's perfect!" he said when I succeeded. Our hands were busy, but he bumped my upper arm with his—kind of like a shoulder high five. I glanced at his arm and couldn't help noticing his muscles. He was lean and wiry, but when it came to arms, he was pretty amazing. Until that minute I never knew I had a thing for boys' arms.

"Is it just me, or is this making you want to eat crab?" I asked.

"It's not just you," he said.

The day seemed incredibly long; we concentrated on our work, but every time I looked up, I caught Marc, George's younger brother, watching us. His expression was neutral; he seemed about our age, and I wondered why he wasn't in school. Music played from speakers in the ceiling. It started out being familiar rock bands, but then it switched, and that's when my mood followed.

The singer was a woman, and the songs she sang were so haunting I felt almost hypnotized. They were sweet and sad, accompanied by a flute, and then, in the background, the unmistakable sound of whales singing.

I stopped, frozen. Then I felt literally pulled away from my workstation to drift across the wide floor and stand under the speaker. I tried to listen to what the woman and the whale were saying. They were each speaking a language different from my own and from each other's, but I felt their words and notes in my bones, my blood. I nearly levitated at the sound of the voices.

A horn sounded—it must have meant the end of work for the day because the machines stopped and everyone began chatting, filing outside. But the music kept playing. Marie walked over to me. She was short and plump, with her black hair pulled back in a ponytail. Her face was very tan and wrinkled.

"Do you like our music?" she asked.

"It's the most beautiful thing I've ever heard," I said.

"That is Alesie," she said. "An Innu singer from Sept-Îles. She's singing in our native language, Innu-aimun. Can you hear the harmony and guess who is making music with her?"

"I hear it," I said. "A whale?"

Marie gave me a surprised smile. "How would you know that?"

"My mother taught me to love whale songs," I said.

"Is your mother Innu?"

"No," I said. "She's not."

"Well, I think I would like her anyway," Marie said. "My son Marc and my nephew Pierre mixed the two voices. Pierre wants to move to Toronto and work in a recording studio, but we need him here."

"And Marc?" I asked. "Does he want to move, too?"

"No," she said. "He is devoted to the community."

She beckoned toward Billy, and we followed her outside the building and along the coast road. We passed a white church with a cross on the steeple and a tepee-like structure— five tree trunks stripped of bark, tied together at the top and emblazoned with a carved eagle. A homemade cross—two pieces of wood held together with a leather cord, stood at the bottom. I stopped to stare. The instant inner knowledge of what it meant sent shivers down my spine.

I knew it was a memorial. Someone had died.

I felt Marie watching me out of the corner of her eye. She took my hand and pulled me past the structure. Inside I was shaking. I could barely swallow. She led us past a row of brightly colored houses. She pointed at a bright blue one, and we filed up to the front door.

George met us at the door. Marc sat at the kitchen table, watching. *"Merci, maman,"* George said.

"De rien, George,*"* she said. *"Vos amis sont trés gentils. La jeune fille aime beauçoup les chants des baleines."*

I understood: *Your friends are very nice. The young girl very much likes whale songs.*

"Merci," I said. *"C'est vrai—j'aime beauçoup la musique."*

"It's good you speak French," Marie said. "We Innu have had to meet others in their languages—the French when they first came to this land, the English and Americans to whom we have always sold our fish, whatever the catch. And whales—we speak to the whales."

"But you don't speak Innu-aimun—Montagnais," Marc said sharply. "Our *real* language."

"French is enough," his mother said. "It is a good effort. Be polite, Marc."

Marc didn't respond; he just frowned and turned away. Marie and George ignored him, but I stared, wondering why Marc seemed angry. Marie took my hands.

"You're very sensitive," she said.

I didn't reply. I wanted to tell her everything: how this was my first time in Canada, how my mother had lived here for three years and I hadn't seen her in all that time, how the sound of Alesie had uplifted me, and how the sight of the tepee made me feel sorrow.

"Ta coeur," she said, touching her chest. "Your heart is very big."

I wanted to hug her, but wasn't sure if it was the custom. She made it easy for me, took me into her arms. My throat ached with everything, especially being hugged by a mom.

Marie dropped her arms, smiled at me, and turned to her son. "Marc, come with me. It's time for dinner."

He got up and without a word left the house.

"He's still young and lives at home," Marie said. "Even though he thinks he's all grown-up and on his own."

She said good-bye to George and Billy, then with a last smile at me, walked away, along the coast road, fifty yards behind Marc.

"That was good work," George said, shaking Billy's and my hands. He reached into his pocket and counted out a hundred dollars.

"Thanks," Billy said. "That's a lot of money for half a day."

"We pay what is owed," George said. "If you'll work for us again tomorrow morning, I'll make sure you get back to Tadoussac in the afternoon. And I'll call my uncle there. He'll take you up the fjord in his boat."

"Thank you," Billy said.

I just nodded. I was afraid to speak; Marie's hug, Alesie's singing, and the way Billy was looking at me overwhelmed me. I was filled with tears of love. I knew that was weird, but I felt that if I cried, the love I was feeling would spill over everything.

We ate dinner with George, and I was really excited

because we were having crab. We sat around the table in his kitchen. It was covered with a yellow oilcloth marked with crayon streaks. I also noticed a Big Wheel, some Legos, and two Barbies in the corner behind the stove. It looked as if they hadn't been played with in a long time.

"This is just for you," he said, serving us big plates of un-cracked crab legs. "I'm so sick of it I can barely look at it, but when we have special workers they're always hungry for the catch."

"My grandfather and I got to the point we couldn't eat lobster," Billy said. "After pulling pots every morning all summer long, then before school in the cold weather, selling it at the local market every day after school."

"You worked hard back home," George said, sounding admiring.

"It didn't feel like work," Billy said. "I was with my grandfather. It was the best time of my life, and I want more of it. I want to work on the water, with a better boat, a faster winch."

George grinned. "It's good you appreciate the benefits of technology, the ways it makes our life easier. I wish Marc would—he's fifteen years younger than me, and he's an old man. He wants to bring back the traditional ways. He thinks the new ones are ruining our culture. Diluting it too much. He'd rather get rid of modern conveniences entirely. But put him in a boat, and he opens up the engine to go as fast as he can. And as much as he talks about how the elders pulled pots with their muscles and complains about the winch, he uses it.

And he loves mixing music with our cousin Pierre. Life is full of conflicts for him."

"Does he like to fish?" Billy asked.

"Of course. We all do. But the thing about lobster fishing, crab fishing: We sometimes forget to appreciate what we have a lot of."

"I think I could eat crab every day," I said. I knew I should love this meal, but the weird thing was, it was hard to take more than a few bites. I was on major overload.

"Yeah, people do forget to appreciate," Billy said. "What they have. And who they have."

"My wife left," George said. "Took our kids with her, too. It gets hard out here. The winters are long and cold. The river often ices over and we have to travel farther east, into the true salt water. That eats up fuel, and the catch might not be there anyway. Money is tight. It's roughest for kids. We have a drug problem here. Huffing, drinking, too. Did you see the memorial out there?"

"Memorial?" Billy asked.

"The tree trunks with the eagle," I said.

George nodded. "That's for my nephew Jacques. He was sixteen years old. Kids at the regional school, they're not all aboriginal there. It's a mix. They bullied him, called him Indian, Eskimo. Threw rocks at him. His mom left the village with someone she met, abandoned him with her sister. Marc tried to protect him, but it wasn't enough."

"What happened to him?" Billy asked.

"He killed himself," I said.

Both Billy and George stared at me, but they didn't ask me how I knew. I had the feeling Billy could see through my skin, know that I had been there, too. I could hear Jacques's voice, as if he were speaking to me.

After dinner, we cleaned up the kitchen. Every move I made felt as if I were swimming underwater. The air felt like the ocean, cold and clear. It was late May, heading toward the longest day of the year, and at this northern latitude the sun stayed high in the sky past nine o'clock.

I couldn't keep my eyes open. George showed us where we would sleep: in twin beds in a small room with one wall painted pink and the other blue. I realized his daughter and son had shared this bedroom.

We were still in our jeans and T-shirts, and Billy climbed into one bed and I into the one on the opposite side. We stared at each other across the narrow space. I thought of all the nights I'd gazed up at the Stansfield Home, waiting to see him through the second-floor window. I'd felt such longing for him. I'd wished I could tell him my secrets and that he could tell me his. I had spent so much time wondering if he was looking back at me.

Now he was.

"Remember how I couldn't trust anyone?" Billy said. "Well, it's been a long time since I felt close to anyone. Or felt as if I belonged."

"They make you feel as if you belong here, don't they?" I asked.

"I meant you," he said. "You make me feel as if I belong . . . everywhere. You do."

"You make me feel that way, too," I said.

Outside the sun had not quite set, and cool blue light came through the window. I could see his straight mouth, the slant of his cheekbones, the way his brown hair fell into his green eyes.

I could see the shape of his body under the blanket, the way his arm looked when he reached across the space between us. And then he held out his hand. And I reached over, and our fingertips touched, and then in the declining light we held each other's hands for a long, long time.

Chapter 16

MAY 26
MITSHISHU-TADOUSSAC

We woke to a bright morning. Even at six a.m., there on the river in eastern Canada, the sun's rays felt surprisingly warm for being so far north.

Small wind-gnarled pine trees grew along the road through the reserve. Walking back to the plant, I couldn't stop thinking of what Billy had said last night, and of holding hands until we fell asleep. We worked half the day, as we'd promised George. I had to really concentrate on doing the job.

I hated to admit it, but going off my medication cold turkey was taking a toll. I'd been cruising through, doing fine, until I'd seen Jacques's memorial. I felt so bad for him. But that morning I realized, for the first time since I had stopped taking my pills, that I was going through withdrawal—exactly what I'd gone through before, what Dr. Bouley had warned me not to do. I felt dizzy, a little sick to my stomach, and in spite of the reasons I should be so happy, sensing the edge of despair. It shimmered just out of sight.

I thought of starting up the antidepressant again, right now. Instead I steeled myself and decided not to. Day three without it, I was at my mental limit, but I knew it would pass if I could just hold on. My brain was scrambling, searching for the neurotransmitters the drug had provided. Now that everything with Billy was changing, and I felt the possibility of real love, I knew I could feel happy forever once my brain chemistry caught up.

I told myself that after another twenty-four hours or so my system would acclimate to being med-free, start producing its own serotonin, and I'd be back to myself, my old self, pre-depression—only better. I was sure that was true. It had to be. The conditions for happiness were in place.

Billy and I had both gotten faster at sorting the catch. I forced myself to keep working hard, and the morning started to fly by. The bad feelings washed over me, retreated, and returned like waves in a big storm. In the moments between them I felt up, hopeful that if I stayed the course I'd get through this.

When work was over, I felt sorry to leave the reserve. We said good-bye to everyone in the processing plant, packed our things, and, bags slung over our shoulders, headed to the spot where George had parked his truck.

It was gone.

No, it couldn't be. Had he lied to us? Had George left us here with no way back to Tadoussac? I couldn't breathe, on the verge of a total hyperventilating panic attack.

Marc walked over, hands in his pockets. His brown skin

looked ruddy from time spent in the sun and on the water, and his black eyes gleamed. He wore thick canvas work pants and scuffed black boots. His red T-shirt was printed with a caribou and symbols I didn't understand.

"George had to leave before sunup," he said. "The shipment was ready early."

"But he said he'd drive us," I said, my voice so strained it barely came out.

"We'll hitchhike," Billy said, giving me a reassuring look. "We'll get you there."

"I'm taking you," Marc said.

I looked around the parking area. There were a couple of rusty cars, an old station wagon on blocks, the way we'd found Billy's grandfather's truck. That left a small blue sedan, so pocked with rust that you could see through the holes.

"What's the matter?" Marc asked, gauging my expression. "You don't want to be seen riding in a junk car?"

"I wasn't thinking that," I said.

"Man, you should have seen the truck we left across the river," Billy said. "It makes your car look brand-new."

Marc gave a half smile, and I was glad Billy had said that, defused the situation.

"We're not taking the car anyway," Marc said. "Come on."

He led us down to the wharf. Most of the fishing boats had left that morning, but there was one medium-size boat tied to the dock. It was white with a small cabin in front and long deck space in back. The boat's name, painted on the transom, was *Wolf.*

"George said you need a ride to Tadoussac and up the fjord," Marc said. "And my uncle there is busy today, so George told me to take you."

"Thank you, Marc," I said, tides of relief flooding me.

"Call me Atik," he said. "That's my Innu name. Around here the older people accept what the Europeans did to us, the English and French names they gave us, but not me. And my cousin Matsheshu didn't, either."

"Matsheshu," I said, pronouncing the beautiful name slowly.

"Everyone called him Jacques," he said. "But he was Matsheshu."

We got into the boat. As Atik started the engine, Billy undid the lines and cast us off the dock. He did it so easily, I could tell a love of boats was in his blood. The water boiled, then rippled into a wide white wake behind us. I stared back at the carved eagle on top of Jacques's—Matsheshu's—memorial. The bird was bold with a hooked beak and spread wings; it looked almost as if it could fly.

Marie, still wearing her blue paper hat and smock, had stepped out of the plant to wave good-bye to us. Atik gave her three quick blasts on the air horn and then, just as George had told us about him, proved his love of speed by opening up the throttle and zooming through the channel.

There was almost no wind, no waves. *Wolf* ran smoothly over the river's glassy blue surface. Atik stood at the wheel, I sat in a high swivel seat with a great view forward through the windshield, and Billy stood between us. I looked at the GPS chart of the area glowing green on the console. We would travel west on the Saint Lawrence River, then take a hard right at Tadoussac and head north into the Saguenay Fjord. It was a very long ride.

Wolf's electronics looked sophisticated—I knew from being on boats with my mom that one was radar and another was a digital fish finder. My mother used one like it to locate marine mammals and schools of fish beneath the water's surface, but it could also determine depth, and if there were any rocks or shipwrecks on the ocean floor.

"Why is the boat called '*Wolf*'?" I asked, wondering why the name wasn't more related to the sea.

"My grandfather dreamed it," Atik said. "*Atik* means caribou; the night I was born, my grandmother dreamed of an entire herd. *Matsheshu* means fox, because the day my cousin was born, his father saw one on the shore."

"But 'wolf' is an English word," Billy said.

"You're right. I'd like to paint it over with *Maikan*, the real name for wolf. But my uncle is just like my mother and thinks the modern ways are better than traditional."

"Why is it more modern to use French or English names instead of Innu-aimun?" I asked.

Atik leaned across Billy to look at me, as if he was surprised and maybe a little pleased that I was interested.

"Aboriginals—Innu, Montagnais—didn't used to live on reserves. We just lived on the land in birch wigwams—our houses. Then the Europeans came. We traded furs and skins and fish with them, and they tricked us."

"How?" I asked.

"Their trading posts were unfair. They took our goods and paid us little in return. Without our goods, our way of living, we became poor, destitute. We weren't immune to their diseases and many of us died from Spanish flu, smallpox, and measles. They took away Manitou and forced their beliefs on us."

"What is Manitou?" Billy asked.

"Our true religion—nature."

I thought of what George had said when we'd first arrived at the reserve and seen the sign: that nature was woven all through their lives.

"The supernatural power that comes from animal spirits, tree spirits, both good and evil," Atik continued. "The Europeans jammed Christianity down our throats to control us and destroy our religion. They built the church. My mother goes to it. You saw the cross by the memorial? She and my aunt put it there."

"Maybe all prayers are good," I said. "And it doesn't matter who you're saying them to."

Atik shrugged, and I didn't know if that meant he wasn't sure and maybe I was right, or if he thought I just didn't get it.

"I'm sorry all that happened to the Inuit," Billy said.

Atik shot him a sharp glance. "We're not Inuit. We're Innu. You think it's the same? It isn't. We're both from the north, and the names sound similar, but our cultures are completely different. They live north of us, mostly in the Arctic. You'd know them as Eskimos, a name we hate. But yes, it happened to the Inuit, too. To all indigenous people."

"I didn't mean to offend you," Billy said.

Atik nodded, but his lips were tight. We cruised for a long time without speaking. I thought of what the Europeans had done and felt sick about the Cartiers, even Laurent.

"What happened to Matsheshu?" I asked.

"He was like his name," Atik said. "A fox—fast, smart, able to hide and wait until he figured something out. But school, and the kids who made fun of him, put him down—he couldn't figure that out. He was so good—not like me, I'm tough and like to fight. If someone attacks my family I don't wait for them to do it a second time. But not Matsheshu."

"How was he good?" I asked.

"Kind. Patient. He believed everyone had a good heart. When kids teased him, he pretended to laugh it off, and when I fought to defend him he'd say, 'Don't do it, brother, it's not worth your anger, they don't mean it.' But yeah, they meant it. There are a lot of whites at our school and they look down on us just like the rest of Canada does—we're garbage people to them. Matsheshu couldn't take it anymore. He filled his pockets with rocks and walked into the river."

I felt stunned into silence, picturing Matsheshu. As soon as I could move, I reached around Billy to give Atik a hug. Billy put his hand on his shoulder. I felt Matsheshu in the circle with us—Atik's love for him was so strong, and even though I hadn't known him, so was mine.

Something I learned at Turner: When someone kills himself, he leaves all his anguish behind for his family, and they have to carry his sorrow. It's a terrible legacy, and I don't believe anyone suffering badly enough to take his or her own life intends to hurt anyone. They just want the pain to stop. As different as our experiences were, I understood that part of Matsheshu. Even though I couldn't know what he'd gone through, I could imagine getting to the point where he did what he did. And that scared me.

All through the cruise I kept watching the water's surface for signs of whales. A horde of seagulls hovered and dove— birds working were sometimes a sign of marine mammals in the area. Whales stirred up small fish, and gulls and terns fed on them. But in spite of the seabirds, I didn't see any spouts or fins.

"Do you hear them singing?" I asked Billy.

"Yeah, loudly," he said.

"Who's singing?" Atik asked.

"Lobsters," I said. "Billy hears them."

"That's kind of Manitou," Atik said, with a touch of admiration in his voice. "George said you're a lobster fisherman."

"I was," Billy said. "And I hope I'll be again."

We continued west, the sun getting hotter as it angled across the sky; it beat down through the windshield. The boat had a sound system, and Atik popped in a CD by Kashtin.

"They're Innu from Sept-Îles, a community east of ours," he said. "The first song is 'Tshinanu'; it means 'what we all are.'"

The music was live and sounded happy—upbeat singers, guitars, people cheering in the background. Atik tapped the wheel with the palm of one hand, and I half danced, the way you do when you're standing still but feeling the beat. Billy moved, too, leaning into me.

"I love this song," I said.

"These guys really made it," Atik said. "They're cool, too. *Kashtin* means 'tornado' in our language, but it's also a dig in English—'cashed-in.' Making money on telling our stories. Good for them, man."

The CD was obviously a homemade compilation with more songs by Kashtin as well as solo songs by the individual members. It lifted me, filled my heart, made me feel connected to something much bigger than me.

For so long I'd felt like a kite that couldn't quite get up in the sky. Depression had made me falter, then crash. But now on the boat, heading to Tadoussac, I felt myself letting out string a little at a time, starting to rise without the help of anti-depressants. With Billy beside me and Atik speeding us toward my mother, I knew I was ready to soar.

Missing, waiting, child, song. I'd be with her soon.

"See those buoys over there?" Atik asked, pointing at a row of three red-and-white buoys floating on the water's surface, along the northern shore.

"Yeah," Billy said.

"They're my uncle's lobster pots. Those are his colors. Let's see you pull them."

Billy looked at Atik, maybe to see if he was serious. Atik didn't say anything more, just handed him a long metal hook.

"No problem," Billy said, beaming.

He hurried out on deck and I followed, while Atik slowed
the engine and eased close to the first buoy. It was made of
Styrofoam, haphazardly bobbing in the current. Billy reached
the boat hook overboard and snagged a rope that ran from the
buoy down to the lobster pot on the river bottom. He threw
the line over a grooved metal wheel hanging off the side of
the boat and pushed a button to start the winch's motor. The
mechanism hummed as it pulled the line.

A minute later, a big green mesh lobster pot came flying up
from the bottom of the river. Billy paused the winch motor
and we peered inside.

"You need gloves?" Atik called.

"Nah," Billy said. He opened the door on the side of
the trap and reached in, pulling out the largest lobster I'd
ever seen.

"It's a four-pounder," Billy said, testing the weight in
his hand.

"That's small for here," Atik said, laughing.

The dark-green lobster clicked its claws, reaching back to
where Billy held it behind its eyes. I cringed, positive Billy was
going to get pinched, but he was an expert. He grabbed wide
yellow elastic bands from a bin on deck, slipped them around
the claws, and dropped the lobster into a blue plastic bucket.
Another pail was full of fish heads, and Billy re-baited the trap
before throwing it overboard.

Atik puttered slowly up to the second buoy, then the third,
and Billy repeated the process—he pulled two equally gigantic
lobsters from each trap. At the third, he held up a lobster that

looked tiny compared to the others. He turned toward the wheelhouse, and without a word Atik tossed him a U-shaped instrument that Billy used to measure the carapace: The lobster was undersize, illegal to keep, so he threw it back in so it could grow some more. The boys' movements seemed graceful, as if they had been fishing together for a long time.

"Won't your uncle mind that we're pulling his pots?" Billy called as Atik eased over to the next set.

"No, that's part of why I'm giving you a ride," Atik said. "My uncle can't work today and he didn't want his pots sitting on the bottom. You know lobsters are cannibals."

"Yeah," Billy said. "If two sit in the same closed space long enough, one will eat the other."

"I thought your family only went crabbing," I said.

"Yes, mostly," Atik said. "But we catch whatever we can to sell and feed our community."

Billy hauled the rest of the pots, and when he finished he was covered with sweat and salt water. He also had the biggest smile on his face, the happiest expression ever. I had a sudden, strong wish that his grandfather could see him like this: He had taught Billy this wonderful skill, and instilled in him a love of fishing. How could he have abandoned him?

"Are you afraid to swim with the lobsters and whatever else is in there?" Atik asked, looking at me.

"No," I said.

"Definitely not," Billy said.

"It's hot in this sun," Atik said. He steered the boat toward the north shore, cut the engine, and threw an anchor overboard.

Leaving home so quickly, I'd forgotten to pack a bathing suit. Billy and I dug through our duffel bags for something to wear, and we took turns changing in the cabin. I pulled on denim shorts and a black camisole.

Billy had on cargo shorts and no shirt. I stared at his chest, his lean muscles, and those arms. Atik came up from below laughing—he'd found his uncle's bathing trunks, dark blue printed with pink palm trees, about three sizes too big.

He hung a swim ladder over the stern. But instead of climbing down, easing ourselves into the water, all three of us stood on the rail. And then we jumped straight in. The rush of cold turned me into an ice cube and I shrieked when I came up for air.

"Hey, I forgot to tell you, swimming's a little different here than down south," Atik called, smiling.

"Feels great," Billy said. It did. I was freezing, but I felt so happy.

"Next time we'll find a glacier and some meltwater and we'll see how tough you are," Atik said, laughing and treading water. "Seriously, that's enough for me. I'm going up, got to call my girlfriend in Sept-Îles. Take your time. If you feel like it, there's an abandoned trading post right over there. You can see where the Europeans set up to take everything they wanted from the land. About twenty yards into the trees." He climbed up the swim ladder.

Tall pines grew straight down to the rocky banks, and Billy and I swam toward shore. The longer we stayed in the water, the more I got used to the temperature; but it felt good to clamber up on the sun-warmed granite ledge. My skin tingled.

We sat there for a few minutes, getting warm. Out on the boat, I could see Atik in the wheelhouse, phone to his ear. Seagulls circled the boat, crying and swooping, hoping to snag a scrap of bait.

"Want to find that trading post?" Billy asked.

"Sure," I said and we got to our feet.

The trail was narrow, so I fell into step behind him.

His shoulders were wide, his back lean and muscular. I'd never thought of Billy as an athlete, but it was obvious he did something to look that way. He had freckles everywhere. I tried not to stare, but there was something about those freckles. I reached out and touched one on his back.

"What?" he asked, smiling as he turned around.

"You have a few freckles," I said.

"Yeah, you noticed?"

I lowered my head, aware that I had turned bright red from the fact that I noticed everything about him, and from having touched his back. He was still shirtless and wet from the swim, and I was in my soaked clothes. I shivered from the air on my skin and from the way he was looking at me.

We had walked through a wooded path along the shore and now stood in a clearing that was tightly ringed with pine trees. A crooked stone tower crumbled and half tumbled onto a rock ledge sloping into a small river inlet. Some charred logs and timbers lay on the ground, and we carefully stepped over them to climb what was left of the tower.

"It feels like such a secret place," I said. "As if it wants to stay hidden. Filled with ancient stories."

"Maia, I . . ." Billy began.

He was standing really close to me. Sunlight slanting through the pine needles made his green eyes shine.

"What?" I asked.

"I love coming here with you," he said.

"Me too," I said. "With you."

He held my hand. We were both facing forward, toward the little curve of river, but then he turned toward me. I moved so slowly, both afraid of what was happening and dying for it to happen. Our movements weren't hesitant, and we weren't upset like in the lighthouse; this was what I'd dreamed of, wanted all along. Billy leaned over to kiss me.

My lips touched his, salty and warm, and my arms went around his neck. I stood on tiptoes. He held me so close. My whole body felt hot, as if I had the strangest fever, one that made me feel wonderful. Stars were running through my blood. He tangled his fingers in my hair, and everything in the world went blank except for the kiss.

I didn't want to stop, ever. I don't think he did either because we kept kissing. Kisses on my lips, then little kisses on the side of my mouth and neck that made me go higher on my tiptoes and lean closer, full of feelings I'd never known existed. No matter how often I'd dreamed of Billy, of really kissing him, not an almost kiss but a real one, it was never as amazing as this.

After a while we sat down on the crooked steps of the old

tower, and put our arms around each other, and then he kissed me again. We stayed there for a long time with his arm around my shoulders. Tiny yellow birds darted around the tops of the trees, and a gray fox ran through the brush, and usually I'd be thrilled with so much inspiring nature, but sitting there with Billy I was only thrilled with him.

"I don't want to leave here," Billy said.

"Neither do I," I said.

"But your mother . . ."

"I know."

"Everything's about to change," he said.

"No it won't," I said. "It doesn't have to."

"It will," he said. "There've been other people along the way . . ."

I thought of them: Darrah and Cleo, Richard and Morgane, Atik and everyone at the reserve.

"But they haven't mattered," Billy went on. "It's been us, Maia, the whole time. We've been on our own. I know we've always been heading to your mother, but in my mind it's been you and me. I even thought . . ."

"Thought what?"

"That maybe when we got close, we'd just keep going."

He kissed me again, and I still had the fever feeling, but this time I also felt a scary shiver run down my spine. I hadn't thought we'd keep going. I'd imagined us living with my mother, in her cabin, finding a school, or having her teach us.

"She's different," I said when the kiss stopped. We didn't

break apart, just leaned into each other, foreheads touching, and his arms around me. "She's not like regular parents."

"She'll send me back," he said. "I expect her to. I'm not her kid."

"She'll want you there, I know she will. Besides, remember the sand dollar? Our pact? We're not going back, no matter what."

"Promises are real when you make them," Billy said. "But they change along the way. It's no one's fault. It's just how it is."

"You'll see. I'll never break my promise to you," I said.

We gazed into each other's eyes for a long time. I felt as if he were trying to memorize me, as if I were going to disappear. I tried, with *my* eyes, to tell him, from the deepest part of my heart, that he could believe me, that our promise was as true and real and eternal as the river, that it would outlast anything or anyone who might want us to break it.

Then we heard three sharp blasts of an air horn: Atik calling to let us know it was time to leave. Billy stood, started to pull me up. But I shook my head and made him crouch down again. The ruined trading post was scattered with broken stones. Many were round, but plenty were flat. We gathered them together, and before we left, we built two tall cairns.

We didn't have to tell each other that the cairns represented us: Billy and Maia, so close together. And we left them standing in the place where we'd had our first kiss. Then we walked down the path and dove back into the cold river and swam out to meet the boat.

Chapter 17

MAY 26
TADOUSSAC

The river was wide and straight. Atik kept the throttle open, but by the time we got to Tadoussac it was nearly dark. We swept along the river, then angled a right turn into the half circle of a bay, and the sun disappeared behind the fjord's soaring rock walls. The sky was indigo, the calm water turned silvery purple, and that's when I saw the first whale.

I heard the spout before I saw the whale. The sound is unmistakable after the first time, a combination of *whoosh* and *pfffft*. I glanced left just in time to see a V of ghostly mist hanging in the air, and then the sleek white back of a beluga.

"Billy," I said, grabbing his arm.

We watched the whale following our boat, a shimmer of pure white just below the surface. It raised its head above water, turned on its side just long enough to look directly at us with its round black eye, filled with unfathomable curiosity and intelligence, and its mouth turned up in what appeared to be a smile. It did a half roll, showing us its small flippers and heart-shaped tail, and then disappeared into the deep.

"Wow," Billy said. "That was amazing." I was so happy, seeing the whale and feeling Billy's excitement.

"Whales are really friendly and love to make contact with humans," Atik said. "You'll see a lot of them in the fjord, but first we have to stop and gas up."

"Where do you dock?" Billy asked, peering at the shore. The distance between the water and the top of the seawall looked too great to climb.

"At the quay," Atik said, pointing. "There's an extreme tide here, fifteen feet between low and high. It's low right now." He looked at his phone—it was already nine o'clock. In May, this far north and barely a month to the longest day of the year, the sky really did stay light until very late. Laurent Cartier had been right about that.

"We should spend the night here and go up the Saguenay tomorrow. It'll be easier to find your mother's cabin in daylight," Atik said.

My heart sank lower than the tide. To be so close to her and have to wait another night seemed almost unbearable. As Atik idled the engine and we slid close to the wooden dock, I jumped off with Billy and helped tie the lines around the cleats.

"You want to walk around town while I call my girlfriend again?" Atik asked. "Then you can come back here to sleep."

"Sure," Billy said. "We'll pick up some food."

"Good luck," he said. "Places around here close early."

"Well, we'll try. We'll bring something back for you."

"I've got some dried fish," he said. "There's plenty for you if you don't find something better."

"Okay," Billy said. I couldn't quite speak; my throat ached with disappointment. I tried to tell myself Atik was right, it made sense to wait until tomorrow, but typical of me, my heart and my mind were in different places. I had wanted to surprise my mother tonight.

A sharply inclined ramp slanted from the floating dock up to the land. It felt like climbing the steep roof at home in Connecticut. When Billy and I got to the top we saw the small town. The massive, old-fashioned white hotel with the bright red roof stood out. It was warmly lit, the windows glowing as the night fell. Beside it was a small chapel, also white with a red roof and steeple.

"Are you okay?" Billy asked.

I nodded, but my heart wasn't in it.

"I know how much you want to see your mother," he said.

That melted my hurt a little because I knew he wanted us to keep moving, that he was leery of what would happen when we saw her. I felt even better when he held my hand, linking his fingers with mine.

"Let's try to find something for dinner," he said. "Although we have to make our money last. Who knows when we'll find another job."

"We can always dive for really big lobsters," I said, feeling okay enough to make a feeble joke.

The street names were in French. As we walked along de Bord de l'Eau, the road that followed the curved bay, we saw that Atik was right: Many places, like the souvenir shops and whale watch office, were closed for the night. But there were bright and lively cafés, filled with people. We passed one that was painted pink with a whale on its sign. Music came through the open door, and I felt the strongest urge to go inside.

Instead we kept walking, in search of a grocery. Billy hadn't let go of my hand. I began to breathe more easily. Once you make up your mind that things are just the way they are, that wishing won't change them, you realize you can live through it. I felt a ripple of weirdness and chalked it up to the third full day off meds.

"Are you okay?" Billy asked.

"Mostly," I said. "It's bizarre, being so close to my mom and thinking really old thoughts."

"Like what?"

"Well, when she first left I went so crazy I wanted to rip my hair out. I wanted to stop existing. The idea of her leaving was so horrible, completely impossible, it didn't seem the earth would keep turning. When the sun came up the next day, it felt wrong."

"Yeah, there couldn't be daylight if she was gone," Billy said. I knew he got it: It had happened to him, too.

"I held on as long as I could," I continued, "but once my dad decided to get remarried it felt as if our family was over. I stopped going to school. I literally couldn't get out of bed."

"That's when you went to the hospital?"

I nodded. "I was like an insane girl in a padded room— well, it wasn't actually padded, but the doors were locked and the windows had bars." I paused, thinking of our fight on the way to the lighthouse. "I'm sorry I couldn't really talk about it before. It's still hard. I thought it would make you hate me."

"Hate you, are you kidding?"

"I feel like the only one, Billy. At least in our school." *Try talking to your friends about your time on a psych ward. Try telling your crush.*

"Just keep getting better, Maia," Billy said softly. "Taking your medication, whatever helps. You can take it in front of me, you know."

"I know," I said, cringing and wondering what he'd say if he knew I'd stopped.

But as we walked through town, with Billy never letting go of my hand, I felt my shoulders drop with a kind of silent relief, and I knew that everything would be okay. Tomorrow would come, and we'd find my mother. She'd be so happy to see me. She'd immediately get Billy, see how both serious and funny he was, how smart and cool. She'd realize he'd survived something terrible, and she'd respect how he'd helped me find my way to her.

"I don't think we're going to find a place," Billy said after we'd scoured the streets around the harbor for an open grocery store. "It might be time to dive for those lobsters."

The air had gotten chilly, a breeze blowing off the harbor. Billy put his arm around me. It felt so good, but it took me a minute to figure out how to walk in step with him. I stumbled a couple of times, and I let out a nervous laugh. He just held me steady until I caught the rhythm. I realized my bones were still chilled from our icy swim, and snuggling into his side felt wonderful. It would have anyway.

As we circled back to the harbor, past the little chapel, the hotel looked so warm and inviting. We climbed a path past a tennis court and a row of white wooden chairs facing the bay. Walking around the hotel's exterior, we saw a fire blazing in the lobby fireplace. We gazed into the restaurant windows. It looked vast and elegant, with white tablecloths and sparkling crystal, like the kind of hotel the Burritt wished it could be. Even though it was late, there were a few people still dining, waiters serving food. Hunger pangs hit me hard, and my mouth started watering.

"Do you think we have enough for dinner?" I asked. "Once we get to my mother's, she'll feed us."

"It looks pretty expensive," Billy said. "But we can try."

"What about that place on the quay? That little pink café. That might be cheaper."

"Yeah," Billy said. "I'm pretty sure white tablecloths are out of our league tonight."

We hurried along, wanting to make sure we got to the pink café before it closed. As we approached we heard music, and I relaxed a little, knowing we'd get in. There was a menu posted by the door, but we didn't even look. By then we were both starving, and we figured we could afford at least a bowl of soup.

A waiter greeted us at the door.

"Would you like to be inside or upstairs on the porch?" he asked.

"Inside," Billy said. I knew he realized I was cold.

The atmosphere was cozy and dark, with strings of white lights around the small stage by the bar; there was a man playing guitar and a woman on accordion. People laughed and chatted, and we heard both English and French.

We sat at a small table by the window. We were just across the street from the bay; a wide beach sloped down to the harbor where house- and streetlights sparkled on the water. The room was really dark, making us feel so private at our table, in our own little enclosed space.

Pizza seemed like a good choice, not too expensive, and when it came, it tasted so delicious I couldn't believe it. I nearly burned my mouth eating the first piece so fast.

"You know what?" Billy asked. "This is our first date."

"Um, we've been on the road together for six days," I said, sounding practical but tingling to hear him say it.

"Yeah," he said. "But things are different. Don't you feel that?"

I did. Everything had changed with our first kiss. The music was cheerful and the room was raucous, but it felt so romantic. We were leaning toward each other, elbows on the table, and then he moved his chair so he was right beside me and kissed me—with everyone all around us.

"See?" he said. "First date."

"You're right."

"We should celebrate it somehow."

"We did—with pizza," I said.

"No, I mean something bigger."

"Like what?" I asked.

"I'll show you," he said. "Stay here, okay?"

"Okay," I said, and he walked out of the café.

It felt weird to see him go, and I nearly called him back. I wanted to follow him, but I'd told him I'd stay. I watched as he crossed the street and disappeared down some steps. The tide was still low; I could see the beach from the window, illuminated by white lights ringing the harbor. Billy walked far out onto the hard-packed sand, and he picked up what looked like a long piece of driftwood. He seemed to be going back and forth, making patterns with the stick. I had to stand up to see what he was doing: writing our initials.

BG + MC

Then he started drawing something around them. At first I thought it was going to be a heart, but it was a circle. Then he made five sharp dashes, almost like rays of light shooting out from our initials.

I had said I'd wait inside, but I couldn't. I ran out the door and met him in the street. I threw my arms around him, kissed him hard. Another first, the first time I'd kissed Billy, started it myself.

"Do you know what it is?" he asked.

"Our initials," I said, my arms around his neck. "You and me together."

"But the circle," he said.

"It's like you drew a star around us."

"No," he said. "It's the sand dollar."

"It is," I said, picturing the five narrow ovals, radiating from a center spot like the points of a star, on the delicate shell. "It's our promise . . ."

I wanted to run down to the beach, see his drawing closer. But we hadn't paid the check yet, so we headed back inside. We stood by the door, peering down the dark bar for our waiter. I'd been so wrapped up in Billy, in just the two of us, I had barely noticed the other people there. There was a group, and some couples, and some people by themselves.

One was a woman with straw-colored hair. She wore a khaki vest, the kind oceanographers sometimes used to hold their pens and notebooks and pocket-size binoculars. She stood at the bar, her back to me. I pulled away from Billy and took a step forward. It couldn't be.

My hand was shaking as I reached up and tapped the woman on the shoulder so lightly I wasn't sure she could feel it. But she did, and she turned around.

"Maia!" she said.

"Mom," I said, and I crashed into her arms.

Chapter 18

MAY 26
TADOUSSAC

I buried my head into my mother's shoulder and cried for a long time. I couldn't have held back if I'd wanted. I wept, clutching her, crying because I felt every minute of those three years without her crashing over us in waves. It didn't matter that Billy was right there, or that all the people in the restaurant could see me. I forgot about all of them—even Billy—until I could control myself enough to stop sobbing.

"You did it," Mom said, holding me at arm's length to look me straight in the eyes. "You made it up here, you really did. I never believed it. Your father said this was where you were heading, but I didn't think it was possible."

"Why are you here?" I asked. "In Tadoussac? I thought you'd be miles up the fjord, on the cliff, in your cabin."

She didn't answer. She just kept staring at me, as if assessing how much I'd grown, how I'd changed. I assessed her, too, but to me she looked exactly the same: our shared blue eyes, the gap between our front teeth, our smile. Suddenly I was wiping my tears and we both had the biggest smiles on our faces.

"This took courage, Maia," Mom said. "I can only imagine how you did it! Only a true Whale Maven could have undertaken this journey. You are a woman after your mother's heart."

"I didn't do it alone," I said.

She looked over my shoulder. Was it my imagination, or did her expression go slightly flat? It bounced back, though, and she gave a warm smile. "You must be Billy."

"Hello, Mrs. Collins," he said, holding out his hand.

She hesitated, then gave it a firm shake. "I use the name I was born with," she said. "Gillian Symonds, but call me Gillian."

"Thank you," Billy said. But I noticed he didn't say her name. I figured it would feel as strange for him as it would for me to call someone's parent by their first name, especially in the instant of meeting them.

"Why, Mom?" I asked. It felt bizarre to me, knowing my mother was using a different last name from mine.

"It's more professional," she said. She made a funny face, her mouth twisting in such a familiar way. "No, that's not the real reason. It just didn't feel right using your dad's name anymore."

"It's mine, too," I said.

"Maia, you were named for one of the brightest stars in the sky. I chose it because the minute I held you in my arms I knew it was the only name for you. You know how much I love the Pleiades, and I know you love them, too. That's part of our forever connection, okay? The last name doesn't matter."

I nodded, trying to see it her way. For a second I felt an awkward pause, as if we were both searching for something to say to each other. But then her eyes lit up, and she jostled my shoulder.

"I want to hear all about your trip," she said. "How did you escape your dad and Astrid? She's got such an eagle eye."

"She does," I said. "I had to climb out my bedroom window—"

"I taught you how to do that!" she said.

"I know, I was thinking of you! And I shinnied down the pine tree—it's gotten so tall, Mom, you wouldn't believe it— and then I drove away in your car. I went to say good-bye to Billy, but instead he came with me . . ."

"Ah, my good old Volvo. I miss her. How is she?"

"She's great, but we figured Dad would have people on the lookout. We hid her behind Billy's family's house," I said, looking at Billy and wanting him to join in, to tell the story with me. But he was silent, his wide mouth set in that way I recognized so well, as if he wasn't sure whether he could trust Mom or not.

"Well, she served you well," Mom said. "Then what?"

"Billy, you tell," I said.

He cleared his throat. "Well, then we took my truck. My grandfather had given it to me."

"That sounds like a phenomenal adventure," Mom said.

"Switching vehicles along the way! How wonderfully diabolical you were. I know it drove Astrid crazy." She put on a pretend-stern face. "Not that that's good."

"I know," I said, smiling with a little shared Astrid bashing.

"But, oh, Maia—I am so glad to see you!" Mom threw her arms around me. Again. Then she looked at Billy. "I'm sure it was good to have a traveling partner. Which one of you drove and who navigated?"

"I drove your car," I explained. "Billy drove the truck, and we took turns navigating. No GPS because we threw out our phones so we couldn't be tracked—we used a paper map most of the way here."

"Well, you were always good at reading charts," Mom said. "I'm just sorry I left before I really taught you how to use a sextant. You never know when celestial navigation will come in handy."

"But you did teach me," I said, wondering why she didn't remember.

"On the roof doesn't count," she said. "You have to be on a boat, rocking and rolling on fifteen-foot waves, to really perfect your skill."

"You can teach me now," I said. "And Billy, too. But, Mom, you didn't tell me, why are you here in Tadoussac? We were going to head up the fjord to find you tomorrow, at the cabin."

"How were you going to do that?" she asked.

"We have a friend with a boat," Billy said.

"You guys are so resourceful!" she said, laughing. "Spectacular. But how would you track down my little hideaway? I never sent you a map, did I?"

I grinned; I had wanted to tell her the whole time. "I borrowed *Beluga and Humpback Whales of Saguenay Fjord*," I said.

"Wait—that's such a rare book! So hard to find."

"That's why I went to Mystic," I said. "Because I remembered you'd made a tiny dot on the map, and I knew that's where your house would be. Is it?"

She nodded, and I saw tears in her eyes. "I never thought you'd remember that. You were so little."

"I remember everything about you," I said.

I stared at her, making sure she took in my words. Did she know how true they were? I could tell her every single thing that had ever happened between us.

"Did you come down here in your boat?" I asked Mom. "Are you going back to your cabin tonight? We can tell Atik, and he can go home, and we can go with you . . ."

My mother wiped her tears away, but she didn't stop gazing at me. She smiled softly, the way she did when I was little, when we would do the most special, secret things together—it was a smile of deep love.

"Why don't we stay on my boat tonight?" she asked.

"Funny, that's what Atik said when I showed him on the chart—he invited us to sleep on his," I said. "I guess your place really *is* a long way from here."

"Yes, very," she said. Then she turned and spoke to the bartender in a low voice so I couldn't hear, and she gestured at the door as if indicating someone about to walk through it. For a second I wondered if she'd been planning to meet a friend here, but when she turned around she said, "Let's go."

"I have to pay," Billy said.

"I took care of it," she said.

That's what she'd been speaking to the bartender about! I grinned at Billy. *See?* I wanted to say to him. *It's going to be great with her, she cares, she likes you already.*

Mom walked down the dock to the *Wolf* with Billy and me, so we could get our things and say good-bye to Atik. He was still in the wheelhouse, leaning back in the chair, feet propped up on the wheel, still talking to his girlfriend.

"Hey, Atik," Billy called.

"Hey," Atik said, lowering the phone.

"This is Maia's mother," Billy said.

"Gillian Symonds," my mother said.

"Hello," he said.

"I recognize the boat," my mother said. "You're related to George and François?"

"Yes," Atik said. "François is my brother and George is my uncle."

"Well, it's a small world," my mother said. "Especially for people who work on the river."

"Yeah, it is," Atik said.

"Thank you for bringing us here," I said.

"No problem," he said. "I'm going to stay for a few days and fish with my uncle. So I'll probably see you around."

"Good," Billy said. The floating dock had started to rise with the incoming tide, so he easily hoisted our bags onto the dock and jumped up after them.

I walked toward my mother, but she took a cell phone from her pocket and gestured for us to go on ahead. I hadn't known she had a phone—it shocked me to see and made me feel weird; she'd been so totally out of touch with me. But then I told myself the reason she hadn't called was that she had no reception in the cabin. And she probably didn't come to town often. Still, I felt strange.

Billy and I kept walking. I heard Mom on the phone. Her voice carried, quiet but urgent. Was she phoning my dad? I stared at her, trying to tell, but couldn't.

Billy and I had reached the half-moon beach, so I turned to look. Waves lapped at the lower part of the circle he'd drawn. Our initials and the sand dollar markings were still there.

"I don't want it to disappear," I said.

"It's okay. If the tide takes it away, I'll draw it again," he said.

I looked up at him and saw resolution in his eyes: our promise. We hugged tightly, but let go fast when we heard my mom approaching. I felt like the biggest dork for not wanting her to see me holding him. But she had left when I was thirteen. I needed a little time to let years and the way I'd changed catch up with how we were now.

"What are you looking at?" Mom asked, following my gaze down to the beach.

"Something Billy drew for me," I said.

My mother stared for a long moment, then shook her head. "I'll have to look in the morning. It's too dark now," she said briskly.

But it wasn't too dark. The streetlights were shining right on the spot, and Billy had drawn our initials and the sand dollar circle so clearly. They were deeply scored into the sand. Why had she pretended she couldn't see it?

"It's a sand dollar," I said.

"What an interesting thing to draw," she said.

"Did you call Dad?" I asked. "Just now?"

"No," she said. "Of course not. You just got here, Maia. We'll sleep tonight and talk about everything tomorrow."

I felt a combination of relieved and strange. But if it wasn't my dad, who had been on the phone?

The three of us headed away from the fishing and whale-watching boats, toward the opposite side of the bay's curve, at the far end of the harbor. The houses got bigger here. We stopped directly in front of one of the largest and most austere, a white mansion that looked like it might have been built by a sea captain.

My mother glanced at the front door. Were the people who lived there friends of hers? A shadow moved behind a curtain in one of the tall downstairs windows. My stomach flipped— was someone watching us?

"Come on," my mother said, leading us down white steps

onto a private dock jutting into the bay. There was no beach here, just deep water. Black and still, it glistened under the harbor lights. We passed a Zodiac inflatable and a sleek, small white sailing dinghy both tied to the dock.

"Whose are these?" I asked. But then we reached *Narwhal*, my mother's research boat. I would have recognized it anywhere, from all the photos she had sent. The vessel was named for the arctic whale with a long tusk, and when I was little she had told me that the myth of the unicorn had started the first time a human encountered a narwhal.

We crossed the deck and climbed down a companionway into the cabin. Mom turned on lights—it was so cozy, with warm wood everywhere, framed watercolors, and red plaid cushions on the settees.

"Are you hungry?" she asked.

"No, we're fine," Billy said.

"We just ate at the café," I said, my words turning into a gigantic yawn.

"But you're tired," she said, laughing.

I nodded. I felt exhausted, as if I had been holding the entire world up for three years, making it spin all by myself, never letting go for a second until the minute I would see my mother again. And here she was; we were together.

She opened her arms, and I tumbled against her. She stroked my hair, just the way she had through my whole childhood. Billy looked around the cabin. He was standing in front of a big poster of whales—the exact one that had been in my mother's whale room at home—and he studied the different species.

"Well, you've had quite a journey," my mother said. "So let's get you to bed."

"No," I said. "Let's stay up, there's so much I want to ask you . . ."

"I know," she said, interrupting me in the middle of another massive yawn—I couldn't stop myself. "But we'll get up early tomorrow and there'll be lots of time to catch up."

"Will we see whales?" I asked.

"Definitely. We'll head out first thing in the morning."

"I saw my first beluga today," Billy said. "It was beyond anything I expected."

"Ahh," Mom said. "And there'll be many more tomorrow. Okay, Maia. You take the forward stateroom. Billy, you take the aft."

"But where will you sleep?" I asked. There were only two separate cabins on the boat.

"Here, on the settee. It pulls out into a bed," she said.

I wanted her to sleep up front, on the wide berth, with me. We'd sometimes fallen asleep reading together side by side when she'd lived at home. But that wasn't going to happen tonight.

"Sweet dreams," my mother said, just as she had every night of my life before she'd left.

"My mother used to say that," Billy said.

"It's in the mother handbook," she said.

"Yeah," he said.

Then my mother hugged me and gave me a little pat on the back, pointing me toward the forward cabin.

Billy stood still, watching me. It really hit me: For the first time since Billy and I had left on our road trip, we wouldn't be sleeping within a few feet of each other. I wanted to go to him, hug him, but everything felt so stilted. We managed to brush fingertips as we walked past each other, but that was it.

And then all three of us went to bed in different parts of the boat.

Chapter 19

MAY 27
UP THE SAGUENAY FJORD

I tossed around for a while, then slept hard until eight a.m. The wake of a passing boat woke me, sloshing against *Narwhal*'s hull. Groggy and disoriented, I got up and walked into the main cabin. I found Billy at the table, eating cereal. My mother was gone.

"Where is she?" I asked.

"I don't know," he said. "She left this."

I panicked a minute before reading her note: *Hello you two. Have breakfast, and I'll see you soon. XXOO*

Billy stood, his spoon clattering onto the table, and put his arms around me. We were both sweaty from boat-sleep in small cabins, and our T-shirts stuck to each other. Billy leaned down and I tilted up, and we kissed, and it was day two of being so close that kissing each other seemed almost normal. But it still sent shivery goose bumps over my skin.

By the time we'd sat back down and finished our bowls of granola, my mother was back. This was typical of her—up early, ready to face the day full-blast, no dawdling. Billy and I heard her hurrying around on deck above our heads. We quickly washed our bowls in the small sink and went up to meet her.

"Hi there," she said, hugging me. "How did you sleep?"

"Great, Mom," I said. *Because I'm with you.*

I'd been right the night before: This was a deep-water dock. Looking down at least twenty feet, the water was so clear I could see the rock-strewn bottom. A starfish seemed to be skipping along. It matched the way I felt—incredibly happy.

Billy and I loosened the bow and stern lines, and my mother drove us into the bay. Morning sun threw diamonds on the water. We rounded the headland, and suddenly we were in the Saguenay Fjord. My heart caught in my throat. Yes, it was spectacularly beautiful, rock walls rising on either side of the dark-blue river, but I barely noticed because this was the spot I'd so long dreamed of seeing my mother again. *This* was the place of my dreams.

And here she was. Here we were.

I stood next to her at the wheel. She gave me a big squeeze. Her smell was so familiar, and so was the pressure of her arm around me. When I was a baby she had carried me around in a blue denim sling, and apparently I'd never wanted her to put me down. I loved her so much, had never wanted to be an inch away. I had cried when I first went to school. It had gotten easier, of course. But being here now, so close, made me remember those early times, and how much I'd missed her, as if part of myself had been torn away, these last few years.

I must have grown since the last time we were together because our shoulders were nearly even. I was almost as tall as she was. I held a secret smile, waiting for her to notice, but she was busy adjusting instruments, peering around.

"Do you see them?" she asked.

"So many!" Billy said.

I'd been so focused on Mom, I hadn't seen: Whales were everywhere.

Belugas swam in clusters down below, the adults as white and glossy as ivory, the smaller juveniles pale gray, almost silver. They came up for air, rolling on their backs, curving their bodies and raising their tails.

Humpbacks, forty-foot gentle giants with long white flippers, were feeding in bubble rings, forcing food—krill, plankton, copepods, small fish—to the surface by the great big bubbles they blew underwater. They swam close to our boat, spy-hopping—lifting their heads clear out of the water to look at us.

I felt ecstatic, overwhelmed. Belugas swam by, white streaks beneath the surface. Reaching overboard I actually touched the head of a female—smaller than the males—knowing she had come to welcome us, to say hello, and I felt the magical connection I'd imagined with whales all these years. They were so emotional and intelligent, and I gazed into this one's deeply beautiful dark eyes, communing with her.

One humpback breached—threw itself totally out of the water—landing with such a huge splash it hit us with a blast of spray.

"Wow, that's amazing!" Billy said. "Why does it do that?"

"She's playing. Feeling exuberant," my mother said.

Another humpback did the same thing, fifty yards away. Three more poked their heads up above the surface, nose-up like tall mountains rising from the sea, all around our boat, gazing at us.

"That's spy-hopping," I told Billy. "They're checking us out."

"You remember the term," my mother said, sounding proud.

"I told you, I remember everything," I said.

We kept going, and every time a whale breached Billy exclaimed, and I felt joy. The belugas were the best, swimming so close, rising straight to the surface as if wanting us to lean out of the boat and pat their heads. Which Billy and I did. He beamed, and I could see he was as full of delight and wonder as I was.

"This is a whale sanctuary," my mother said, "and boats are supposed to stay four hundred meters from any whale. Belugas are endangered, so it's really important to protect them. But the whales know me, and they refuse to stay away! I never feed them, of course, but they are such social creatures. I'm sure they're coming over to meet you."

"That's what I was thinking!" I said, totally blown away by it all.

"How many different kinds are here?" Billy asked.

"Belugas, minkes, humpbacks, fin whales, North Atlantic right whales, sperm whales, the occasional rare blue," Mom explained. "Some species are endangered, and others are vulnerable. The North Atlantic gray whale is now extinct. There used to be bowheads here, but no sightings since I arrived."

"What happened to them?" Billy asked.

"Humans," she said bluntly. "The north is the first place to feel climate change. Melting sea ice alters salinity, causes algae blooms in some places, and kills food sources. Whales starve." It broke my heart to think of them suffering, not having enough food.

"Nature needs protecting," I said.

Her eyes twinkled as if she was proud of me for saying it.

She idled the engine and more and more belugas came up to see us, heads out of the water nearly levitating until she touched each one. Mom beckoned me over, indicated I should hold out my hand, and sure enough—whale after whale rose up to touch my hand.

"That's Blue, and that's Crescent, and that's Euphotic—he takes the deepest dives . . ." Mom glanced at me to see if I remembered what the aphotic zone was, and I did: six hundred and sixty feet below the water's surface, where no light could penetrate. "And that's Phyto, for phytoplankton, and that's Polaris, and that's Preemie, because she was born so early."

She had always named whales, even on our family trips, and I'd loved the way she recognized them as individuals, noticed little differences in their appearances: a deeper V in one's tail, a bite taken out of a flipper by a predator, a scar on the top of one's head from a close encounter with a ship's propeller.

"I'm looking for Persephone," Mom added. "One of my regular belugas. I've known her since she was still with her mother, and now we're waiting for her to deliver a calf. She has the most beautiful song of any whale I've ever heard, and I'm missing her. I'm hoping the next time I see her she has her baby."

"Maybe we'll see her today," I said, wondering why my mother's words sounded familiar, as if they'd swum up from a dream, and made me feel dizzy, the deck tilting under my feet.

"Does Persephone have a favorite spot?" Billy asked.

"No, she could be anywhere. But I'm sending out my own song to her, and I hope she hears it and comes to find me."

"I did that," I said. "I heard your song and came to find you."

My mother stood at the wheel, and I was surprised to see she had a grave expression in her eyes—it seemed so odd for the wonderful time we were having. "Daughters do that," she said.

We cruised farther north, up the fjord. Whales still surrounded us, but there was no sign of Persephone. The morning passed quickly, and at noon we anchored in a deep inlet on the fjord's western shore.

My mother had packed us a beach picnic. The wicker basket was filled with my favorites, almost as if she'd expected me: Granny Smith apples, carrot sticks and hummus, and *pan bagnat*—the most delicious sandwiches ever and a tradition for our family to have on the water: a crusty baguette stuffed with really good tuna, the kind from France packed in olive oil, and chopped artichoke hearts, fresh tomatoes, basil, and lemon juice.

She'd even left out the red onion because she knew I didn't like it.

"This is delicious, Mrs.—I mean, Gillian," Billy said.

"I'm glad you like it," she said. "I wanted Maia to have her favorite boat picnic food."

"I love it," I said. "Mom, tell me the truth—did you know I was coming?"

"How could I have?"

"Because this picnic . . . it's the best."

"I'm so glad you like it, sweetheart," she said. "I ran out while you were sleeping to fill the basket."

"The grocery store in Tadoussac must open early," I said.

"I didn't go to a store," my mother said.

"Where, then?"

"You know me, Maia. I'm resourceful."

She used a big bread knife to cut the last section of *pan bagnat* in half and gave them each to Billy and me. Then, without asking for help, she went forward and started to raise the anchor.

"Let me do that!" Billy called, heading toward the bow.

She gave him a long, steady look, and even from the cockpit I could see the steel in her eyes. I should have warned him: He'd made the cardinal error.

"I know you mean well," she said. "But I can handle the anchor, Billy. I'm not the biggest fan of chivalry."

He walked back toward me, and I could see his freckles standing out against his skin, bright red, as if he'd been slapped.

"I'm sorry," I whispered. "She was like that with my dad, too."

She started the engine, and we continued north. I knew Billy's feelings were hurt, but he was incredibly great about it. He just shook it off, grabbed my hand, and pulled me to the rail.

"We have company," Billy said, looking overboard. I saw the great shadowy shape of a humpback—its black back and those unmistakable white flippers that had always reminded me of wings—following us. A smaller whale seemed nearly attached to her side.

"That's Gray Girl," my mother said. "And her daughter Aurora."

"Is this the time of year whales have babies?" Billy asked. "Like Persephone?"

"It varies," my mother said. "We first saw this child a month ago, the morning after a wild display of the northern lights. So I named her for that."

"Aurora borealis," Billy said.

Mom nodded. "Gray was childless for so long. The other females would give birth to calves and she would keen. Her song was so high-pitched and mournful, full of grief."

"What happened after she had Aurora?" I asked, staring at the small calf nearly glued to her mother's side.

"Well, mothers miss their daughters—even before they've had them. There's an empty space just waiting to be filled. So after so much waiting, she finally found peace."

"Did her song change?" Billy asked.

"Listen," my mother said. She flipped a switch on the console, and suddenly whale music filled the boat, coming from speakers overhead. There were chirps and trills—long, lingering notes that ranged from high to low and reminded me of my mother's favorite Celtic fiddle music combined with the low notes of a horn, maybe a saxophone. The whale sounded peaceful, happy.

"That's live," my mother said. "The hydrophones beneath the boat are picking up the sounds of Gray Girl's contentment. She's changed since she became a mother. This is a recording of how she sounded before Aurora was born."

Mom turned a dial, pushed a button, and a very different sound came out.

She was right: It sounded like crying. The whale screeched, and screamed, and her voice finally fell into a low, low sobbing sound.

The whale's grief had jostled something in me. Gray had wanted to have a baby so badly, and now that she had one, her entire being had changed. And my mother loved these whales. And she was missing Persephone, waiting for her, loving Gray's child and waiting for Persephone and hers, listening to their songs.

Missing, waiting, child, song.

I froze. Could Morgane's vision of my mother's love have been about whales, not about me?

"Turn it off," I said. "Please?"

But my mother didn't, and that feeling of dizziness overtook me, flipped me over. I lost my balance and crashed against the console. I must have hit the audio switch because the sound stopped.

"Maia!" my mother said. I'd messed with her electronics, and she busily reset every dial I'd accidentally turned, every toggle I'd flipped.

"What's wrong, are you okay?" Billy asked, coming to me, holding me in his arms. I pressed my face into his shoulder. Was this attack a symptom of stopping my medication? The daggers were back, that falling feeling scary and strong. I heard my mother hurrying across the deck to us.

"Let her go," she said, but Billy didn't. He held me closer, and I rocked against him.

My mother grabbed my shoulder, pulling me away from him.

"Hey!" Billy said.

"Maia," my mother said, ignoring him. It would have been almost okay if she'd hugged me, if I'd been able to glue myself to her like that baby calf, but she wasn't letting me.

"You erased part of the recording, and could have destroyed a lot more research there," she said sharply.

"I'm sorry," I said.

"What got into you?"

"I feel sick," I said.

"You don't get seasick," she said. "You never have. Just stare at the horizon. That will steady you."

And it did. Eventually. It helped that Billy was holding my hand, just out of Mom's sight. Why hadn't she wanted him to hug me? I guessed I'd been right the night before, that the sixteen-year-old me was very different from the thirteen-year-old, and the contrast was hard for my mother to handle.

I had hoped I was over the withdrawal from the meds, but I still felt really bad. Mom wheeled the boat around, and we began heading south. She seemed upset with me—for messing with her console, getting dizzy? I was glad when Gray and Aurora dove out of sight, and I had the crazy, uneasy, unshakable feeling that I didn't want to see Persephone and, if she'd in fact given birth, her newborn baby. It was bizarre, because no one had ever loved baby whales more than I did.

"Wait, aren't we going to your cabin?" I asked when it hit me that we were going in the opposite direction, back to Tadoussac.

"No, Maia. We're not."

"But why? Are we going to stay on the boat? Do you live aboard? You don't really live in your cabin?"

"No," she said. "I don't live in the cabin."

My head exploded. The place I'd been picturing her for three years—did it even exist?

"Is the cabin real?" I asked.

"Of course—you saw the photos I sent. But it's a very hard place to live with the work I do, the electronics I need. There's no reception, and I always lose power—the receiver goes dead, and all the data from the hydrophones can be lost. You see how I get when I lose data," she said, trying to make a joke about my nearly erasing the recording. But I couldn't laugh.

"That cabin is in the back-of-beyond," she continued as we drove on over the water. "There's no Wi-Fi up there, so I couldn't even email the oceanographic institute—the people who fund my grant. Wait till you see my office, my studio. It's fully equipped, state-of-the-art. You'll understand why I had to leave it."

"Where? Where did you move?"

"Tadoussac. You probably saw. That big white house above the dock."

I felt stunned. My mother lived in a mansion in Tadoussac, not in a remote cabin up the fjord. She had a cell phone. She had reception. She had power. She emailed the grant people.

But she'd never called or emailed me. We wrote letters. Letters that took forever to send and receive.

I tried to push the bad feelings away. We returned to the harbor and tied up. As Billy, my mother, and I walked down the dock, I told myself, *I'm with my mother, we're together again, she took me and Billy out in her boat to see whales.*

I wondered, a little, why I had to tell myself those things instead of feeling them. Was it because Mom was striding down the dock with the intense purpose I'd sometimes seen her do with my father, without a glance back at me, or without chatting or touching my shoulder, playing with my hair as we walked?

And then there was the house.

It was huge, painted white, with granite steps leading up to a wide porch. It had a steeply pitched roof and about a hundred dormer windows on the second floor. It looked very old, but pristine, the maritime equivalent of the mansions where the rich industrialists lived back in Crawford. The kind of house my mother had always disdained.

We paused at the doorway.

"Maia," she began.

"What?" I asked.

She just shook her head. "Come inside. You'll see."

This was the kind of town where doors could be left unlocked. My mother opened the door—as if the house belonged to her—and held it open so we could walk inside.

My stomach churned. Everything felt so wrong.

Missing, waiting, child, song.

I had to admit the truth: Those words had referred to my mother and whales, not her and me.

I'd thought that realization was the worst thing possible, but I was wrong.

Chapter 20

MAY 27
TADOUSSAC

A man stood just inside the door. He was tall with graying brown hair and a beard, and he wore a blue button-down shirt and khakis—the kind of clothes my dad wore.

My mother walked over to him, and the man hugged her, and she stood in the crook of his arm.

"Maia, this is Drake. And, Drake, this is my daughter and her friend Billy."

"You made it," Drake said. "Wow, Gillian said your dad told her you might be coming, but I don't think either of us fully believed it. What a trek you've had."

I couldn't speak. I don't know why I'd never expected to see my mother with someone else, not when my father was with Astrid, but I didn't. I tried to smile, but my mouth wouldn't move.

"Maia would have done anything to get here," Billy said, shaking Drake's hand.

"This is really where you live?" I asked, facing my mother.

"Oh, Maia."

"Why didn't you tell me last night? Why did we stay on the boat?"

"I knew . . . all this would be hard for you."

All this: her lies? The fact that she'd woven a tale about a magical cabin in the wilderness? Or the fact that she was with Drake? We stood in a foyer gleaming with polished wide-board floors. I knew from history class that only the richest people from earlier centuries could afford floors made from such broad planks, that the wood came from the hearts of live oak trees.

My mother and Drake huddled next to an antique grand-father clock, speaking quietly. The clock chimed five times slowly, drowning out their words.

"Is this all right with you?" Billy asked me, very quietly.

"I'm not sure."

"Drake," he said. "You didn't expect him."

"That's putting it mildly."

I wanted to hug Billy, have him hold me close. It slammed into my mind that he'd been right—everything *had* changed the minute we'd gotten here. I wished we had kept going.

The last chime rang in the air. I felt my mother's and Drake's gazes on us.

"Let's sit down," Drake said.

"Yes, please come in here," my mother said, leading us forward.

The living room was lined with bookcases. Massive gold-framed paintings of sailing ships—looking as if they belonged in a museum—flanked a large fireplace. Antique brass marine instruments shared space on the mantel with framed photos of people I didn't recognize. Red leather armchairs, two sofas and a love seat covered with expensively faded red-and-blue paisley fabric, and valuable-looking Persian rugs and mahogany tables were everywhere. It was a room straight out of one of Astrid's house magazines.

For a moment I felt reassured. There was no way my mother would like a place like this. Maybe she stayed here, for cell reception and Wi-Fi, but this would never be her home.

Windows with four panes over four panes faced the harbor. There was the private dock out front with the three boats tied to it: a Zodiac, a dinghy, and my mother's boat. I figured the inflatable and small sailboat belonged to Drake. My mother, no matter what he thought, was really just visiting here.

"You have a great view," Billy said.

"Thank you," Drake said. "My grandparents built this place. We go back pretty far in this part of Canada. Both my grandfather and his father were ship captains."

Nailed it, I thought. The minute I'd seen this house, I'd known.

"What kind of ships?" Billy asked.

"My great-grandfather carried furs and timber from Eastern Quebec up the Saint Lawrence through the Great Lakes or down to New England."

Perfect, I thought. Drake was descended from the trappers— the Europeans—who had subjugated the Innu, brought disease to their communities, and tried to destroy their culture.

"And his son, my grandfather," Drake continued, "captained a steamer that carried goods from here to Boston."

"Are you a captain, too?" Billy asked.

"Well, I have my license," Drake said. "But I'm like Maia's mom. I'm a scientist."

"What kind?" Billy asked.

"Marine biologist. I fell in love with the sea when I was a kid."

"So did I," Billy said. "I was a lobster fisherman with my grandfather."

My mother had been standing aside, listening. But now she stepped forward, right in front of Billy.

"I wonder what your grandfather thinks of you leaving school and taking this trip," she said. "I wonder if he's as worried as Maia's father and stepmother have been."

"He's not," Billy said.

My mother and Drake waited for him to say more, but he didn't.

"We have to have a talk," my mother said.

I prepared myself. She was going to tell me she'd called, or was going to call, my father. She was going to tell me she loved me, and was glad to see me, but she had to do the right thing and send me back to Connecticut.

But she didn't.

"I know this is all coming as a surprise to you," she said, walking across the room to face me, to look me straight in the eye. "It's not how I wanted you to find out."

"I dreamed of you in the cabin. I thought that was why you couldn't contact me."

"I know. Every step of the way I thought, 'I should tell Maia.'"

"Every step of what way? You mean when you met Drake?"

"Well, I've known Drake a long time. We were in grad school together, and we did our first big oceanographic project together."

Okay, that was a long time ago. I did the math and remembered that I was in sixth grade when she'd gone away for weeks to do her fieldwork near the floe edge on Baffin Island, in the Canadian Arctic.

"So then what do you mean? Every step of what?"

"Oh, Maia," she said, as if she felt total pity for me. Drake stood behind her, and the expression in his eyes was pure sympathy. It was so extreme I froze in fear. Was my mother sick? Were they about to tell me she was dying?

"Tell me, Mom. What is it?"

Billy had his eye on the door to the foyer, and I saw his mouth drop open. He walked close to me but didn't touch me. He just stood by my side, invisibly propping me up.

A young woman walked into the room. She looked a few years older than me and was nearly as tall as Drake, with braided brown hair and gold wire-rimmed glasses. And she was holding a baby—not an infant, but maybe a one-year-old. My mind did a million things in ten seconds and computed that the young woman was Drake's daughter, and the baby was his grandchild, and that my mother knew I'd be upset because there was another daughter-like person in her life.

"Maia, this is my daughter," my mother said.

"No." I almost laughed. What a joke—the girl must have been in her twenties. I would have known about her. Unless— was it possible my mother had given her up for adoption? Had she had her before she met my father, before or during college, and known she wasn't ready for motherhood? Where had the girl been all this time? Could it be like those stories you hear about where the child searches the mother out? Had this person found her up here in Tadoussac?

The young woman handed the little child to my mother. My mother cradled her—I could see now that she was a girl, with curly blond hair and blue eyes, wearing a white T-shirt imprinted with a little pink whale, hearts coming out of its spout.

"This is Merie," my mother said. "Your sister."

"My what?"

"Maia, we named her thinking of you," Drake said. "For Merope, another star in the Pleiades."

My mother held her out to me, and I blindly took her into my arms. Merie gurgled, and clutched my hair with her tiny hands. Looking into her blue eyes, staring at me with fascination, was like seeing myself as a baby.

I kissed the top of her head. I gave her my index finger, and she gripped it with stunning strength. Her tiny fingernails were just long enough to scratch me slightly. It didn't hurt. She didn't want to let go.

When I handed her back to my mother, she had to pry Merie's hand off my finger. Merie fussed as if she'd wanted to stay with me, and my mother bounced her and sang a song she'd sung to me:

> *"Wynken and Blynken and Nod one night*
> *Sailed off on a wooden shoe*
> *Sailed down a river of crystal light*
> *Into a sea of dew . . ."*

I must have been in a trance because I certainly didn't want to sing but heard myself joining in on the next part, a kind of familiar harmony my mother and I had perfected when I was about four, my voice coming out of my mouth:

> *"Where are you going and what do you wish?*
> *The old moon asked the three*
> *Well, we're going out fishing for herring fish*
> *That live in the beautiful sea . . ."*

"You loved that song," my mother said, and Merie relaxed, gazing at me with a kind of sisterly wonder I'd never seen in anyone's face before. She cooed now, reaching for me again. I let her take my finger, accidentally smearing blood on her hand.

"Oh, Merie, my little sea star, did you claw your sister?" my mother asked Merie in her right arm, comfortably slung against her side. "Let's go to the sink and wash it off, Maia.

Merie doesn't know her own strength. You were exactly the same as a baby. You were a little powerhouse."

She and Drake began walking toward the kitchen, but when we reached the foyer I took Billy's hand and pulled him out the front door. He didn't ask any questions. We ran across the wide porch, down the granite steps, and when we hit the ground we tore as fast as we could away from the sea captain's house, away from my mother and Drake, away from the cutest baby I'd ever seen.

Away from my sister.

My half sister.

My sister.

I tried on all the names, but it didn't matter. I'd loved her on sight, but her existence turned my mother into the world's worst liar. Not living in the cabin was *nothing*, having a cell phone turned out to be no big deal, not compared with the fact that she'd had a baby and didn't even tell me.

She couldn't stand the boring comforts of suburban life, the restrictions of our family, but here she was living in a fancy house with her new husband and daughter.

Billy and I ran toward the quay, where Atik had been docked, but when we got there, the boat was gone. Two fishermen were unloading their catch a few slips away from where the boat had been.

"Hey, do you know if *Wolf* left for good?" Billy asked.

"No," one of them said. "They're out pulling pots. They'll be back before dark."

"We can wait that long," I said to Billy.

"And then what?" he asked.

"Just like you said. It was a mistake to come here. Everything changed. Only in a completely different way than I expected."

"Kind of a shock," Billy said, watching me carefully.

"Kind of," I said. The whole thing was so ridiculous and surreal, I started to crack up, laugh uncontrollably.

Billy grabbed my shoulder to steady me. "Don't lose it on me now."

"I'm not. It's honestly funny, don't you think?"

"Not really," he said. He had a question behind his eyes. "Should we go back home, to Connecticut? Now that you've seen your mother? Because I don't think staying here is going to work out."

"You're totally right about that. But we're not going back there. Sand dollar," I said.

"Sand dollar," he said. That finally got him to smile.

I glanced over my shoulder, down the quay, expecting my mother to come barreling after us. The last thing I wanted was to return to her house, to have her try to explain everything again, or in a different way. "Let's get away from the harbor till Atik comes back."

"Okay," Billy said.

And he was good at this: getting us out of a place we didn't want to be. There was no one better. We ducked behind a boat shed and angled up a pine-needle-strewn path. We headed west toward the late-day sun, still high enough in the sky to paint the bay and the treetops the same shade of butterscotch.

We were traveling light, considering we'd left our stuff on my mother's boat. But I felt light in other ways, too. The top of my head felt as if it might float off. At the top of the path we stood in the coastal forest that rose behind the town. Tall pines spiked around us. I felt if we walked another hour we'd be far enough away, and we could just keep going—just as Billy had wanted to do in the first place.

"Where are we going?" he asked.

"Heaven and back," I said. "Except not back."

"That sounds good," he said.

Around the next bend we came to an open hill leading down to a few houses—the kind of hill that, if covered in snow, would have been perfect for sledding. A wooden ladder was attached to the trunk of a tall tree, but even better—a swing hung from one of its rambling, crooked branches.

The swing's wide seat was made of a splintery plank. It looked old, as if it had been there forever. I wondered if kids in the houses below still used it. Billy tested the long ropes, tugging on them to make sure they were safe.

"Get on," he said.

"We're too old for swinging," I said. "I wonder what's up that ladder."

"Get on," he said again.

So I did. He pushed me, softly at first. *Tap*, his hand on the small of my back, *tap*, and I'd lazily drift out and back. The out part was okay, but back was best because I loved feeling his fingers touch my back. *Tap*, a little harder, and I went out a little farther. From here I saw the inn's red roof from above, and the harbor spreading out into the Saint Lawrence River.

Billy's taps turned into solid pushes, both hands on my waist every time I came back. And I swung farther up and out, too. The river reminded me of where we'd come from, all the way east. It reminded me of the reserve and there—I saw it returning to the bay, its wake rippling in a frothy white V behind it—was *Wolf.*

"Atik's on his way in," I said.

"Good," Billy said. But instead of me getting off so we could head down to the quay, Billy held the swing steady and eased himself onto the board beside me. We barely fit. He held both ropes, one arm around me, and his legs moved us forward, then back, until we were swinging. Not as high up as I'd gone before, but still getting air.

I glanced up at him. His freckles seemed to be standing out more than ever, and his eyes fixed on me; he was smiling a funny, lopsided smile.

"This is it," he said.

"What?" I asked.

"Something you always look for but never know when it's going to happen."

"Finding a splintery old swing way above a little town in Canada?"

"Exactly," he said. "What I've always dreamed of."

"Seriously, what?"

We went back and forth, back and forth, another minute.

The sun turned orange and went down a little more, glancing off the fjord's high rock walls, making the bay look like fire.

"The best moment of my life," he said.

"This, right now?"

"Yeah," he said and kissed me. His lips were soft, and the kiss was gentle, but I felt energy pouring off him, as if he wanted to fly, or run a million miles, or swim across the river. Or maybe that energy was coming from me.

"It's a good moment, true," I said when we stopped kissing. "But there are going to be better ones. They'll be so much better. Away from here, away from her."

He listened to me, and I wasn't sure why he didn't agree out loud. I could hear his thoughts, the way he could hear lobsters singing, and he was planning our route, our escape. All those days on the lam with his father had taught him so much. He'd proven it on our trip so far—even today, finding the path up this hill to this swing.

"Where will we go next?" I asked. "We'll have to sneak onto her boat and get our things. Even if she locked it, that's okay. She always uses the same combination, 1-9-0-7, the year Rachel Carson was born. But after that, what? Back to the reserve with Atik?"

"You liked it there, didn't you?" he asked.

"I loved it," I said. "If we hadn't had to come here, I would have wanted to stay. Did you?"

"It was good," he said.

"We could work there. Go to school where Atik went and kick the butts of all those bullies."

Billy smiled. "My tough girl Maia."

"So tough," I said, glowing because he'd said "my." *My tough girl Maia.*

"I think we should head down now," he said. "Before it gets too dark."

"Okay," I said, and we began to walk. The way down seemed steeper, the pine needles underfoot more slippery than they had been on the climb up. Billy and I held hands, making sure we didn't fall. That was our way: looking out for each other. I felt exhilarated; he was right: We were living the best moment of our lives.

So far, I told myself. Imagine the rest of our lives. We'd always be together, we had to, and life would get better and better from here.

"Do you think they planned it all along?" I asked.

"Who?"

"My mother and Drake," I said. "Ha-ha."

"What do you mean, 'ha-ha'?"

"Just, it's funny to think about. She's known him so many years and she just happens to wind up here, in the same town where he lives? It's so far from Connecticut, so far from anywhere. She didn't just leave my father and me—she left us for him. Don't you think?"

"It occurred to me," he said.

We had to concentrate, scrambling down a scree of rocks—boulders, really, much bigger than they had seemed going up, when the light was better.

"I feel sorry for Merie," I said. "If Mom could do this to

me, she'll do it to her. That's the worst. She's that kind of a person."

Billy didn't answer. I could tell he was concentrating on getting us both safely down the rocky part. There was a slight cliff edge I hadn't noticed, an almost sheer twenty-foot drop. My dizziness came back. I half swooned. I wasn't sure I could make it the rest of the way down.

"We're exactly alike, you and I," I said. I clutched his hand.

"You know it," he said.

"Even more than I knew."

"Yeah?" he asked. "I didn't think more was possible."

"We both have bad parents. I mean, really bad. Your father, what he did to your mother. And my mother . . ."

"At least she didn't kill anyone," Billy said.

I heard the words in my mind: *missing, waiting, child, song.*

They weren't for me, they weren't even for the whales: They were for my mother's new child. They were for Merie. The four words were for my mother's other daughter.

Everything inside me broke. All my bones and organs crashed into one another. My heart exploded. My body collapsed, and I crouched to the ground, feeling my blood stop in my veins.

Then I heard a voice echoing off the fjord's rock walls, the cliffs rising and falling around us, the wide-open water. The voice was keening, weeping, loud, and insane. The voice was screaming, and it was mine.

"Yes, she did, Billy! She killed me, she killed me, my mother doesn't love me, she killed me!"

Chapter 21

MAY 28
TADOUSSAC AND ONWARD

Well, that was embarrassing," I said the next morning. Billy had gotten me down the hill to Atik's boat. I didn't remember my feet moving. I think he might have carried me. I couldn't stop crying, so he and Atik had tucked me into bed—the single bunk down below—and Billy had watched me all night. I didn't exactly fall asleep—I passed out.

And now, still lying there with Billy sitting beside me, I was trying to sound normal, carefree, as if a girl howling into a crevice, having to be put to bed by her boyfriend, was the most normal thing in the world.

But I knew I was in that place again: the real depression, the black hole.

Billy had left me on *Wolf* with Atik and gone to my mother's boat to get our things. Just as I'd suspected, her combination was the same: 1907. He'd returned with our duffel bags, and I dug through them and found my medication. I knew I wasn't supposed to take the pills all at once, to make up for all the days I'd missed, but I popped four, hoping they would work fast, deliver serotonin to the receptors and make me well right away.

Atik's bunk was narrow, but Billy perched on the edge beside me, holding my hand. I was smiling, but my lips quivered with the effort, and tears leaked from my eyes.

"I'm so sorry I acted that way."

"It's okay," he said.

"No, it's horrible. It'll get better. The meds will kick in. I shouldn't have stopped . . ."

"You went off them? Maia."

"I know," I said. "I was stupid." And it had been stupid to hide them from him in the first place.

He said nothing to that, making me think he agreed with me. That hurt. Everything did.

"Did you see her? My mother?" I asked.

"No," he said.

"Or Drake?"

He shook his head. "Atik said they came by last night, right about the time I was on board your mother's boat, but he told them he hadn't seen us. He gave them the idea we'd gone off on our own."

"I'm surprised they even looked."

"You're still her daughter."

"Whatever that means," I said. "I feel bad for Merie." It was easier to think of my curly-haired baby half sister than to think of myself. My mother *had* killed me. Or she might as well have.

It was a trauma reaction. I'd learned about them in Turner. When something hurts or shocks you terribly, you check out of yourself. You have another part living inside you, and it takes over. Memories of what happened are slippery or even wiped out. One part, stronger than the others, deals with the pain, anger, or sorrow, protecting the more fragile part.

That's how I felt in the bunk: scraps and seconds of yesterday, of last night, my mother's revelations, Merie staring into my eyes, my voice screaming on the mountainside, floated in and out of my mind. But the whole picture was too hard to deal with.

It was easier to sleep, so I did.

I don't know how much time went by. It was one of those sleeps of drifting in and out, dreaming and then realizing my eyes were open, closing them and going through the same cycle. In every dream I was struggling. Hiding with mythological winged beasts, driving at high speed down a mountain, fighting with a woman in a mask.

I woke up again. The boat had been rocking gently on the waves and tide, but suddenly it thrashed, bobbing, as if someone had stepped heavily aboard.

"Maia?"

I heard someone call my name.

The voice was very familiar, but I wouldn't let myself face it.

Ten seconds later, my father climbed down the ladder and crouched beside my bunk. I lay there, feeling like stone.

"Come on, sweetheart. Let's go," he said.

I wouldn't move.

But then he held my hand as if I were six years old, and I

very slowly pushed myself out of bed and went up on deck with him. The bright sun blinded me and hurt my eyes, and I blinked at shadows standing there in silhouette.

Once my eyes adjusted, I saw my mother, Drake, Astrid, and Billy standing on the quay. Atik stood off to the side with a man I assumed was his uncle. My father and I climbed the long, steep dock up to them.

Billy broke free of the group, came to me. He put his arms around my shoulders, and I buried my face in his chest.

"See what I mean?" my mother said. "It's as if she's brainwashed. She's given him all her power. And he has a criminal record, I'd like to have him arrested, I can't stand that she's done this, I raised her to be strong, independent . . ."

"Gillian," my father said.

"Andrew, if you'd been paying attention you wouldn't have let this happen," my mother said. "You and Astrid, too wrapped up in each other to notice your daughter is so miserable she has to take up with . . ."

"Enough," my father said, more loudly.

I expected Astrid to jump in and defend herself and my father, but she stood there, uncharacteristically silent.

"Let's give Maia a chance to talk," Astrid finally said.

I felt furious at her for intruding. What business did she have even being here? This was the first time my parents and I had been together in years, I thought. Only we weren't together—not really. Not at all.

"I don't want to talk," I said. "I just want to get out of here. Billy . . ."

"Hey, guys," Atik said. "I gotta get back to the reserve."

"Take us with you," I said.

"We can't go with him, Maia," Billy said.

"I'll see you," Atik said.

I tried to pull Billy so we could go after Atik. I watched as he and his uncle untied the lines, hopped into the boat, and drove east. Billy held me tighter. I wanted us to escape, the way we had been doing for so long. We had run away from my house, away from my mother, and now I wanted to get away from everyone here. I felt as if we'd missed our best chance, fleeing with Atik. I couldn't stand what my mother was saying about Billy.

"Get your hands off her," my mother said, coming closer.

"Gillian," Drake said. "Let's stay calm. It's all going to work out."

"So help me," my mother said, glaring at Billy.

"Why are you blaming him?" I asked. "I'm the one who started this. I wanted to find you. That's the whole reason we came here. Yesterday you were saying how great it was, how we were so resourceful to have made it here . . ."

"Frankly, Maia," Drake said, "your mother didn't know what to think or say to you. She was concerned about your instability and wanted to make sure you didn't bolt."

"You could have told me about Merie," I said, staring into my mother's eyes. "Before I got here."

"Maia, I was afraid how you would take it. I could have done it better, but I was afraid you couldn't handle all this," my mother said. And she was already vindicated because clearly I couldn't.

"Where is she now?" I asked. "Are you going to abandon her, too?"

"She's with the nanny," Drake said.

"I didn't even know she existed!" I said. "You had a baby a year ago, and I didn't know!"

"Okay," my mother said. "You've said that."

"I think Maia deserved to know she has a half sister," my father said.

"You stay out of this, Andrew! What goes on between Maia and me has nothing to do with you."

"It's the same as ever, the two of you, you're always fighting," I said, my voice rising. I felt the panic, hysteria building, just like on the cliff path.

I pressed even tighter against Billy, took deep breaths to calm down. I wished we could just disappear. I reached into my pocket and felt the sand dollar—when he'd gone to get our things, he'd wrapped it in tissue and put it on the pillow next to me, where I'd find it when I woke up. I held it now, as if it were a magic talisman and could transport us somewhere else.

"Please, get us out of here," I whispered to Billy.

"Maia, I can't," he whispered back.

I handed him the sand dollar. He let go of me long enough to unwrap it, look at it.

"Our promise," I said. "We're not returning."

"Oh, Maia," my father said, sounding sad.

"Andrew, it's time, you're all going to miss your flight," Mom said.

"You called him," I said, wheeling toward her, my face

turning red. "You couldn't wait to get rid of me. You just couldn't wait."

"That's not true," my mother said.

"It is," I said. "I felt it the whole time, how much trouble I was to you. And all you did was lie to me about everything. Nothing I've believed about you is true! And now you just want to get rid of me, so you called Dad, and . . ."

"She didn't," Billy said.

"What?" I asked, looking up at him, into his green eyes. "How do you know?"

"Because I called him," he said.

"No!" I couldn't believe it. In that second, I thought I would die. He held both my hands. The sand dollar was pressed between our palms. Tears blurred my eyes. Billy's betrayal filled my whole body like poison. "Why?" I asked. It was all I could manage.

"Because I was so worried," he said. "When we were on the cliff, and you started screaming, I was so afraid for you. And when we got back to the boat, and all you could do was sleep . . . there was nothing I could do."

"I'm getting better," I said. "The medication will start working again."

"I hope so, I want it to," Billy said. "But I wasn't sure. I couldn't watch you suffer that way. You need help, Maia. More than I could give."

"Well, there's something," my mother said to Billy. "You did the sensible thing, but you also brought her to this point. She wouldn't have taken this trip if you hadn't been encouraging her. When this is all over, I want you to stay away from—"

"Lay off him," a deep voice said, from behind where we were standing. An old man came toward us, limping with a cane.

Everyone turned to look. He had pure white hair, a ruddy face, and sun lines around his eyes and mouth, as if he'd spent his life on the water. He wore khaki work pants and a plaid shirt. And he had green eyes.

"How dare you?" my mother asked. "This is a family discussion, so please stay out of it."

"I *am* family," he said. "I'm Billy's grandfather."

The man's gaze bored into Billy's. I thought Billy must have phoned him, too, but Billy looked completely shocked, rooted in place, unable to move.

"Grandpa," he said. "What are you doing here?"

"I got a phone call," his grandfather said.

"Who called you?"

"It doesn't matter, Bill. Come with me."

"I didn't think you wanted me." Billy's voice broke. In his face I saw the little kid he'd been, the boy who still needed his family and couldn't quite believe his grandfather, the man who'd abandoned him and sent him to foster care, was actually here.

"I made a mistake," his grandfather said, sounding gruff. "A big one."

"Grandpa, it's okay."

"No, it isn't. But let's fix it now. We're going home."

"No!" I said, clutching Billy's hand. "You can't. We have to stay together. You were right, everything changed here, but we can get it back. It can be the way it was again. Our pact!"

Billy held me and leaned his forehead against mine, and we looked into each other's eyes the way we had along the way.

"I want you to keep the sand dollar," he said. "For us. We need to do this right now, Maia. You have to get well. I don't know who called my grandfather, but he's here now, and . . ."

"You're going with him," I said.

"Yeah," Billy said. "I am."

"You can make things right with each other later," I argued. "But we need each other now!"

"Maia," he said, his face full of pain.

"What will happen?" I asked. "To us?"

He shook his head. He had tears in his eyes. "Everything good in life was gone, but you brought it back. It killed me, calling your dad, but I did it for you. There was no other way."

"But there is," I said. "You trust me, right? You said you did. So why can't we stay together? Just trust it will all work out?"

"Because it won't," he said. "Not right now."

Billy kissed me, right in front of my parents and step-mother and step-whatever Drake was, and his grandfather. It was only the third day of us kissing, and my knees went weak—not because of that feeling of closeness that had enveloped us, kept us in our beautiful, private world, but because it felt like the end.

"Let's go, Billy," his grandfather said. "We have a long trip ahead of us."

"Okay, Grandpa," Billy said, then walked away. He didn't look back. I had the feeling he couldn't. I heard his grand-father's cane thumping down the quay until they were too far away for me to hear it anymore.

"You'd better go, too, Andrew," my mother said to my dad. "The three of you are going to miss your flight."

The three of us: me, Dad, and Astrid. Not me and her. I wasn't even part of her family now. I felt every single thing I loved and cared about washing away faster than Billy's draw-ing in the sand.

"You haven't changed, Gillian," Dad said. "You want us out of your life; you can't wait to get back to whatever you're doing."

"You know nothing about me," she said. "You never have."

"Because you don't let people . . ."

I heard Drake join in to defend my mother. The bickering went on, and then it was just a roaring in my ears. I didn't remember moving my feet, but suddenly I was at the end of the quay. The river blurred.

I felt an arm around my shoulder. I smelled Chanel No. 5. I knew if I turned around I'd see the off-white cashmere sweater, the heavy gold necklace.

"Maia?" Astrid asked quietly.

She was trying for an embrace, but I wrenched out from under her arm.

"I'm so sorry," she said. If she started criticizing my mother I would lose my mind, I'd push her into the water.

"Just don't, Astrid," I said.

"For what you're going through," she continued. Her voice was gentle. I didn't want her to see, but I couldn't stop the tears leaking from my eyes. I steeled myself for the next part: She'd tell me she'd seen this coming, she'd known I was getting depressed again, and of course I should have known better than to expect anything from my mother. But then came the shocker.

"You're in love," she said.

I felt stunned and stared at her. No one else had said that to me. No one else seemed to understand. This was Astrid; there had to be something more coming, a twist of the I-told-you-so knife. She had to be setting me up.

"And he's in love with you, too," she said.

"How can you tell?" I asked, my voice shaking, backing away because I didn't trust her and couldn't bear what might come next.

"Oh, Maia," she said, smiling sadly. "Anyone who looks at him, at either of you, can tell." And I knew she was speaking the truth.

I saw Billy's freckles, his wide smile, his green eyes. My love had started before this trip, at home, sitting at my bedroom window and looking up the hill toward Stansfield. I realized my hand was empty. I patted my pocket—the sand dollar wasn't there, either. I must have dropped it when we had stepped apart.

"It feels over," I said. I heard the words echoing in my ears and couldn't believe I was saying something so gut-wrenching to Astrid.

"No," Astrid said. "If you could have heard what he said to your father when he called. We both knew—we both could feel how deeply he cares, how he wants the best for you. It was a sacrifice he made. Giving up his time with you to make sure you got help."

"But he called his grandfather, too," I said, my voice breaking. "So he could get away from me."

"No, Maia," Astrid said softly. "I made that call. Without you, I knew Billy would feel so alone. I found his grandfather online and told him everything. And you know what? He wants Billy with him. He wants that very much."

At that, thinking of all Billy had lost, how he'd been stuck in an institution missing his old life, lobster fishing with his grandfather, I began to sob. I thought of how much I'd wanted us to stay together, how horrible I'd felt last night, finding out about my mother. It all came crashing in on me.

Astrid pulled me into a strong hug. I started to resist—my mind told me to push her away. But somehow I didn't, and then I was leaning into her, holding on tight, not wanting to let her go.

"Take me to Turner," I said, weeping. "I think I need to go there."

"Of course, Maia," Astrid said. "We will. We'll take you there right now."

Chapter 22

JULY 12
TURNER INSTITUTE

Good work, Maia, good work," Simone said, half teasing and half meaning it.

"Why do the doctors always say that after sessions?" I asked, sitting on the edge of my bed.

"I don't know, but they always do," Simone said. "I guess because it really does take work to get better. Depression is a bear."

I nodded. Therapy was intense, and I'd had a lot of it these last six weeks at Turner. So had my roommate, Simone.

Tall, thin, with black hair that swept her shoulders, she was both gorgeous and brilliant: She'd come here from Harvard. Her mother was African American, her father Cuban, and they were both college professors in New York City. Last fall, Simone had started freshman year thinking that one day she would teach Women's Studies like her mother. But it had been hard to adjust, and she was homesick. Her courses were grueling. She'd been valedictorian in high school, but now she was afraid of failing. Midway through spring semester she crashed.

She had stopped getting up in the morning. For the first time in her life she was both skipping and barely passing classes. When she tried to read an assignment, all the words ran together. She felt as if English had turned into a brand-new language and she couldn't speak it. She had lost her ability to think, and she realized she was a fraud. Walking to the T, with a vague idea that she needed to get to South Station and take a train to New York, she nearly got hit by a truck.

The driver stopped, and although Simone wasn't hurt, she sat down on the curb and couldn't stop weeping. Police arrived. They drove her to an ER, and within hours both her parents arrived, and arranged for her to be admitted to Turner. And she was healing here. It really was the best place, as much as I sometimes didn't want to admit it.

"I've loved rooming with you," I said.

"Back at you. I can't believe you're leaving me."

"You'll be getting out soon."

"If I keep doing the *work*," she said, and we laughed: just a little inpatient humor.

"In September we'll both be back at school," I said. I was actually going to be able to attend high school as a junior, along with the rest of my class, as long as I went to summer school when I got home.

"Yeah," Simone said. "*Hasta la vista* Cambridge, hello living at home."

"I know, but NYU."

"I'm actually looking forward to it," she said. "They have great Psychology and Women's Studies departments. Harvard said I could transfer back if I want, but I doubt I will."

"Don't project. Can't you just hear Dr. Hendricks? 'It's good to have goals, but ground yourself in the present.'" I quoted our psychiatrist in her English accent, gentle and melodic. Not only had Simone and I been roommates, but we'd shared the same psychiatrist, bonding us further. We often rehashed our therapy sessions into the night, trying to better each other's imitation of Dr. Hendricks, even as the night staff did checks.

I'd told Simone about Dr. Bouley, whom I still loved and would see when I went home, and she told me she had no idea who her doctor would be in New York—that scared her a little, but I assured her she could always try someone different if the first wasn't a good fit. Over the years I had become something of an expert on such things.

"Will you visit me in the city?" Simone asked.

"Definitely," I said.

"Yes, I seem to remember you have a friend who knows his way around the city," she said, teasing.

"I do," I said.

"What will you miss most about this place?" she asked. "Other than me?"

I thought about it. It seemed strange to say I'd miss Turner at all, but the truth was, this time I would. It had been safe, a cocoon, protecting me from the outside world until I was strong enough.

"Not checks," I said.

"Right—it will be nice to sleep through the night."

At first they had me on two-minute checks—when the staff looked in to make sure I was safe, i.e., alive and not harming myself.

They weren't wrong to do that, because when I first got to the hospital, thoughts of suicide were strong. For the first few days I wished I'd jumped off the cliff the night I'd started screaming. It was very hard to want to go on. I felt I'd lost my mother twice: once when she left us, and again now, when I'd left Canada never wanting to see her again. The idea of continuing to live with that reality stopped making sense.

Here's the thing about wanting to die: You think nothing will ever be good again. The therapists and doctors and psychiatric nurses all tell you that it will, that if you hold on and get some perspective, a certain happiness, even joy, will return.

And if I wasn't all the way there yet, I was starting to be. Every session with Dr. Christine Hendricks had taken me back to Tadoussac and the truth of my mother's life.

Dr. Hendricks had listened to me describe how happy she had looked to see me, that first night in the harborside café, how she had hugged and kissed me. How I'd still believed that *missing, waiting, child, song* had been for me.

I had found it easier to talk about the whales: how their haunting songs expressed their own emotions, how they had complicated lives and relationships just like humans. They longed for connection, like Gray Girl and Aurora, and they disappeared from their homes, like Persephone.

I wondered if Persephone had reappeared, if she'd had her baby.

Eventually we talked about the real baby in my life: Merie. How much I loved her, in spite of being shocked that she existed. Then we finally got to my mother: her lies and omissions, the reality that she was nothing like I'd imagined—or wanted—her to be. Dr. Hendricks said that someday I'd be ready to write to her again, even see her, but I didn't have to rush it. I could do it when I was ready.

I was ready for a lot of things, but not for that. *Not yet*, I told Dr. Hendricks. I'd save the real truth for Dr. Bouley: I was never going back to see my mother. It's just that if I said that at Turner, they might never let me out.

Turner really wasn't that bad. They called the grounds "the campus" as if it were a college instead of a hospital. It did resemble an Ivy League university with a thousand acres of lawn and woodlands, including a gigantic oak tree that had been there since the Revolutionary War. The famous landscape architect Frederick Law Olmsted, who had designed Central Park in New York City, had figured out a way to create his gorgeous grounds around that ancient tree, and I loved him for it.

If possible, I loved him even more when I found out he had some kind of a mental breakdown and wound up in a hospital a lot like this one. It comforted me to think that the man who had conjured up such a peaceful, inspiring setting had not been immune to the demons of misery. If mental illness could affect him, it could happen to anyone.

The hospital, which used to be called "The Turner Insane Asylum"—*nice, right?*—when it opened in 1820, had large brick mansionlike buildings with towers and turrets, leaded windows, slate roofs, and many chimneys. Some rooms had fireplaces from the old days, the marble mantels adding a nice touch, but the plastered-over openings reminded us that there was no escape, even up the flue.

Mostly I loved sitting in the shade of the spreading branches of the oaks and maples, walking the trails with staff and Simone and other patients. They let people smoke on the walks. Patients weren't allowed to have lighters or matches, so they could only light up when staff was there. One girl, Calista, was really smart and pretty in a geeky short-brown-hair-with-heavy-black-glasses way, but she was so nervous and full of anxiety she'd carry two cigarettes, one in each hand, and take turns puffing on them.

"Maia, your ride's here." Natalie, one of my favorite nurses, poked her head into the room.

"Okay," I said, looking around to make sure I had everything. These four walls, painted soft yellow, had held me safely this last month and a half. My duffel bag was full of everything, including the notebooks I'd filled with notes and drawings. I'd started turning them into a graphic novel. Maybe I was inspired by the fact that Turner had helped many writers. Or perhaps it was just my need to make sense of what I'd been through.

Simone and I hugged, and I hoisted my duffel. Natalie and I walked out to the nurses' station.

He stood right by the elevator, waiting for me. I approached him, feeling waves of both shyness and excitement. This was our first time seeing each other in six weeks.

"Hey," Billy said.

"Hey," I said.

"Ready to hit the road?" he asked.

I nodded. Michele, another of my favorite nurses, gave me a hug and handed me my discharge papers, a sheaf of prescriptions, and enough meds to hold me over till I could get them filled. She unlocked the elevator, and Billy and I were on our way.

When we got down to the parking lot, I caught sight of our ride and gulped a deep breath: the rusty red truck.

"No way," I said.

"Yeah," he said. "My grandfather and I picked it up last week." He took my duffel bag and loaded it behind the seat. He faced me. We still hadn't touched.

"It seemed right . . . coming to get you in it. I was pretty sure your dad would want to drive you home himself," he said.

"I guess he trusts you."

The trust word.

"Maia, I know how badly I hurt you when I called him."

"You did the right thing."

"I wasn't sure . . ."

"Let's just go, Billy," I said.

And we went.

Driving south to Connecticut, we basically retraced the route we'd taken on our way north. This truck had been our home away from home. We'd sought escape from real life and the ache of our missing mothers, filled in as each other's family and so much more.

Billy reached across the seat as if he wanted to take my hand, but he didn't. Maybe he felt as awkward as I did. All those days driving to Tadoussac, we had gotten so comfortable together. I'd started to feel as if I knew how it felt inside his skin. But right now there were six weeks of time between us, and everything was brand-new again.

"You're really better?" he asked.

"Yeah," I said.

"How'd you do it?"

"Talking a lot, getting my meds stabilized, and writing."

"Letters," he said, nodding.

"Not only," I said. "I started a graphic novel, too. It was part of art therapy, but I want to keep going."

"You didn't tell me. What's it about?"

I hesitated. It was so hard to sum up my writing because it wasn't linear, it wasn't a list of themes or characters or settings. "A road trip, whales, and . . ." I said. I held back the last word: *love.* I couldn't say it out loud. Billy and I were different now.

"I want to read it," he said.

"You will," I said. "Someday." In the hospital I'd drawn pictures and told the story of Billy and me running away with each other, the story of us. But now, sitting with him in the same truck that had become so familiar, where we'd shared so much, I felt hesitant, as if I needed to keep some things inside, just for myself.

"I'm glad you finally wrote back to me," he said.

It had taken a while. The first two weeks I'd been so crazed with the agony of believing that he'd given up on me in Canada, turned me over to my father, that I couldn't even read his letters. But eventually I thawed enough to open them, along with the box he'd sent with the last one, and read his words:

> *I'm sending you a sand dollar. It's not the original one we found, but it means the same thing. Don't think we broke our promise, Maia. The truth is we didn't go back—not to where we were, anyway. I came to a different place—to my family, a home with my grandfather.*
>
> *We were never going back without each other. You're at Turner now and you'll be home in Crawford soon and I'll be living in Stonington. But we can be apart and still together. Can't we?*

Could we?

Dr. Hendricks had told me to be careful with absolutes, with the idea of forever. She was very wise and knew so much, and she wanted me to proceed with caution. I glanced across the seat at Billy, and at the same second he looked over at me. The sight of his green eyes made me feel shy. Weird, after all we'd been through. Maybe this was how it would be.

It seemed impossible that I wouldn't be seeing him in class every day. I wouldn't be able to look up at the Stansfield Home and see his light burning on the second floor, in the far-right window.

"You seem far away," Billy said. "Tell me where you are."

"Right here."

"You sure?"

"Stonington is far from Crawford," I said.

"That's what the red truck is for," he said, shooting me a glance. "The rest of this summer and weekends once school starts."

"It won't be the same."

"Nothing ever is, Maia. You know that more than any-one." Change didn't have to be sad, Dr. Hendricks said. It might pierce your heart at first, but if you let go, it could carry you to a better place.

"I'm going to visit my father in prison," Billy said after a while.

"Really?" I asked, shocked.

"Yeah," he said. "His lawyer's putting my name on the visitors list."

"What does your grandfather think?"

"He told me I'm my own person, not just my father's son. He understands I need to look my dad in the eye."

"But why?" I asked.

"Because of you," Billy said. "You did it with your mother. Nothing could have been harder, Maia. You were really brave."

No, I'm not, I wanted to say. But I could see that he believed it, and that made me think. Traveling so far to see my mother had been brave, a little. Leaving her at the end had been, a lot. Seeing her as she was, really was, and not as I'd dreamed her to be had taken more courage than I'd thought I had.

"You helped me be brave," I said.

"No, it was in you the whole time. I was just there, in awe of you."

I laughed, because *awe* was such an un-me word. As in, nothing about me would inspire it. In one of Gen's letters, she'd said she was in awe of Tiler Peck, principal dancer of the New York City Ballet. Gen said that she, Clarissa, and I should go to New York to see Tiler in *The Nutcracker.* I thought about inviting Simone and having a worlds-collide moment. That could be nice.

But right now my only world was this truck and Billy. I glanced over at him. What would it have been like if we'd just kept going? Why did missing someone have to include so much hurt? Had he been thinking about Helen, maybe even talked to her?

"Are there other people?" I asked.

"In the world?" he asked, smiling. "Yes."

"I mean in your life. New ones, who you have met? And old ones?" I couldn't bring myself to say her name.

"Helen?" he asked.

My stomach dropped. How would he have known if he hadn't been thinking of her?

"No. Not now, not ever. Another thing this trip did for me . . . it let me put the old things behind me."

"She's an old thing?" I asked.

"The oldest. I haven't thought of her since . . ."

"Since?"

"You."

We drove along in silence at that, goose bumps on my arms because what he'd said was true for me, too. For me, there was only Billy.

Just then we passed the turnoff for Crawford, the way to my house.

"Did you forget the way?" I asked.

"No, I didn't."

"Then where are we going?" I asked.

"Do you have the book?" he asked.

I knew exactly what he meant: *Beluga and Humpback Whales of Saguenay Fjord.*

"The green book," I said. "I do."

"Then I think you know."

I didn't even answer, but I felt the start of a smile. Instead of taking the highway, the most direct route, Billy drove us along back roads. This was our territory. We stopped at a gas station, and he filled the tank. He had plenty of money this time, because he'd spent the last six weeks lobster fishing with his grandfather.

Of course we stopped at the mini-mart and bought snacks—gummy bears and orange cheese crackers. Munching as we drove along, I tuned the radio to one of our stations at the low end of the dial. We picked up WBRU, crackling over the air from Brown University, and I remembered our walk on Thayer Street. The road wound through eastern Connecticut's woods and fields. We flew along. The music kept playing.

"Is it?" Billy asked, when the song came on.

"I can't believe it," I said.

I felt shooting stars in my chest, remembering the last time we'd heard the Old Crow Medicine Show blast into "Wagon Wheel." And here it came again.

Billy pulled the truck over to the roadside, and stopped right in front of an old lichen-covered stone wall surrounding a sprawling farm. Rows of corn grew tall, bright green stalks reaching into the blue sky. A red barn stood in the distance, and a herd of black-and-white cows headed home to be milked.

To the sound of exuberant fiddles, Billy grabbed my hand and pulled me into the field. We started to dance. He twirled me around, and just as we'd done seven weeks ago, in the wilds of Canada, we held each other close, moving to the music. He sang the chorus, his mouth against my ear:

"So rock me mama like a wagon wheel . . ."

"I will," I said.

"And I'll rock you back," he said, laughing.

When the song ended, we kept dancing. The music changed, and so had we, but we couldn't stop singing "Wagon Wheel." Far away from the barn, we heard the cows lowing. Summer clouds floated through the azure sky. We held each other, and for the first time since Canada, we kissed.

Then it was time to go.

Leaving the field, I spotted a flat rock that had tumbled from the granite wall. I crouched beside it. Billy collected a handful of stones. We piled them on top of each other, one at a time, until we had a perfect cairn. Then we got into our rusty red truck and set off again.

There were many miles to Mystic. We had something important, earth-shatteringly crucial, to do. I wondered if the little library would be unlocked. If it wasn't, I hoped Charlie the security guard would let us in. I thought he probably would.

Tell me where you are, Billy had asked. I was right here beside him. We had changed but we were also the same, we were living in different towns but we were still together, we had traveled hundreds of miles and we had come home. In spite of everything, that turned out to be okay.

And now it was time to return the little green book. Afterward, maybe we'd go to the beach. We could walk the tide line. We could stand with our feet in the waves of Long Island Sound, our native waters, and listen to the lobsters. We could remember the whales of Tadoussac.

And then Billy would drive me home.

AUTHOR'S NOTE

I wanted to write about a teen girl with depression because I know so well what it's like. I'm not sure exactly how old I was when it first started. I do know that beginning in fourth grade I used to miss about half the school year because I "didn't feel good." It was hard to figure out just *where* I didn't feel good—it wasn't exactly a sore throat, or a stomachache, but it was both of them and more besides. (My throat hurt because I was holding back tears and words. I couldn't seem to tell anyone that I was sad and worried all the time.)

There were reasons. My dad drank and often didn't come home at night. I would wait up for him, sometimes until dawn, and I'd be too tired to go to school. I was shy and felt different from other kids. I thought if they knew the truth of my family that everything would fall apart. In spite of family pain, I loved my parents and sisters and felt very protective of them.

Writing helped me survive. I wrote short stories and poems. They were always about people who loved one another, who stayed together no matter what, whose lives were happy. I was the opposite of Sylvia Plath: While Sylvia wrote poems ripped straight from her heart, about feeling depressed and self-destructive, I kept those feelings locked deep inside and wrote from dreams of a different reality from the one I was living in, from desperate yearning for everything to be okay. I wanted so badly for my family to be like the happy "normal" people I wrote about.

In high school I got very lucky. My homeroom teacher noticed my absences (nowadays schools would investigate, but back then many psychological and behavioral issues were totally considered to be family problems) and suggested I see a counselor. My parents said okay, as long as I didn't talk about our home life. Crazy, right, when that was the source of my feeling so bad? But my counselor was wise and creative, and she helped me express my anguish by having me draw pictures. In that way, although I didn't literally "talk" about anything, it was a huge relief to have someone care and understand.

Things got better, then worse, and then better again.

Like Maia, I spent time as an inpatient at a psychiatric hospital, and I found a wonderful therapist. It took a while to find the right medication, but eventually I did. All this has helped me so much. Depression is nothing to be ashamed of. It's an illness and can be treated, talked about, and dealt with. I have to be careful and make sure I take care of myself.

The times I haven't, it has come back. But as long as I remember there's help, and reach out for it, life gets so good.

If anyone reading this feels very sad, as if something is wrong, or as if you want to hurt yourself, please tell someone you trust. It could be your parents, or siblings, or best friend, or favorite teacher, but whatever you do, don't keep it to yourself. So many people care about you, including me.

XXOO

Luanne

HERE ARE SOME PLACES TO FIND HELP

National Suicide Prevention Lifeline: 1-800-273-TALK (8255)

This toll-free, twenty-four-hour, confidential hotline will connect you to a trained counselor at the nearest suicide crisis center.

The Trevor Project:
1-866-488-7386, www.TheTrevorProject.org

The Trevor Helpline is a suicide prevention helpline specifically for lesbian, gay, bisexual, transgender, and questioning (LGBTQ) teens, but anyone who needs help can call—all young people, but also parents, family members, and friends.

The Jed Foundation: www.jedfoundation.org

The Jed Foundation works toward mental and emotional health in college students, and also to reduce the stigma some might feel about having emotional issues or seeking treatment.

McLean Hospital Adolescent Acute Residential Treatment Program (ART): www.mcleanhospital.org/programs/adolescent-art

McLean's ART is an inpatient program in Belmont, Massachusetts (near Boston), for teens and young adults affected by illnesses such as depression, anxiety, and bipolar disorder. They also offer help for young people suffering from a co-occurring substance disorder.

ACKNOWLEDGMENTS

For bringing *The Beautiful Lost* into the world, I thank everyone at Scholastic: my brilliant and sensitive editor Aimee Friedman, Ellie Berger, David Levithan, Jennifer Abbots, Tracy van Straaten, Rachel Feld, Lauren Festa, Betsy Politi, Sue Flynn, Nikki Mutch, Anna Swenson, Elizabeth Parisi, Kerianne Okie, Olivia Valcarce, Lizette Serrano, Emily Heddleson, and many more.

For his knowledge regarding the Innu, I would like to make special mention of Lee Francis IV.

I am so fortunate to have been with my agent, Andrea Cirillo, since the beginning of my career, and I'm thankful to her and all the extraordinary people at the Jane Rotrosen Agency: Jane Berkey, Meg Ruley, Annelise Robey, Christina Hogrebe, Amy Tannenbaum, Rebecca Scherer, Jess Errera, Chris Prestia, Julianne Tinari, Michael Conroy, Donald W. Cleary, Jill Krupnik, Danielle Sickles, Peggy Boulos Smith, Ellen Tischler, and Sabrina Prestia. And of course, Don Cleary Sr.

My love of whales goes very far back, but my curiosity and learning about them grew even more during my time aboard the schooner *Westward*, researching humpbacks and their songs. I am grateful to the Sea Education Association of Woods Hole, Massachusetts, for that opportunity.

I send love and hope to everyone who is or has ever been depressed or suffered other forms of mental illness, and deep thanks to the people who care, treat, and try to understand all that they are going through.

ABOUT THE AUTHOR

Luanne Rice is the *New York Times* bestselling author of 32 novels, which have been translated into 24 languages. The author of *Dream Country*, *Beach Girls*, *The Secret Language of Sisters*, and others, Rice often writes about love, family, nature, and the sea. She received the 2014 Connecticut Governor's Arts Award for excellence and lifetime achievement in the Literary Arts category. Several of Rice's novels have been adapted for television, including *Crazy in Love* for TNT, *Blue Moon* for CBS, *Follow the Stars Home* and *Silver Bells* for the Hallmark Hall of Fame, and *Beach Girls* for Lifetime. Rice is an avid environmentalist and advocate for families affected by domestic violence. She divides her time between New York City and Old Lyme, Connecticut. Visit her online at www.luannerice.net.